Without Reser

by J.L. Langley

Copyright

Editing by Desi Chapman, Blue Ink Editing, LLC
Cover Art by Tiferet Design

Prologue

"*Brooom-brooom....* Mommy, if I'm a wolf like Daddy, why can't I change into a wolf?"

Lena Winston looked up from her mixing bowl and smiled at her four-year-old son.

Chay had a toy car in each hand, his wide brown eyes staring up at her expectantly.

"Because you haven't reached puberty yet, Chay." She went back to stirring the chocolate cake batter.

Chay made "*brooom-brooom*" noises again, and the toy cars clicked against the floor. "Mommy, what's pooberty?"

Oops. Maybe she should have worded that differently. Lena turned, grinning at him. Chayton was the most inquisitive child she'd ever known. Of course he would ask that. "Umm, it means when you are older. A teenager."

His little forehead wrinkled. He sat quietly for several seconds, then cocked his dark head. "Mommy, when am I going to be a teenager?"

She set the mixed batter on the counter and dug out a pan from under it. "In about eleven years, when you're fifteen or so."

"But thirteen and fourteen comes before fifteen, and they say *teen* too. Won't I be a teenager when I'm thirteen and fourteen?"

Lena shook her head and poured the cake mix into the pan. "Chay, you are too smart for your own good. Yes, you will be a teenager then too." She held out the mixing bowl and spoon toward him. "Do you want to lick the bowl?"

1

"Yes, yes, yes," Chay dropped his cars, jumped to his feet, and bounced on his toes. "Yay, I get to lick the bowl. I get to lick the bowl." He danced in place.

"Sit on the floor, and I'll give it to you."

Chay sat so fast he practically rebounded when he hit the linoleum. Their dog, Roscoe, ambled into the kitchen, licked the boy across the cheek, and flopped down beside him.

Lena set the bowl between Chay's outspread legs and handed him the spoon. "Try not to make a mess. I'm going to start on dinner while the cake is in the oven."

Chay took the big plastic spoon and shoved the whole end of it into his small mouth. Cake mix oozed from the corners of his lips and spread across his nose and cheeks.

Deciding that keeping him clean was a lost cause, Lena put the cake in the oven and proceeded to the pantry. She brought the spuds to the sink and began rinsing them, when she heard slurping or... licking sounds? Without even turning around, she knew what was going on. "Chayton Montgomery Winston. What have I told you about sharing your food with the dog?"

"But, Mommy, Roscoe likes to lick the bowl too."

"Chay...."

He sighed. "Oh, all right. No more, Roscoe. Mommy says I can't."

Lena heard the dog's toenails click on the linoleum as he left. She shook her head. Chay thought absolutely nothing of letting the dog lick his spoon and then putting it back into his own mouth. *Yuck.*

"Mommy?"

Lena turned the faucet off and dug through the drawer to find her potato peeler. "Yes, Chay?"

"How did you know Daddy was your mate if you aren't a wolf? Daddy says that wolves know their mates when they meet them."

"That's true, but the wolf's mate also knows. We feel it too." She started peeling potatoes. "Wolves don't pick their mates, sweetie. God picks them. But when mates meet for the first time, they know it. It's like destiny tapping you on the shoulder." Lena smiled, thinking about her husband, Joseph.

"Who is destiny? Does she know everyone's mate?"

Oh, brother. With a giggle, Lena tossed one spud into the pan and got another. "Destiny isn't a person. Destiny means what is supposed to happen. Like God's plan for us."

"Oh. Okay. Mommy, my mate will have hair like the sun and eyes like the sky. He will be like a prince."

"She. And it's a princess, honey, not prince," Lena corrected automatically. Then what he said about hair and eyes sank in. She felt like someone sucker punched her. She took a deep breath and reminded herself that he was a child and didn't know any better. "No, Chay. Your mate will be one of our people, *not* a white woman. She will have long beautiful black hair, brown eyes, and lovely tanned skin. She may not be Apache, like I'm not—I'm Lakota—but she'll be one of us."

The spoon scraped the sides of the bowl a few more times. "But you said we don't pick our mates. God does. How do you know that my mate won't have hair like sunshine and eyes like the sky?"

Lena rolled her eyes and heaved a sigh. "Because God wouldn't do that to us, Chay." She finished the last potato, turned toward the refrigerator, and stopped dead in her tracks.

"Chayton Montgomery Winston. What did I say about sharing with the animals?"

Chay's eyes sparkled up at her. He glanced at the family cat, which had cake batter all over her whiskers, then back to his mother. "You said not to share with Roscoe, Mommy. You didn't say anything about Fluffy."

Chapter One

"Dr. Winston?"

Chay finished the stitch on Bitsy, Mrs. Preston's cat, then looked up at his receptionist. "Yes, Cheryl?"

"The game warden is here. He brought a wolf in, and he wants to speak to you. He says it's urgent."

What in the world did Frank Red Hawk want? He normally dropped off the wounded animals and left. "Okay, I'll be right there." He smiled over at his veterinary assistant, Tina. "Can you finish up here?"

Tina's brown eyes twinkled over her surgical mask. "Sure thing, boss."

Chay chuckled at her exuberance and stepped aside. Tina loved her job. She'd have done the entire surgery by herself if he'd let her.

He washed up and went into the reception area.

The game warden paced on the other side of the counter, worrying his bottom lip.

Crap. Something must be really wrong. Chay walked around the counter.

Frank practically ran to him. He grabbed Chay's shoulders and leaned in, whispering so only Chay could hear. "Chay, I brought you a wolf. One of your assistants put it in a room. But I need to talk to you." He raised his eyebrow meaningfully and looked around. When his gaze landed on Cheryl, he cleared his throat. "Can we go into your office?"

"Sure. Right this way." Chay led Frank into his office and shut the door. He crossed to his desk and propped his butt

5

against the front of the big mahogany surface. "What happened, Frank?"

"The wolf is one of us, Chay. I was out this morning, looking into a call about poachers. I found several shell casings before I heard a whine. There was a wolf lying in the shallow ravine just north of the pack's marked territory. So I ran back and got my tranq gun. I shot it before I realized it was a werewolf. But the thing is, Chay, the wolf isn't pack. The wolf is white. I mean, the fur... it has white fur and is really small... maybe a teenager." Frank frowned and rubbed his chin. "Really strong for a teenager, though."

Chay pinched his bottom lip between his thumb and index finger. "Why didn't the poachers take the wolf?"

Frank shrugged. "I don't know. Probably got scared off would be my guess."

"What condition is it in now?"

"It has a head wound but doesn't appear too serious. I didn't see a bullet. It looks like a nick. You know how bad they bleed, but it doesn't look to have gone very deep. I'm pretty sure it didn't penetrate the skull, but I suspect there's enough blood loss to make it difficult to shift back."

Chay nodded. That made sense. It could also be disorientation, though. Changing to human form would heal the wounds, but a blow to the head would cause confusion, and one needed focus in order to shift back.

Frank leaned on the black leather chair in front of Chay's desk, gripping the upholstery so tight his knuckles turned white. "I'm going straight to the rez police from here. Afterwards I'll go report it to John Carter."

Chay nodded. John Carter was their pack leader. He had to be told of such things. "Yeah, you do that. I don't like the sound of this. We damned sure don't need poachers on pack land. The fact that last night was the full moon makes it even more disturbing."

"Yeah, that was my reaction too."

"All right. I better go check on my new patient." Chay pushed away from his desk and offered his hand to the warden.

Frank shook it. "Thanks a lot, Doc. Let me know how our little patient fares."

"Will do, Frank." Chay opened the door and showed Frank out. He stopped at the reception counter. "Cheryl, where is the wolf the warden brought in?"

"Exam room four, Dr. Winston. Tommy put a muzzle on it, but it's pretty out of it, so I doubt it needed it."

"Good. I'm going to check it out."

"Dr. Winston?"

Chay turned around. "Yes?"

"Bob McIntyre called and wants you to go out to the rez and check on his new mare. He thinks she might be pregnant."

He nodded and checked his watch. It was almost noon. Today was his short day, so he'd get off at twelve thirty. He glanced at the empty reception area and back at Cheryl. "Do we have any appointments?"

She looked down at the open book in front of her. "No. We're done unless someone else comes in."

"Okay. Go ahead and flip the Closed sign and call Bob. Tell him I'll be out on my way home."

"Yes, sir."

Chay left the reception area. He had a wolf to check on.

Tina stepped out of the surgery room as he rounded the corner. "Hey, Chay, Bitsy's in recovery."

Chay gave her a high five. "Good deal, Tina. You can leave for the day. But first, will you go give Mrs. Preston a call and tell her that Bitsy is fine and she can pick her up tomorrow morning?"

"You got it, Chay. See you tomorrow." Tina winked and jogged off toward the reception area.

"Oh, wait, Tina."

She spun around so quickly, her dark ponytail swung into her eyes. She blinked and brushed her hair back. "Yes?"

"Don't forget you have the five o'clock and midnight shift tonight to come check on the animals."

"Gotcha. You coming back up here tonight?"

"Yeah, I'll swing back by at three thirty and eight, since we had three surgeries today. But Tommy will come back and stay all night."

"Coolio. Later, Chay."

"Later, Tina." He grinned at her retreating back and continued down the hall to exam room four.

His teeth stung his gums, and his canines extended. *What the heck?* The closer he got to the room, the more bizarre his body reacted. He got a euphoric feeling, like flutters in his stomach but not quite. It wasn't nerves, more like butterflies rushing to life. His eyes blurred as he reached for the doorknob. He blinked, seeing in black-and-white—his wolf vision. He stood there for a few moments, ignoring the anxious, exultant feeling, and contemplated the strange reactions. He hadn't lost control of his wolf instincts since he was a young wolf.

Then it hit him. *My mate is on the other side of this door.*

How was this possible? He'd never heard of a female were-wolf. It was a genetic trait that exhibited in males. Women could carry and pass on the werewolf gene, but they did not become wolves. Could his mate have been turned as the result of an attack? Was *that* even possible? Werewolf attacks were very rare. He'd never heard of a woman being changed, but just because he didn't know about it, didn't make it impossible.

He closed his eyes, resting his head against the cool wood of the door. His heart pounded in anticipation. At thirty years of age, he was more than ready for this. He'd figure out how it was possible that she was a wolf after he met her. Right now, excitement bubbled up inside him. He'd finally found his mate.

Taking several deep breaths, he willed his body under control. Not that it would bother his mate if she were awake, but if one of his staff came in, he'd terrify the crap out of them. After a few seconds of deep concentration, his teeth receded. He opened his eyes, and they were once again human. Unwilling to wait any longer, he pushed open the door.

The small white wolf was wrapped in a dark blue blanket, lying on the exam table, with her back toward the door. The clotted blood was obscenely garish on the pale fur. The coat not matted with blood had a golden cast to it, and Chay would be willing to bet that pale fur turned into platinum blond locks in human form.

Somehow he'd always known his mate would not be Native American, as his mother had assured him she would be. He'd always been partial to blond hair, even though his mom didn't believe in mixing races. Mom was going to flip her lid when he brought his mate to meet them. Chay grinned. *Oh well.* She had absolutely no say in this. A wolf didn't pick his mate; he was born to her. It was destiny or God's will or whatever. It just was. Fortunately his dad wasn't a prejudiced man.

The dark straps of a muzzle stood out against the light fur, drawing Chay's gaze. He groaned at the indignity and stepped up to the exam table. Quickly he unfastened the contraption and tossed it to the floor. He felt the carotid artery with his fingers, searching for a pulse. It was faster than it would be in human form, slower than an alert wolf, but not slow enough to indicate extreme distress.

He ran his hands through the pale fur, enjoying the softness as he searched out the head wound. Frank was right, it didn't appear too bad, but Chay needed to clean it to make certain. He turned to the cabinet behind him and got out the gauze and antiseptic he needed to tend to the wound. After determining it was only a nick, he bandaged it.

Chay didn't need to bother with an antibiotic or a tetanus shot. Werewolves didn't get infections or viruses. His kind had an extremely efficient immune system. After shifting back to human form, the head wound would heal completely. In normal cases, it would have already healed, but his mate's blood loss slowed his healing.

Chay leaned forward and buried his nose in his mate's neck for a few seconds.

The scent was spicy and... woodsy? It was sort of musky. That was strange; most women had a sweet floral smell to them. The odd scent was actually very nice. Intoxicating. His cock twitched, making him groan. He stood and told himself to behave. He needed to finish taking care of his mate. There'd be time enough later for other exploration.

He stepped back, smiling like an idiot. "Okay, Little Bit, let's get rid of this." Chay grabbed the edge of the blanket and began gently removing it. "Gotta make sure there are no other injuries." He finally got the blanket untangled and tossed it off the still body.

He studied his mate's form, starting at her head. Smiling at all the platinum fur, he gazed farther down the slim frame. "I bet your eyes are—"

He gasped and stumbled backward. His hand flew to his mouth. No, that couldn't be right. He was seeing things—*things* that shouldn't be there. Chay blinked and looked again. No, it *was* there. It had to be some sort of mistake. His body, his senses, they must be confused. This wasn't his mate. It couldn't be....

Chay closed his eyes and took a deep breath. It couldn't be, but it *was*. He couldn't deny what he felt. This *was* his mate, but how? It didn't make sense. Apparently, he'd been right to begin with. Females were not wolves, and his mate wasn't a female.

His brain hurt.

Chay had gone through every possible scenario he could think of, trying to come up with another valid excuse for his body's reaction to the white wolf. None of them made as much sense as the mate hypothesis. Even more puzzling than his response was the fact that he wasn't as disturbed as he expected. There was something really appealing about the little wolf. That more than anything supported his feeling that this was truly his mate. He'd never found men *that* appealing before.

He'd looked at other men, sure, but everyone did. Didn't they? A beautiful person was a beautiful person... right?

When everyone else had left for the day, he'd closed up shop, changed out of his scrubs, and even gone and warmed up his truck. The day was a little cool for early fall, and he did not want his mate to be cold. And after all that, he *still* had a hard-on. *Oh well.* His jeans concealed it enough, and his coat reached midthigh.

Chay packed his bag to take out to Bob McIntyre's place and loaded his mate in the back seat of his quad cab. He tucked the blanket around the small body and pulled the seat belt over him. After giving the pale fur one last gentle caress, he closed the door and climbed behind the wheel. Once he got on the road, he picked up his cell to give his old man a call, then transferred the call to hands-free.

Joe Winston answered on the second ring. "Hey, son. Whatcha doing?"

"I really wish you wouldn't do that. It's creepy."

"What?" His father's voice was laced with amusement.

"Starting our conversation before you even say hello."

Joe laughed. "But that's what the caller ID is for. So I know who's calling before I answer it, but if it's that important to you... hello?"

Chay chuckled. They'd had this conversation a dozen times. "Hi, Dad. What are you doing?"

"Watching TV. What are you up to?"

"Going out to Bob McIntyre's place. He thinks his new mare is expecting."

"Ah. Are you still coming over Wednesday night for dinner?"

"Yeah, probably." The question was, would it be just him or would he be taking his mate to dinner too? Chay winced at the thought.

"Your mother will be disappointed if you cancel." His father's tone made it clear he would be too.

Chay grinned. It was nice to be loved, but sometimes being an only child put a lot of pressure on him. He adjusted the rearview mirror and checked on his... the wolf. "Listen, Dad, I have kind of a serious question for you."

"Okay, shoot."

"How do you know when you've found your mate?"

"Why?"

"Come on, Dad, just answer the question."

Joe sighed. "Chay, you'll find your mate. You aren't that old. I didn't meet your mother until I was thirty-two."

Thank goodness his dad didn't read more into the question. He wasn't ready to tell his parents, not yet. Sadly, he suspected the fact his mate was white was going to be the least of his worries when his parents found out.

"When you do find your mate, son, you will feel it."

Yeah, he'd already figured that much out. "But how do you feel it?"

"It's like an intense longing... sort of. Kind of like an adrenaline high at first. Your body will respond before you even realize it's your mate. I don't really know how to describe it, son. You'll know."

Chay sighed. That's what he thought. And his dad was right; he *did* know. It was.... "Dad, has anyone ever gotten confused? And think they found their mate but they didn't?"

"None that I'm familiar with. It's not something you can mistake or confuse with anything else. It's an instinctual sort of reaction."

He gave a quick peek at the mirror and saw pale fur in the back seat. "I wanted to make sure it's not something I can miss by accident."

"You'll know, son."

"All right. Thanks, Dad." Chay took a deep breath, willing himself to relax. He couldn't help it if nobody liked the idea. It's not like *he* chose his mate. This was a good thing, not a bad thing. Why did he feel like it was such a huge obstacle?

"You have got to be the only man alive who has wanted a mate since he was four. Son, you'll find her, I promise."

Him, not her, Chay corrected mentally. He pinched the bridge of his nose. Lord, why did this have to be difficult? There were too many variables. What if his mate woke up and wanted nothing to do with him? Or what if he was a teenager like Frank thought? Chay didn't think so, but his mate was awfully small. How would his parents react? "Listen, Dad, I'm almost to the McIntyre place. I'll talk to you later."

"All right, son. Good luck and let us know about Wednesday."

"Yeah, I'll do that. Bye, Dad." Chay pushed End on his phone as he pulled into Bob's drive. He started to turn off the truck, but he didn't know how long he'd be. Would it get too cold? Chay rolled his eyes at his own idiocy. How cold did *he* get in fur? Not very. He cut the ignition, unfastened his seat belt, and turned sideways, resting his arm on the seat back and his chin on his arm. With his other hand, he reached back and stroked the wolf's shoulder. "What am I going to do with you, Little Bit?"

His mate was still out of it. The wolf hadn't moved from where Chay had put him. He looked very sweet and peaceful... innocent. He was a handsome wolf. Actually, he was more pretty than handsome. Not that he was feminine exactly, but his size wasn't all that masculine. In human form, the top of his head would probably only come to Chay's chin. Chay ran his fingers across the snout and over the closed eyes. He'd be willing to bet those eyes were a pale sky blue.

He should've called Frank to come get this Little Bit as soon as he'd patched him up, and he could've pretended like nothing was different. Even still, he should send the man on his way when he woke. But Chay knew he wouldn't. He had no earthly idea what to do with a male mate, but it didn't stop him from wanting to keep him.

A knock on the window startled Chay out of his thoughts. He rolled the window down to provide air for his mate, even though this would be a quick stop, opened the door, and grabbed his bag off the front floorboard. "Hey, Bob."

"I see you're taking work home." Bob tipped his salt-and-peppered head toward the back seat.

Chay glanced at his mate and smiled. "Yep. He's headed home with me. Bandaged him up right before I headed out. Hopefully he's going to wake up sometime tonight." After shutting the truck door, he clapped Bob on the shoulder and started walking away from the truck. "Let's go see this pretty lady and find out if she's gonna be a mama."

Chapter Two

His head was going to explode. What the heck had he done? It felt like he was moving, but he knew perfectly well he was lying still. He'd never been a big drinker, so he hadn't tied one on last night, but his head sure felt like he had. There was a nervous flutter in his stomach and the sense that something important had happened. And why was he still in wolf form? *Wait a minute.* He really was moving... in some sort of vehicle. *Uh-oh.*

Keaton blinked his eyes open. He lay in the back seat of a car.... No, it was bigger than a car. A truck. He tried to push himself into a sitting position. *Ouch.* His head ached something fierce.... *Oh, yeah.* He'd been shot.

"You're awake. Hang on a few more minutes, Little Bit, and I'll get you inside so you can shift."

Keaton's head snapped up—*ouch*—at the deep sexy voice. *Little Bit? Who in the...?* The man had a lovely head of black hair, high cheekbones, and a tanned complexion. He was obviously Native American and fairly young, but that was all Keaton could see from his point of view. He raised his snout and sniffed, trying to see if the man's scent seemed familiar, and damn if his cock didn't throb. *Good God Almighty, what a wonderful scent.* The butterflies in his belly got worse. Even so, he discerned the man was a wolf and he definitely didn't know him.

He dropped his head back down on the seat and relaxed. Apparently he wasn't in any danger. This man must have rescued him.

It was Keaton's first full moon here in his new home, and he hadn't even met the local pack yet. Maybe he should have made more of an effort so he could've hunted in a protected area. He knew the rules. He'd stayed out of the pack's marked territory. At least he'd managed to hunt on the unmarked pack land so someone had been able to rescue him.

The truck stopped. The man cut the ignition and turned around to face him. If Keaton had been in human form, he'd have gasped, but as a wolf it came out as more of a whine.

The man was gorgeous. Big eyes—probably brown—and full lips, and his smile.... Keaton blinked. Good Lord, he'd been rescued by a walking wet dream. He'd always had a thing for tall, dark, and handsome men.

"I knew you'd have blue eyes." The man stopped smiling, his face becoming very serious. "We're here. Are you ready to go in?" He didn't wait for a response. Instead he got out of the truck. He stayed away for about a minute, then came back and opened the back door. "Okay, this is how we're going to do this. You're going to try to be very still, and I'm going to be very careful and try not to jostle you around a lot." He unbuckled the seat belt and slid his hand underneath Keaton's side. After pulling him out gently, the man picked Keaton up and kicked the door shut.

Thank God. Keaton's head ached so much he didn't even want to attempt walking. The man carried him to a nice little ranch-style house. The door was open, so Keaton supposed that's where the man had disappeared to after he got out of the truck. He walked right in and laid Keaton, still wrapped in the blanket, on the floor, then shut the front door.

Keaton lay there for a minute, taking everything in, or trying to. He couldn't seem to keep his eyes off the man. Tall and wide-shouldered... and his hair.... The man's hair was a little longer than shoulder-length. It was sexy as hell.

The man turned, catching Keaton staring, and smiled. "Yeah, kinda weird, huh? You feel it too, right? Like fate tapping you on the shoulder."

What? Keaton cocked his head to the side automatically, then wished he hadn't. He had a headache from hell. But how did the man know how Keaton felt? Fate was exactly how it felt. Like he was supposed to be right here, right now with this man. When in reality he should be a bit panicked being in a stranger's house. Wait, if he felt it too, then it wasn't just the trauma of being shot. What did that mean? Keaton's heart began to pound.

"Why don't you go ahead and change so we can talk."

Yeah, change... good idea. It'd probably stop his head from hurting too. But how in the heck was he going to hide his nakedness from this gorgeous man?

Keaton shifted, managing to keep his bottom half covered by the blanket. Fully human again, he sat up, stomach still in knots, heart still pounding, but no fear. He looked up at the man, and suddenly it hit him. "Omigod. You're my mate."

My God, was right. Little Bit was absolutely the prettiest man Chay had ever seen. Although to call him a man might have been stretching it a bit. He looked legal, but barely. And it wasn't only his slim build that gave the impression of youth. His features were lovely. His nose was narrow and straight, slightly upturned at the end. Chay had never understood what the term peaches-and-cream complexion meant until now. Little Bit had flawless skin. His short platinum locks lay in waves, where it wasn't matted with blood.

Chay squatted next to his mate and pulled the gauze away from the sunny-colored hair, knocking a hank of it down to obscure huge sky-blue eyes. The wound had healed completely—not even a scar on the pale skin.

He peered up at Chay in astonishment and pushed the hair back with a slim, elegant hand. "What's your name?"

Chay smiled at the thick Southern accent. "Chay... Chayton Winston. What's yours, Little Bit?"

A light brown eyebrow arched. "I assure you it *isn't* Little Bit."

Oh-ho. Little Bit had teeth. Chay raised a brow of his own.

Bit blushed and cleared his throat. "Sorry. I just get tired of all the cracks about my age and size. I guess I'm a little sensitive about it. My name is Keaton." He held out his hand. When Chay shook it, he added, "Dr. Keaton Reynolds."

Chay's mouth dropped open. "How old are you?"

Keaton sighed. "Twenty-five. And before you ask, I have a PhD in history."

Wow. Very impressive. Smart and much older than he looked. Chay grinned and sat on the floor. "You obviously aren't from here. What brings you to New Mexico?"

"Work. I teach Ancient Civ at NMSU." Keaton smiled and slid on the wood floor to get closer. "What about you? What do you do?"

"I'm a vet."

"Yeah? Thanks for rescuing me, Dr. Winston."

"I didn't. The game warden did. Shot you with a tranquilizer dart and brought you to my clinic. I only cleaned your wound."

Keaton moved, practically scooting into Chay's lap. "Thank you," he whispered.

Chay stared, hypnotized by the smattering of freckles he'd just noticed across the bridge of Little Bit's nose. "You're very welcome."

Keaton's breath fanned over his face, but Chay didn't move back. *Who would have thought freckles could be sexy?*

Keaton blinked. He had eyelashes any woman would kill for—long and curled at the ends. Up close, his beauty became more apparent. Keaton leaned in and pressed his lips against Chay's.

Chay pressed back without thought.

Bit's lips felt warm, right. His tongue teased Chay's lips, seeking entrance. Kissing him didn't feel any different from kissing a woman. Chay pulled back. "Uh, I'm not gay."

Keaton looked like someone slapped him. He blinked several times and turned away, sinking back onto his heels. "I'm sorry. I thought.... Never mind." He gathered the blanket around his waist as he stood. "Do you have some clothes I can borrow? And a phone? I'll call someone to come get me. I'll, uh, get out of your hair." He sounded unsure of himself, embarrassed.

Chay felt like a real ass. "Look, I'm the one who's sorry. You don't have to go, but I'll find you something to wear, okay?" He got up and went to his room.

Keaton followed him. "Listen, Chay. I think it's probably best if I just go. I can call a taxi to come get me."

Chay snagged a pair of black sweatpants off a hanger and pulled out a T-shirt. When he turned, Keaton was standing in the middle of the bedroom with the blanket clutched around him, seeming for all the world like a kicked dog. Chay felt about two inches tall. He sighed, walked over to Bit, and gave him the clothes. "Here you go. The bathroom is right behind you. Go ahead and take a shower and we'll talk. There are towels in the cabinet above the toilet."

Keaton took the clothes and strode into the bathroom without a glance at him.

Chay leaned against the wall. What was he going to do? He should just let Keaton go, and then they could get on with their lives. This could be a good thing. He could pick his own partner, and Keaton could pick his.

He squelched down panic. His chest felt tight at the thought of not seeing Keaton again. No, they'd have to work something out. Letting Bit go didn't feel right. Chay'd wanted a mate for as long as he could remember, and he'd be damned if the fact his mate wasn't a woman kept him from claiming his mate. He tapped on the door. "Hey? Are you hungry?"

"No." The curt answer bordered on hostile, and the sound of the water being turned on followed.

Chay squeezed his eyes shut. Bit had to be hungry. He'd spent all night in that ravine. Chay shoved himself off the wall and went to the kitchen. He didn't know what Bit liked, but hell, he was a wolf; he'd probably eat any kind of meat. He gathered stuff to fix two bologna sandwiches and got two sodas.

When Bit came to the kitchen doorway, Chay'd just opened a bag of chips. Bit stopped in the doorway, his hair damp and a frown on his face. "I said I wasn't hungry. I need to be leaving."

Chay grinned. His clothes were way too big. They made Keaton appear even younger. The petulant frown and those full lips weren't helping matters any. "Come on, Keaton, give me a break. I'm sorry I hurt your feelings. We need to figure this out. Sit down and eat. I know damned well you've got to be hungry."

Bit stood there for several seconds before the set of his shoulders relaxed. "All right. I'm not sure what you think it is we're going to work out, but I'm listening." He sat at the small round table across from Chay and took a bite of the sandwich. "Umm. Thank you. You're right. I'm starved. I got shot before I could hunt, and after that I couldn't seem to focus."

The tightness in Chay's chest eased a little at the sight of Bit eating. He ate some of his own sandwich and washed it down with a swig of soda. "So, you're gay?"

"Yeah, you got a problem with that?" Keaton set his sandwich down and got up. "Look, this is stupid and an obvious waste of time. Thank you for patching me up. I'll get your clothes back to you tomorrow." He turned and walked out of the kitchen.

Chay sat there in stunned silence until he heard the front door open and close. "Shit." What the hell had he said this time? He'd only asked the man if he was gay. Damn, Bit was sensitive.

Chay ran into the living room and threw the door open. Keaton stood in the front yard with a hand on his chin and his bottom lip between his teeth. He looked left and right. When he caught sight of Chay, he waved and started walking down the street.

Good Lord, the man was stubborn. It became obvious Keaton had no clue where he was. And to top it off, he had no shoes. Chay sighed and jogged into the house to get his keys. By the time he got in his truck and caught up, Keaton had made it to the end of the street. Chay drove up beside him. "Get in and I'll take you wherever you want to go."

"No, thanks."

Chay gritted his teeth to keep from yelling but wasn't entirely successful. "Get in the *damn* truck."

Bit glared at him, his eyebrows pulling low over his eyes, and gritted his teeth right back. "No." He snapped his head forward and kept right on walking.

"Keaton, get in the truck... please. We've got to talk."

Bit threw his hands up and let them fall. He came over to Chay's truck and leaned in the window. "I'm gay. You aren't. What the hell is left to say? So long, have a nice life? Gee, doesn't fate suck?"

Interesting, his Southern accent grew more prominent with anger. How endearing. "Please get in the truck. Do you have any idea where you are or where you're going?"

Bit sighed, opened the door, and got in. "No, I've only been here a month. I live close to the Walmart Supercenter. Do you know where that is?"

"Yeah. I know where that is. Where are you from, anyway?"

"You mean it's not obvious? I'm from Georgia."

Chay nodded. "I knew it was somewhere in the Deep South, but I didn't know where exactly." They rode along in silence for several minutes, and then Chay decided he'd better get to the important topic before Bit got all pissed off again. "We're mates."

Keaton's forehead furrowed, and he crossed his arms over his chest. "Look, I didn't have anything to do with it. It's not my fault, okay?"

Chay blinked. *What?* Out of everything Keaton could have said, *that* he hadn't expected. "I know that. I come from a long line of wolves. I know all about how the whole mate thing works. I never anticipated having a male mate. You know?"

"Fuck you. You aren't exactly what I expected either."

Chay's mouth dropped open. *Whoa*, someone had quite a temper. Chay snapped his mouth shut. "I didn't say I was pissed off or anything. I.... Hell, I'm surprised."

"Yeah, I think you made your feelings on the subject quite clear. And for the record, I don't have any kind of communicable disease. Kissing me won't give you rabies or anything." Sarcasm laced the deep Southern drawl.

So that's what he was all bent out of joint over—the kiss. "Hey, I thought you should know, okay? I didn't mean anything by that. It was a nice kiss. It was just—"

"Yeah, look, I'm sorry. I'm being an asshole." He pointed left. "Turn here. My apartment complex is the next left. It's the second building."

Chay pulled in and slowed the truck. "Here?"

"Yeah, this is fine. I'll have to go get the manager to let me in. I'm right up there. Listen, if you want to wait, I'll run in and change and bring you your clothes back. The apartment manager lives directly across from me. Or I can wash them and bring them to you tomorrow after I get off work. It's up to you."

Chay smiled. *You aren't getting away from me that easy, Bit.*

Keaton got out of the truck and shut the door. "Well, do you want to wait, or do you want me to bring them to you?"

"What time do you get off work tomorrow?"

"My last class is at three o'clock."

"What time do you usually get home?"

"About four fifteen. Why?"

"I'll get them tomorrow when I come for dinner at six. You have a preference of pizza toppings?"

Keaton frowned. "Look, I think it's best we part ways here and now. You don't want me, and I'll be damned if I—"

"Okay, then. Pepperoni it is. See you tomorrow, Bit." Chay pulled away with a satisfied grin and glanced in the rearview at an astonished Keaton. The man would eventually figure out that Chay was every bit as stubborn as he was.

Chapter Three

Keaton pushed his glasses up on his nose, looked back at the book, and read the same sentence for the third time. Who was he kidding? He slammed the book shut, pulled his glasses off, and set them on top of the textbook. The clock on the microwave read 5:45 p.m. He did not care if Chay showed up. He didn't. The man didn't even like him.

Keaton groaned and got up from the kitchen table. *Damn Chay anyway.* Not only did the man have the audacity to be straight, he had to be Keaton's type. He was gorgeous, smart, and obviously a kind, considerate man. Keaton rolled his eyes. Chay had practically run from the house screaming yesterday when Keaton had kissed him, but it didn't stop him from trying to feed Keaton's skinny ass and from making sure he got home safely. To complicate things, even after being so soundly set down, it hadn't stopped Keaton from imagining Chay last night when he'd jerked off. Oh, what he wanted to do to that man. He could practically feel that nicely muscled body, moving over his....

A straight man. He could not do this again, not after Jonathon... and Jonathon wasn't even his mate. This had the potential to be much worse. Keaton groaned and paced back into the kitchen. This entire situation seriously sucked. He had to stop this before it even started. It was better that way. Better for Chay and definitely better for him.

He smelled Chay before hearing the knock at the door. Keaton rolled his eyes. Even Chay's scent called to him. Damn if his idiot cock didn't jump up and take note of Chay's arrival too. *Stupid sensitive sense of smell. Damned pheromones.* Keaton sighed, stomped to the door, flung it open, and glared.

Chay smiled—damn him—and held out a pizza box and a six-pack of beer.

"I don't drink."

Chay chuckled. "Hi, Bit. Nice to see you too. Gee, thanks, I'd love to come in."

Keaton growled and stepped aside, letting Chay in. "My name isn't Bit."

The pizza box was shoved at him again, giving him no choice but to take it this time.

Chay set the beers on the kitchen counter and started wandering from room to room.

Keaton's lips twitched. The man had balls, he'd give him that. Most people would've been scared off by now. "Why are you here, Chay?"

"Because you are mine. I haven't figured out what the hell I'm going to do with you yet, but it doesn't change the fact that you're my mate."

"How about you just leave and pretend we never met. Go find yourself a nice girl, settle down, get married, and have babies. No one but you and I will ever know I'm your mate."

Chay turned around from inspecting Keaton's bedroom and looked him square in the eye, his gaze boring holes in Keaton. "No." His eyes changed, the whites almost disappearing.

A thrill shot through Keaton, and his own eyes started to shift, but he fought it off. He glanced down and noted Chay's tented scrub pants. At least Chay's body and his wolf instincts responded to Keaton, even if his mind didn't. Keaton wasn't sure whether to be happy or to be pissed off about that too.

This was a no-win situation. The more Chay hung around, the more Keaton found to admire about the man. And that wasn't even counting the physical pull. Chay was gorgeous, there were no two ways about that, but damn it, the man was likable too.

Not many people stood up to Keaton. It wasn't like he was some intimidating big bodybuilder type, but he was a very powerful werewolf. The fact was, wolves steered clear of him when he wanted them to. But not Chay. The man wasn't the least bit intimidated. Somehow he doubted much did deter Chay. Keaton could fall for Chay, if he let himself. But to what ends? To always be his best bud? His pal? The thought didn't hold much appeal, because somehow he knew his feelings for Chay would be much more, given half a chance. And what were the odds that Chay's feelings would ever progress to that point?

"Come on, Bit, let's eat. I'm hungry. I got extra pepperoni." Chay walked past him, grabbing the box out of Keaton's hands on the way to the kitchen. He set the box on the counter and started going through the cabinet.

Great. Keaton stormed into the kitchen and pulled down a couple of plates, then handed them to Chay. He *was* hungry. Maybe after they ate, he could explain why this was a bad idea.

"You wanna sit at the table? Or on the couch? Looks like you have work set out on the table."

"Couch. You want a glass for your beer?"

"Nope. I'm good." Chay settled himself on the couch and the food on the coffee table, then filled his plate with pizza. He popped the top off his beer and took a long swig.

He had a nice strong neck. A neck meant to sink teeth into, to lick.

"You gonna eat, Bit? Or are you going to stand there staring at me with a glass in your hand?"

Keaton closed his eyes, more pissed off at himself for staring than at Chay's smug remarks. He filled his glass with ice tea and joined Chay on the couch.

They ate in silence. As soon as they finished, Keaton took their empty plates and the empty pizza box to the kitchen. When he came back to the den, Chay had stretched out on the couch with his arms over the back and his feet out in front of him. The man had long legs. He had to be at least six inches taller than Keaton. Keaton had always liked tall men.

Keaton sat on the other end of the couch. He was supposed to be getting Chay out of here, not admiring the man's bod. "Listen, Chay. I appreciate you trying to make things work, but it's not going to. It would be best if we didn't see each other anymore."

Chay leaned forward and caught Keaton's chin in his hand.

Keaton was so stunned, he just sat there.

Chay drew close enough Keaton could feel his breath on his skin. "This is about the kiss, isn't it? I'm sorry. It caught me by surprise. I've never kissed a guy before."

He nodded, his chin still in Chay's grasp. "Yes, but that's not—"

Chay kissed him. Closed his mouth right over Keaton's.

He couldn't do this. He had to stop, but his body refused to listen. The next thing he knew, Chay's tongue probed at his lips. Keaton moaned and opened up for him, sliding his own tongue out to play. He felt Chay's canines with his tongue, then felt the sting in his gums signaling his fangs elongating.

Chay moved away a tad, nipping Keaton's bottom lip as he did. His eyes were once again wolf eyes. "That wasn't bad. Not bad at all."

Keaton blinked, his vision going monochrome. He whimpered, leaning forward, practically begging. How pathetic was that?

"That's it, Bit. Don't fight it." Chay's grin turned feral as he slanted his mouth over Keaton's again.

God, he didn't want to, he *needed* to, but.... Maybe Chay could develop feelings for him.

Keaton pulled back and scooted away from Chay. "Okay, listen. You wanna be friends, get to know each other, okay. It's against my better judgment, but okay."

Chay smiled and slid closer to him.

Keaton held a hand out. "But no kissing. No touching, no... no... nothing physical."

"Why?"

Yeah, why? his cock wanted to know. "Because we aren't getting involved. We're only friends."

The look on Chay's face said, "Wanna bet?" but he nodded. "Okay, Bit. If that's how you want it."

Keaton's prick chimed in too, telling him to shut the fuck up. He ignored it and frowned at Chay. "My name's not Bit."

Between the two of them they'd finished off an eighteen-inch pizza, and Keaton was stuffed. Apparently Chay suffered from the same feelings, because he was spread out on the couch, with his ankles crossed and his arms resting on the back of the couch. By the looks of him, he had no intention of moving.

Keaton couldn't decide whether to be irritated or relieved that Chay was actually trying to get to know him. He crossed his own arms over his chest and asked, "You aren't going anywhere anytime soon, are you?"

"Nope," Chay said with a smirk and reached for the remote sitting on the coffee table in front of them.

Frowning, Keaton made a grab for the remote. "No, just no."

Chay raised his brows and his grin turned into a full-fledged smile. He raised the remote over his head and shifted it to the hand farthest away from Keaton. "What? There is a Cowboys' game on. Kickoff starts in five minutes."

"You cannot grab another man's remote."

"Why not?"

Yeah, why not? "Well, because there are rules. And who says we're watching football?"

"Oh my God! You don't like football? That is sacrilege!" Chay's brow wrinkled, and he gawked. That was the only way to describe the look. As if Keaton had announced he were a serial killer or something. Lowering his hand, Chay held it out way past the arm of the couch, out of Keaton's reach.

Chuckling, Keaton held out his hand and wiggled his fingers. "I never said I didn't like football. I just don't like the Cowboys."

Chay's mouth dropped open, and his free hand clutched his chest. Slowly he shook his head and *tsked* as if he were shaming a child, but he was smiling the whole time. "Bit, Bit, Bit. I don't think this thing between us is going to work out."

A full belly laugh bubbled up inside of Keaton, but he didn't drop his hand. He snapped his fingers impatiently as the commentator's voice came on the TV, announcing that the Cowboys had won the toss for the kickoff and were receiving. "That is exactly what I've been trying to tell you."

"For shame. I may even have to put you on my dead-to-me list."

"You have a dead-to-me list?"

Chay nodded solemnly.

Keaton lost it. He started laughing so hard he could barely talk. "That is why I don't like the Cowboys; you fans are all the same. A bunch of fanatics who don't think any other team exists."

Gasping in disbelief, Chay said, "That's why we're called America's Team!"

"But you aren't even from Dallas—wait, are you?" Sadly, he knew next to nothing about Chay other than he was gorgeous, kind, and completely stubborn. Add a sense of humor to that too, because this was kinda fun.

"Nope, born and raised in New Mexico." Chay shook his head. "So, see, you have no excuse not to be a Cowboys fan."

"You're definitely fanatical." Keaton lunged for the remote, landing on Chay, but Chay deftly managed to keep the remote out of reach. They both laughed even harder and ended up rolling around and off the couch, tangled together, wrestling like Keaton and his brother had done when they were kids.

Cheers from the TV sounded as the kickoff started.

On the floor, practically under the coffee table, Chay paused long enough to watch the return, all the while holding Keaton at bay, which made Keaton laugh even harder. Sheesh, so much for werewolf powers; it was like he was powerless. He finally gave up and climbed off of Chay, out of breath, and stood with his hands on his hips. "Fine, you can watch the stupid Cowboys."

"We are going to have to do something about your irrational Cowboy hatred. I think it might be against the law or something. It's at least against common decency." Chay propped himself on his elbows as the ball was marked at the twenty-second yard line.

Shaking his head, Keaton reached down and offered Chay a hand up.

When Chay took his hand and stood, Keaton made another grab for the remote, which set off another round of laughter.

"Who is your favorite team?" Chay asked as they sat back down on the couch.

"The Falcons of course."

"Okay, I'll cut you some slack, since you're from Georgia, but I'm going to make you a Cowboys fan as well. You'll see." Chay winked at him. It should have been corny, but instead was utterly charming.

Keaton decided if it would get him a smile and an occasional wink, he'd learn to like the Cowboys. Wait, what was he saying? He was not getting involved—well, other than as friends. But in his defense, if they were going to be friends, they should have something in common, right? "What kind of music do you listen to?"

"Mostly country and classic rock. You?"

Football wasn't the only thing they had in common. "Country. But I like oldies as well."

Chay nodded. "Movies?"

"Action. You?"

A blush stole up Chay's cheeks. *Interesting.* He shrugged.

Keaton grinned and waited.

The blush got deeper.

Oh boy, this was going to be good. "Chay?"

With a sigh, Chay glared at him. "Romantic comedies are my favorites."

Oh, that was priceless, and Keaton decided he now had ammunition for when he didn't want to watch the Cowboys, though he had to admit, the quarterback was kind of cute, so maybe he could tolerate watching the games.

Chay pointed at him. "No laughing."

Biting his lip, Keaton shook his head. His silence only lasted for a few seconds before his mirth took over.

This time it was Chay who tackled him.

Maybe this being friends wouldn't be so bad after all. It had been a long time since Keaton had a friend.

After three hours of idle chitchat and watching the dratted Cowboy game, Chay looked at his phone. He got up and stretched. "I hate to leave, but I have the ten o'clock shift to check on animals."

"Check on animals?" Keaton knew Chay was a vet, but....

"Yup. Gotta go up to the office and make sure everyone is right and tight. I had a surgery this morning and delivered some puppies. They're so cute. The owner is out of town, so they are still there. Ya wanna see them?"

Ooh, he liked puppies—kittens too, actually—but he shouldn't press his luck. It had been a nice evening despite his efforts to derail it before it started. He shook his head.

Chay chuckled, grabbed his hand, and pulled him up. "No, you don't, Bit. I saw that look on your face when I mentioned puppies. You're coming with me."

"Chay, really, I can't. I have an early class tomorrow. And quit calling me Bit."

Chay just smiled, damn him. Something told Keaton he'd better get used to the nickname.

"All right, I'll go with you to your office, but afterward I have to come home and go to bed."

One of Chay's dark eyebrows lifted, and a grin tugged at his lips.

Keaton laughed. *Good Lord, the man is going to be the death of me.* "Alone."

"I didn't say anything." Chay tugged Keaton out the door.

"Wait. Gotta get my keys."

"You could always spend the night at my house if you get locked out."

"Ha-ha. Will you quit flirting with me?" Keaton grabbed his keys and followed Chay.

"That another one of your rules, Bit? No touching, no kissing, no flirting?"

"You forgot no calling me Bit."

"Yeah, I don't like that one. I don't think I like the no flirting either." Chay opened his truck, clicked the button to unlock the passenger side, and got in.

Oh, brother. If Chay was going to disregard rules he didn't like, Keaton was in big trouble. He slid into the truck and put his seat belt on as Chay started the truck and backed out. "How does that work? You ignore rules you don't like?"

Those full sensual lips quirked. "Well, yeah. I mean, it's worked so far. Annoys the crap out of my mom, but hey...."

Keaton smiled. The man was something else. His good humor and carefree attitude was catching.

"Speaking of my mother...."

Uh-oh!

"What are you doing tomorrow night?"

Okay, this could be a case of opening his mouth and inserting his foot, but he didn't want to lie to Chay. If they were going to have any kind of a relationship, it needed to be founded on honesty. And up until this point it had—brutal honesty, actually. "Same thing I do every night. Finish up my lesson plans, grade any tests that need grading, and then read or watch TV. So basically nothing. Why?" *Dare I ask?*

"I'm having dinner with my folks tomorrow evening. I want you to go with me. Meet my parents."

He did a mental eye roll. He knew that was coming. "Do you really think that's a good idea?"

Chay nodded. "I think it's a great idea."

Keaton snorted. "Yeah. Hey, Mom, Dad. This is Keaton. I know I'm straight, but he's my mate. Don't know what the hell I'm going to do about it yet, but deal with it."

"We really have to work on your pessimistic attitude, Bit. You are definitely a 'glass half-empty' kind of guy." Chay laughed. "I will introduce you as my friend."

"Well... okay, I guess." Yup, it had definitely been an "open mouth, insert foot" situation. What the hell had he agreed to?

Chapter Four

When Bit walked down the stairs of his apartment the next evening, headed for Chay's truck, the first thing that popped into Chay's head was *mine*. The second was *damn, the man is a looker*. After spending the evening with Keaton and getting to know him, and seeing him "ooh" and "ahh" over those puppies... no way in hell was Chay going anywhere. Bit was his, and the man was going to have to deal with it. Chay wasn't about to give up his mate—the one and only mate he'd ever get—just because Bit was a guy. However, he had to admit, that although the instinctual physical pull of a mate was still present, he was convinced that wasn't the main reason he was sticking around. Chay genuinely liked Keaton and was intrigued by him.

Chay grinned as Bit slid into the truck and shut the door.

Keaton wore a pair of khaki pants and a blue pullover shirt, and damn, he smelled good. Chay's cock perked right up at the scent. Actually his prick had started getting hard from the thought of seeing Keaton again. He should probably be embarrassed, knowing Keaton could smell his arousal, but he wasn't. It was fate. For some reason or another, he'd been given a male mate, and he was going to enjoy it. Who was he to question the powers that be? He was lucky; some wolves never found their mates.

"Hey, Bit. How was your day?"

Keaton chuckled and shook his head. "I can see I'm going to have to find an equally annoying nickname for you, aren't I?"

"Why do you say that?"

"Because you insist on calling me Bit. And my day was good, thank you. How was yours?" Keaton looked Chay over from head to toe, then grabbed his seat belt and put it on.

Chay glanced down and noticed a distinct tenting in Bit's slacks. Somehow it felt better knowing he wasn't the only one affected. The fact that, for once, Bit wasn't snarling at him, felt pretty damned excellent too. "It was fine. You're in a good mood."

Keaton shrugged. "The thought of home-cooked food, I guess."

"Hmm, the thought of my mother's potato salad gives you wood?"

Bit's eyes widened comically, the heart-shaped lips parted slightly, and then he burst into laughter. And boy, those sky-blue eyes crinkling at the edges and sparkling with humor was a pretty sight. "Well, I'm not the only one." Bit glanced down at Chay's lap. "Apparently it's some damned good potato salad."

Chay laughed. This was fun. Bit was a pleasure to be around when he wasn't grumbling about not getting involved with a "straight man." "Oh God. I hope like hell we don't have it tonight. I don't think I can keep a straight face if we do."

Bit nodded, still giggling. "Me too. I don't think I want to explain that one to your parents." He dabbed the tears out of his eyes. "Hi, Mr. and Mrs. Winston, nice to meet you. It's not the food that's funny.... Chay wants to fuck the potato salad."

"Not the potato salad, Bit."

Bit blinked at him, wide-eyed, and cackled even harder. "Don't want to explain that either."

Yeah, neither did he. Just the thought of telling them who Keaton was—to him—was a nightmare. Why was he laughing so hard?

Finally they stopped enough for Chay to put the truck in gear and get on the road. "You know, Bit, that might not be a bad way to break it to them. The lesser of two evils, so to speak. I mean, which is worse, your mate being a man or the idea that you have a hard-on for food?"

"Good point." Keaton got quiet for a minute. "You aren't planning on telling them, are you?" A slight quiver laced Bit's voice.

Chay glanced over at him. Bit shifted uncomfortably. "Nah, not yet. Relax. I told you I'd take it slow, and I meant it. You have my word. I won't say anything until you decide it's okay." Honestly, he wasn't sure how his parents would take the news. His dad would deal with it, but his mom.... Chay suppressed a shudder. Yeah, he was definitely okay with waiting till Bit was ready.

The tension on the other side of the truck seemed to ease a bit. "I'm not trying to be a hardass, Chay. I just.... It's.... You don't like guys that way, and now you *do* want me that way? It's a little hard to believe. Hard to trust, ya know? Not saying you're lying, but...."

Chay did understand. He'd had a hard time figuring it out himself. One thing he knew for certain, though—the thought of being with Keaton, making love to him, *didn't* repulse Chay. The opposite, actually. "I don't know how to explain it. You're my mate, and that is all that matters. We can work around the rest." Thinking about it now, the idea of sex with a man had never disgusted him; he'd just always preferred women.

But with Keaton? Keaton was everything he'd ever wanted in a mate. More, actually. Bit had extra... well, bits. Chay's lips twitched, but he gained control quickly. Somehow, under the circumstances, he didn't think Keaton would share his amusement. "When I was little, I used to dream about you."

"Me?" Bit's voice squeaked.

Chay nodded. "I knew my mate would have blue eyes and blond hair." He smiled fondly. "My mom used to tell me no way, no how was I getting a white mate. She insisted my mate would be one of us, Apache or maybe Lakota like her. But I knew. I wasn't a bit surprised when I walked into that exam room and saw that pale blond fur."

"You are so lying through your teeth." Bit chuckled.

"No, I'm not. I used to dream of my mate. Hair like sunshine, eyes like the sky.... That's what I used to tell my mother."

"Not that. I believe that. I can't say I've ever dreamed of you, but I've always had a preference for men who look like you. I meant lying about not being surprised. I bet you freaked. I mean I know damned well I'd have freaked if I rescued my mate and it turned out to be a woman."

"Yeah, okay, fine, I was a little startled at that. I kept trying to figure out how there were female wolves and I'd never heard of any. But I wasn't surprised that you had blond hair."

"I would have left," Bit whispered.

"Huh?"

"I mean, if my mate was a girl, I'd have left. Well, maybe not left. I'd have made sure she was okay, but I'd never have waited around for her to wake up and realize I was her mate."

Chay raised an eyebrow. He had considered it briefly, but he knew he never could have walked away. He didn't think

Keaton could either. The attraction was just too strong. "Are you sure about that?"

Bit nodded. "Yeah, I... think so."

He grinned, not believing it for a second. The mate bond was stronger than he'd ever imagined. "This your way of telling me if I were a girl, you'd kick me to the curb, Bit?"

Keaton shook his head, smiling. "You don't believe me? You're a *guy*, and I'm trying to kick you to the curb."

"Touché. But guess what? You aren't going to. I won't allow it."

Bit got pretty quiet after that, but he didn't argue. Chay took that as a good sign. It gave him hope that Bit would eventually realize this was the real deal.

As they drove onto the reservation, Keaton started asking questions. The man had a real interest in tribal history, not all that surprising since he had a doctorate in history.

"Do you have shovel-shaped incisors?"

"Huh?" Chay blinked. How had they gone from the history of his tribe to his teeth?

"Your teeth. Run your tongue over the back of your incisors and see if they curve in, like a shovel."

"I know what incisors are. I meant why?"

"It's a trait of indigenous people, that's why."

He ran his tongue over his teeth. Oh, hey, he did have incisors that dipped in, didn't everyone? "Yeah, they do."

"Cool." Keaton practically bounced.

Chay liked how excited Bit got. He filed it away in his memory. Keaton plus history equaled excited-happy-bouncy Keaton.

After that, Bit rattled off all sorts of questions. Did he speak the Apache language? Did he ever participate in any of the tribal dances and ceremonies? On and on it went. By the time they got to Chay's parents' house, Chay feared being dissected and put under a microscope.

They pulled to a stop in front of his parents' house, and Bit got quiet again. Chay turned off the truck and pocketed his keys. "'Sup, Bit?"

"What if they hate me?"

"They won't. Come on." He opened his door and exited. Out of habit, he walked around and reached for the handle of Bit's door.

Bit frowned at him and opened the door himself. "I can open my own door, Chay."

Chay chuckled, half expecting Keaton to tell him this wasn't a date and he wasn't a girl. But Keaton only shook his head and went up the walkway ahead of him. Chay's attention zeroed in on that tight little ass in front of him. Bit had a nice ass. *Shit.* He couldn't be noticing things like that, unless he wanted to clue his parents in to who Bit was to him.

Bit turned his head as he stepped up onto the porch. "Chay? You comin'?"

Not yet, but you keep teasing me, I bet I can get pretty close. "Yeah." He gave Bit's ass one more fond glance and jogged up the steps. He took a deep breath, willing himself to relax, and opened the door.

"Chay." Joe Winston got up from the recliner and grabbed his son in a big bear hug, pounding him on the back.

Chay wheezed at the crushing embrace but returned the gesture. "Dad, this is Keaton Reynolds." He stepped back and indicated Keaton. "Bit, this is my dad."

Bit gave Chay a quick glare, then turned to Chay's father. He offered his hand as he lowered his eyes and tilted his head to the side, showing his neck out of respect. "Nice to meet you, Mr. Winston."

Joe's eyes widened. "Son, from what my senses tell me, I should be baring my throat to you. You are the stronger wolf, but it's nice to meet you too. Please call me Joe. You must be the wolf Chay patched up the other day."

Chay frowned. Why did his dad think Bit was the stronger wolf? His dad was beta of their pack. He was very strong.

Wait. He hadn't told his dad about Keaton, had he? "How'd you know about that?"

His dad's brow rose and furrowed ever so slightly. "Frank Red Hawk told me about it." He glanced back at Keaton and smiled. "So, Keaton, where are you from?"

"Georgia, sir."

"You're planning on staying here now?"

"Uh, maybe. I mean for the time being anyway. My job is here."

Joe patted Keaton on the back and led him to the couch. He pushed Keaton down and took a seat across from him. "Tell me about yourself, son. How's the head? Shot didn't go too deep did it?" He glanced up at Chay.

Chay shook his head. What the hell was his dad up to? The man was always friendly, but he'd never taken this kind of interest in Chay's friends.

"Good, good. You aren't a teenager, are you?"

Keaton blinked. From the looks of him, Bit was as confused as Chay. "No, sir. I'm twenty-five."

"You're only a little younger than Chay. What do you do, Keaton? And please call me Joe. We're family, after all."

"What?" Chay wasn't sure who squeaked louder, he or Bit. Chay cleared his throat and tried again. "What?"

Keaton just stared, wide-eyed.

His dad looked at him, a huge smile on his face. "He's going to be pack, right? I mean he said he wasn't going anywhere." He looked back at Keaton. "Right?"

Bit nodded, relaxing a little. "Right, si—Joe."

Yep. The old man was up to something, but damned if Chay knew what. No way could Dad know Keaton was his mate. Chay sat next to Keaton, watching his father closely.

They sat there for several minutes, Bit answering questions about himself, until Chay's mom popped her head out of the kitchen. "Chay? Where's your new fri—oh." Her gaze landed on Keaton, then snapped up to Chay. "I thought...." She shook her head, looking puzzled as though she were expecting someone else. "Your father thought that.... Never mind."

Chay frowned in puzzlement. What had she thought?

Keaton stood, holding out his hand. "Mrs. Winston, pleasure to meet you. I'm Chay's friend Keaton."

Lena looked startled but shook Bit's hand. "Nice to meet you, Keaton. I admit, you weren't what I expected."

"Someone a little taller?" Keaton asked, a chuckle in his voice.

"Someone a little darker."

"Mom." Chay gasped and jumped to his feet.

So did Joe. "Lena."

"Supper is ready." Lena turned and left, going back to the kitchen.

Chay touched Bit on the shoulder. "Sorry, Bit. I have no idea what came over her. She's not usually like that."

Joe patted Chay's shoulder, then Bit's. "Don't worry about it, son. You're welcome in our home. I'll have a talk with Lena. She'll come around. Now... let's eat." He sauntered to the kitchen, leaving Chay alone with Bit.

Bit raised a light brown eyebrow. "You could have warned me."

"Sorry. I didn't know. I mean she doesn't really have any white friends, but...." Chay frowned.

"What?"

"Well, she doesn't like my friend Remi's mom, but I thought that was because she didn't like the fact that Remi's mom doesn't stand up for him with his dad. She absolutely loathes Remi's dad, but she adores Remi and his little brother."

"Remi is white?"

"He's half. And well... he probably doesn't really count. He looks Apache."

"Come on, boys. Brisket's getting cold." Joe's shout echoed through the house.

Bit grinned. "I like your dad."

Chay tried to dispel the unease over his mom's comment. He'd known his mom would have an issue with Keaton being his mate, but he'd never dreamed she'd have an issue with him being white as Chay's friend. Banishing the thought from his mind he nodded. "I like him too. Come on before he eats all the food."

Even with his mom's standoffish attitude, the evening went well. Keaton seemed to relax and enjoy himself. The man could be real charming when he wanted to be. Chay caught himself staring more than once over dinner. He couldn't help it. Keaton drew him like a moth to a flame. He couldn't wait to run his hands through those blond curls. He wanted to know if that hair was as soft in human form as it was in wolf. And those eyes... damn, he had nice eyes. They actually sparkled when Bit smiled. And dimples. Bit had dimples. Chay hadn't noticed them before. Of course, that could be because he hadn't seen Bit smile much.

"I like your family, Chay."

He glanced to the passenger side of the truck, gaze zeroing in on that angelic face. "Good. I think they like you too. My dad does, anyway. But my mom... she will too, eventually." *I hope.*

"You think? I tell you, I don't think I helped my own cause any when she asked if I wanted any potato salad and I laughed in her face."

They both shared a quick laugh. "You may be right. But eventually she'll get over the fact that you're melatonin-chal-lenged."

Keaton chuckled. "Yeah, maybe, but something tells me when she finds out we're mates, she's going to have a bigger problem with my penis than she does my pigment."

Chay winced, but refrained from telling Bit how right he was. He pulled into the parking lot of Bit's apartment and drove around to Keaton's building. He parked next to Keaton's car.

"Thanks, Chay. I *did* enjoy it."

"Me too, Bit. Me too."

Bit reached for the door handle, but Chay grabbed his arm and tugged him back. Before Bit could protest, Chay did what he'd been dying to do all night. He cupped Bit's head in his hands, threading his fingers through those pale locks, and slanted his mouth over Bit's. And yes, his hair felt as soft in human form.

Bit hesitated for half a second before he relaxed and let Chay in.

Chay took complete advantage. His tongue thrust into Keaton's mouth, touching, tasting, devouring. Keaton tasted intoxicating and, God, could the man kiss.

He consumed Chay right back, giving as good as he got, even sucking on Chay's bottom lip.

Chay's cock grew harder than a fucking rock. He couldn't remember ever getting this turned-on this fast. Maybe as a teenager, but not recently. If he didn't stop now, he wouldn't. Not that that was a bad thing, but he'd promised. He drew back, gasping for air.

Bit followed suit, laying his head on Chay's shoulder, breathing heavily.

Chay gave in to one last temptation and ran his fingers through Bit's hair. "Sorry about that, Bit. Kinda lost my head there."

Keaton nodded. "Yeah, th-th-this is.... We aren't supposed to be doing this."

Chay smiled. A stuttering Bit was really cute. Chay wanted to push and see if he could make Bit stutter some more, but he was pretty certain Keaton wouldn't allow him to kiss him again. He settled for a caress of that smooth pale cheek.

Bit leaned into the caress for a second, then opened the door and got out.

Chay rolled down the window. "Tomorrow night, poker game."

Keaton stopped midturn. "Huh?"

Chay grinned, put the truck in reverse, and backed up. "I'll see you tomorrow around six o'clock. I'm going to take you to dinner, and after, you're going to a poker game with me."

Bit shook his head as Chay started rolling up the window. No way was he going to let the man say no. "Six o'clock. Be ready, babe." He hauled ass out of the parking lot, a huge smile on his face. Eventually Keaton would get wise to his schemes, but damn, it was fun while it lasted.

Chapter Five

When the knock sounded at the door, Keaton smiled, then groaned. He'd told himself he wasn't going to get excited every time Chay came over. But he couldn't help it. Every single time Chay showed up, it felt like a small victory—not to mention the fact that Chay had followed through on his word and actually came when he said he would. Jonathon never had. Heck, Chay had already proved himself to be several cuts above Jonathon. He'd told Chay he'd give him a chance, and by gosh he would, and that included not comparing him to that ex-scumbag boyfriend.

The knock came again. "Bit. I know you're in there."

"Coming." Keaton tried to control the little excitement he felt and went to the door. He really liked that Chay wasn't easily dissuaded. It gave him some measure of hope. Maybe Chay would stick around. Keaton shook his head. He hadn't just fallen off the turnip truck. They had a long way to go, and he knew it. Chay liked him right *now*. It didn't mean the man would want a relationship once his friends and family began to put pressure on him.

Keaton opened the door, and Chay nearly fell in on top of him.

"Hey, Bit." Chay smiled and grabbed the back of Keaton's neck and pulled him into a kiss.

Keaton melted, tangling his tongue with Chay's until his brain kicked in. Unfortunately so did his dick. The kiss, the scent of Chay, everything conspired against him. His cock grew hard in seconds flat. He pushed back, a little breathless. When he looked up, Chay's eyes had changed to his wolf eyes. "Chay."

"Huh?" His hand caressed Keaton's cheek, but his eyes never left Keaton's lips. "You have such pretty lips, Bit."

Keaton's cock twitched. *Damn.* How could he remain strong against that? The man couldn't fake his eyes shifting or an erection; Chay did want him. And Keaton's idiotic overhormonal body reacted. His own eyes blurred as Chay tried to kiss him again. He moved back with a groan and blinked several times, trying to regain control. He'd never felt such a physical pull for someone. "Chay, I thought we were going to go get a bite to eat?"

Chay blinked and drew back, a dazed look on his face. "Oh, yeah. Yeah. We need to eat. At the poker games, we usually sit around and drink. So it's best to have something in your stomach before you go." He stepped aside and let Keaton exit, then shut the door and checked to make sure it locked.

"I don't drink, remember?"

"At all?"

Keaton shook his head. "Nope. I do stupid things when I drink."

Chay grinned and opened the passenger side door of his truck for Keaton. "Like what?"

Keaton rolled his eyes at the open door but didn't argue. He felt ridiculous having his door opened for him, but it also felt kinda nice too, so he decided to shut up and go with it. "I giggle. And you know that dizzy feeling drinking gives you? Well, I'm terrified of falling over, so I crawl."

"You crawl?" Chay shut his door before jogging around to his side and getting in. "Like on the ground, on all fours?"

"Yes. Is there any other way to crawl besides on all fours?"

"Uh, no, but the vision of you crawling around with that nice little ass of yours in the air...."

Keaton swallowed. Chay thought he had a nice ass? Well, hell, he wondered what Chay would do if he just offered it up? *No. Bad.* He was supposed to be taking things slow. "Uh, Chay?"

"Yeah?"

"Lay off."

"Yeah, good idea, sorry. Guess I need to get a grip. Don't think the guys would appreciate me coming to poker night with a boner."

Yeah, that's what Keaton was afraid of, and damned if he wasn't hard too. God, what had he gotten himself into? Poker night, with a bunch of straight men. *Oh goody.* "This is a bad idea."

"No, it isn't. You are going to have to meet my friends eventually."

"Chay, I'm socially awkward. I don't mingle well with others."

"You got along great with my parents."

"Yeah, but they are older. And I didn't exactly win your mother over. Anyway, I've always gotten along with older people. But people my own age.... I'm a nerd. I'd rather be home reading or watching a documentary on Civil War military campaign tactics. I make people uncomfortable."

Chay chuckled. "Are you trying to tell me you're missing a show on the Civil War?"

"No. I'm recording it."

"You'll be fine, Bit. And for what it's worth, you don't make me uncomfortable."

Keaton snorted. "Yes, but you're weird. You're even a wolf and I don't intimidate you."

"What do you mean?" Chay glanced at him, his eyebrows furrowed.

"Chay, most wolves steer clear of me. Didn't you notice your dad's reaction?"

He shrugged. "He said you were strong."

True, but he *had* mentioned it. Most wolves sensed Keaton's strength and avoided him. Chay was an exception. "Are these friends of yours pack members?"

"Nope. Only one of them—Bobby. The rest have no idea that werewolves exist."

Keaton sighed. He wasn't sure if that was a good thing or a bad thing. At least wolves wouldn't pick on him.

After dinner they drove by the store to get a couple of six-packs of beer and some water for Keaton, then straight to Chay's friend's house. Following a quick round of introductions, they sat down to play poker. There were five of them. Bobby, the only other wolf in attendance, Simon, the guy who owned the house, and Remi.

Bobby had been polite, but definitely reserved and watchful when they'd been introduced, which was how most other wolves treated Keaton. Simon seemed nice, although kind of quiet, but Remi... Remi was, well, he was something else. He looked Apache, with his shoulder-length black hair, high cheekbones, and beautiful tanned skin, but he had the lightest green eyes Keaton had ever seen. They reminded Keaton of peridots. And his body.... He was about Chay's size and build. *Yum.* In fact, the man could be Chay's clone from the back. He was simply gorgeous. Unfortunately he was one of the biggest assholes Keaton had ever met. It was kind of fitting that Chay's mom adored him.

They were playing Texas Hold'em and talking sports when Remi put his poker chips on top of his cards, going out for the round, and leaned back in his chair. His attention zeroed in on Keaton. "So, Keaton, you ever date any of the college girls you teach?"

He'd known it was coming—not *that* specifically, but a question regarding his sexuality or rather fishing for answers in a roundabout way. Remi had been sizing him up all evening, making snide remarks here and there. Keaton glanced at Chay.

Chay shrugged and looked back at his cards.

"No, I have not, nor will I. It's unethical for a professor to date students. They can fire me for it."

Remi snorted. "Come on. Okay, but you've thought about it, right? I mean how could you not?"

Keaton rolled his eyes. "Never. I like my job."

"I knew it. You're a fag."

"Remi!" Chay, Bobby, and Simon yelled at once.

Keaton smiled. He'd known from the moment he agreed to come with Chay that this would be brought up. It wasn't like he acted any different from anyone else, but his size and youthful appearance always made macho straight guys think *gay*. Which he was, but... well, yeah, he was, therefore it was a moot point.

He had every intention of answering in the affirmative, but before he could, the table rattled slightly.

Remi jumped up, glaring at Chay. "What the fuck did you do that for?"

Chay came to his feet, glaring right back. "Stop being a dick. You've been giving Keaton shit since we got here. First you called him a pussy for not drinking, now.... Quit being a dickhead."

Simon tossed his cards on the table and cocked a brow at the two men. "Give it up, Chay. He's been a dick since elementary school." He looked over at Keaton. "Sorry, man. Just ignore him. Don't take it too personal. Remi is an asshole to everyone."

Bobby shot Keaton an apologetic glance and cleared his throat. "Uh, Chay? Remi?"

"What?" they both answered. Neither of them moved an inch. They continued trying to stare each other into the floor.

"We gonna play or what?" Bobby asked.

Chay sighed and sat. "Yeah."

"Hey, I *was* playing. Chay's the one who assaulted my shin." Remi took his seat. He gave Keaton one last good glare and took a swig of his beer.

Things calmed down for about three more hands after that, and then Remi started in again. He upped the ante a dollar and looked from Chay to Keaton. "Where did you meet Chay?"

Keaton glanced at Chay and back to Remi. "At his clinic. I brought a wounded, uh, dog in to him."

Bobby shifted a little in his seat. "You're the wo—dog... I mean you're the one who brought the dog in? My brother mentioned it the other night. He heard from the game warden that someone shot a dog and Chay patched it up. Glad he made it. The authorities need to look into that. We can't have people going around shooting dogs."

Keaton nodded. First, Joe Winston, now Bobby. Apparently, Chay's pack liked to gossip like his did. "That was me."

"Have you met Jasmine yet?" Remi asked with a smile.

"Jasmine?" Keaton raised a brow.

Chay cleared his throat and opened his mouth to speak, but Remi interrupted him. "Chay's girlfriend."

What? Keaton tried not to react, but he wasn't sure how successful he was, because it felt like someone punched him in the stomach. He couldn't get air into his lungs. Could a person pass out from sorrow? He didn't look at Chay. He couldn't. He shook his head and smiled at Remi. "No, I haven't. Maybe after Chay introduces me, we can double date sometime." Okay, yeah, it was petty, but he wasn't happy with Chay at the moment. He could have told Keaton about a girlfriend.

"No, we cannot, because Jasmine is *not* my girlfriend. We dated exactly twice. That hardly constitutes a relationship."

"But you fucked her." Remi smiled so big his pretty white teeth gleamed, and then he glanced back and forth between Chay and Keaton.

Oh God. Keaton felt sick to his stomach. Logically he knew Chay wasn't a virgin. He even knew it had been with women, but why did it hurt so much hearing about it? He had no claim on Chay... not really. Had Chay been getting serious about this woman before Keaton showed up on his exam table?

Chay leaned back in his chair and took a drink of his beer, acting for all the world like the conversation wasn't important. Even though Keaton could smell the underlying scent of unease coming off him. It was irritating. "Are you practically engaged to everyone you fuck?"

Remi shrugged. "Okay, point taken." He picked up his cards and looked at them again, his eyes twinkling over the top of his cards at Keaton.

He had no idea what Remi's problem was, but the man obviously had it in for him. Which didn't bother Keaton too much, until Remi and Chay started reminiscing—at Remi's instigation of course—making it clear the two had been friends for a long time.

By the time they left, Keaton felt downright dejected, and to make matters worse, the ride home was silent. *Not good.*

Keaton knew Remi had purposely set out to upset him, and damn it, it had worked. The man had brought to light what he'd known from the beginning. He didn't belong in Chay's world.

Somehow, after meeting Chay's parents, he'd kidded himself into thinking everything would be smooth sailing, assuming Chay could get over the whole "gay thing." Which was stupid on several counts. Number one, he actually cared about Chay. Chay was a good person. No way was Keaton willing to watch the man's life go to shit because of him. Number two, Chay would be miserable being an outcast from his friends and family. Unlike Keaton, the man was a social being; he liked people. Number three—hell, number three didn't really matter, because number one and number two made Keaton change *his* mind.

"Bit, I'm sorry. I don't know what got into Remi tonight. He's not usually so... obnoxious."

Keaton sighed. Damn, he was going to miss Chay calling him Bit. How screwed-up was that? "Don't worry about it, Chay."

The truck stopped next to Keaton's car. "How about tomorrow we just get something to eat here and watch the documentary you recorded?"

He closed his eyes and pressed his forehead against the window. It would be easy to agree to a date and not be here tomorrow when Chay got here, but he wasn't a coward. "No. I don't think that is a good idea." He looked at Chay. "This isn't working, Chay. We need to move on."

"What? No fucking way, Bit. You are not going to brush me off because my friend was an asshole to you."

Why couldn't this be easy? Keaton should have known any mate destined to be his would be his equal when it came to being stubborn. Then again, he'd have thought his mate would be gay too. "Chay, I'm not going to argue with you about this. I don't want to see you again. Goodbye." He got out of the truck and didn't turn back. He made it all the way into his apartment and leaned against the door before he started questioning his decision.

He hoped like hell he was doing the right thing, because damn if his heart didn't ache. He barely knew Chay, but the thought of never seeing him again cut like a knife.

Keaton slid down the door and pulled his knees up, resting his head on them. Why did everything in his screwed-up life have to be complicated? Why couldn't Chay have been gay? Why did he have to care for the man after such a short time? God, his chest hurt... bad. His nose was stopped up, making it hard to breathe, and his stupid eyes were blurry.

Fuck. He was actually crying.

Chay sat there dumbfounded for about five minutes before anger took over. He was *not* going to do this every time Bit got upset over something. The sooner Bit understood that the better. Chay got out of his truck and stormed up the steps to Keaton's apartment. He didn't even bother knocking. He knew Bit could hear him, smell him. "Keaton, open the damned door."

The locks clicked, then the door flew open. Bit's frowning face appeared in the crack of the door. "Why are you still here?"

Were Bit's eyes red? Did he smell tears? Chay pushed him back and walked into the apartment. "Because my mate is throwing a temper tantrum."

"What?" Bit shut the door, spun around, and leaned against it. "I am *not* throwing a temper tantrum. Damn it, Chay. Can't you get it through your thick head…. You don't want me."

"What? You don't have any clue what I want. You may be a goddamned genius, Dr. Reynolds, but you don't know everything. Why don't you get *that* through *your* thick head." He grabbed two handfuls of those glorious platinum curls and pulled Bit's face up to his. He was a little rougher than he should be, but he was pissed and wanted to prove to Bit that he did want him. He slanted his mouth down over Bit's. His tongue plunged in, seizing Keaton's mouth, staking his claim. *Let Bit digest that.*

Surprisingly, Bit kissed back. He clutched Chay's forearms and made this sweet little whimpering sound that went straight to Chay's dick. *Damn, what a sweet sound.*

He broke off the kiss, staring down at his mate. Keaton *had* been crying. There were tear streaks on his face. Chay relaxed his hold on Keaton's hair a tad. What else could he say to the man to get through to him? He finally settled on the truth. "I have always wanted you. I've wanted a mate since I was four years old. And it's always been you. I didn't know it at first, but I do now." He ran one hand down that angelic face, feeling Bit's cheek. "I dreamed of *you*. Of *this* face." He bent and kissed Bit's cheek, where he'd caressed. "Of *these* freckles." His lips brushed over the bridge of Keaton's nose. "*These* stunning blue eyes. *This* pretty blond hair. It was *you*. God, you're beautiful."

Keaton whimpered again and slid his arms around Chay's neck.

Chay groaned. Fuck, he was so hard. His cock strained against his jeans, making him uncomfortable as hell. Before sealing their lips together, Chay nipped Bit's bottom lip. This time the kiss was sensual, meant to explore and savor. He traced every inch of Bit's mouth before seeking out his tongue. He took and Keaton gave. It was sweet and arousing.

Chay smelled tears again and pulled back, looking down at Bit. Keaton's eyes brimmed with tears. Chay blinked, realizing everything appeared black-and-white—his eyes had changed.

"You don't want me." Bit shook his head. "And I don't want you. Go home, Chay." Bit tried to push away, but his words lacked heat.

Damn, the man was stubborn. His body and heart said one thing, and his mind said another. He was too analytical for his own good.

Chay smiled. Bit was perfect. Abso-fucking-lutely perfect. Stubborn, beautiful, funny, smart—he embodied everything Chay had ever wanted. "If you don't want me, why are you so fucking hard?" Chay grabbed the harder-than-nails prick through Keaton's jeans, proving his point. He wasn't sure who moaned louder. Keaton *was* hard, and oh damn, Little Bit wasn't small there. Chay squeezed, then started rubbing.

Bit's eyes closed, and he pushed into the caress. "Because of your stupid pheromones. I hate your pheromones."

Chay chuckled and leaned into Keaton, pressing his small body up against the door. "My pheromones hate you too." He nuzzled Bit's neck, nipping and licking.

Bit nuzzled back, and there was that sweet little whine again. Letting go of Keaton's cock, he fumbled with his pants. Chay had to feel that hard, hot prick with no barrier. He got the jeans unfastened and pushed them down past Bit's hips.

Keaton gasped, drawing back and blinking up at Chay.

He pulled back too, looking down at the thick cock he'd revealed. He moaned, unable to help it. Keaton was every bit as big as he was, and Chay wasn't a small man by anyone's standards. He couldn't decide if that was a good thing or not. It was very aesthetically pleasing, though. He'd never considered dicks pretty, but Bit's was—long, thick, an enticing reddish tint to it and curving toward his belly just slightly. His pubes were the same beautiful platinum color as on his head.

Chay wrapped his hand around the pretty prick and slid it up and back down, lightly, before gripping it more firmly. His own cock jerked inside his too-tight jeans.

Bit's cock throbbed in his hand, already leaking precum.

Knowing Bit was this hard all because of him was a powerful aphrodisiac. Hell, Keaton himself was a freaking turn-on. Everything about the man called to Chay.

Bit squirmed, his eyes wide, the whites swallowed up by blue, his wolf eyes. "Chay?"

Chay kept stroking. Slow and easy at first, then faster as Bit's hips surged forward, fucking his hand. He captured Keaton's mouth, his tongue pushing deep, plunging in and out to the rhythm his hand set. His teeth stung his gums as his canines lengthened. He needed relief bad, but he wasn't going to let go of Bit long enough to get it. He had Keaton right where he wanted him—squirming, panting, and moaning. It was the sexiest thing Chay had ever witnessed. He couldn't remember being this hot for anyone else... ever. He'd never lost control of his wolf side with anyone but Bit. No woman had ever made his teeth and eyes change. He pressed himself to Keaton's side, grinding his cock against Keaton's hip as he continued to pump Bit's dick.

Bit was getting close. His movements were erratic, his heart had sped up, and his moans grew louder. Finally, Bit moved back. His eyes locked to Chay's. His back arched against the door, and a guttural groan ripped from his chest as he came.

The sharp scent of semen filled the air as Bit spurted on Chay's hand and wrist. Bit slid down the door and sat, panting.

Chay bit his bottom lip, his balls drawing impossibly tight at the sight of Keaton sprawled at his feet, jeans open, prick hanging out, drops of cum still clinging to it... to his jeans and the bottom of his shirt as well. *Fuck, the man is sexy.* Chay rested his head against the door. He was too close, and he did not want to drive home in squishy pants. He took a deep breath and closed his eyes, concentrating on the cool door beneath his head.

He wasn't sure how long he stayed there, but a rustling sound below him caught his attention, and then Bit's fingers started working the fastenings on Chay's pants. "Bit, what—"

Keaton tugged Chay's pants and boxers to his knees in one motion. Then his cock was engulfed in moist heat.

"Oh shit."

Bit grabbed his ass, encouraging him to move. Bit slipped half of him into his mouth, and pulled back before taking more in. It felt damned good. This was going to be the shortest blowjob in history.

He looked down to find that angelic face turned up toward him, the smooth cheeks hollowed out as Bit sucked. Those big sky-blue eyes held his. Then Bit did the most amazing thing—he took every inch of Chay's dick into his mouth and swallowed. The sight of that pretty little freckled nose buried in the dark curls above his cock was the straw that broke the camel's back. Chay lost it. His balls squeezed tight, his prick jerked in Bit's mouth, and he came and came and came. "Keeeeaton!"

Bit swallowed every drop, and bless him, he didn't release Chay's cock until it became limp. Chay decided then and there the man was a fucking God.

He slithered to the floor and ended up lying in a sprawl next to Bit. Chay drew him into his arms, holding him tight, and kissed the back of his neck.

"I guess this means you aren't leaving?" Bit snuggled in, getting cozy.

"Nope. You better get used to me in your life. I'm here to stay."

"It's not going to be easy. You are probably going to end up hating me."

"Nothing worth having is ever easy." Chay kissed the back of his mate's neck again and squeezed him. "I could *never* hate you, Bit. My pheromones, on the other hand, can't stand your ass."

Chapter Six

Keaton finally gave in to the insistent tugging on his pant leg and closed his book. Chay would be here soon anyway. He pushed his glasses back up his nose and scooted away from the table to look down at the newest gift. He smiled at the big gold eyes peering up at him. Chay had dropped off the little golden retriever puppy yesterday after he got off work.

In the week after their episode—as Chay called it—Chay started bringing him presents. Keaton had told him to stop, but as usual Chay didn't listen. He brought a book on Apache history and culture. Then it was a book on Sioux history and culture. Keaton had in turn taken to getting things for Chay. He'd bought him the new mystery book in a series he had read and a new lab coat, because his was, well, it was just yucky, stained with God only knew what. And last night Chay gave him a puppy.

The night of their "episode," he had reluctantly agreed to forget the possibility of their relationship not working. In turn, Chay had declared it a done deal; they were a couple. So now Chay was back to wooing—which was silly, considering the man himself said this wasn't a trial relationship but the real thing—and Keaton in turn was wooing Chay. Chay thought it would help them get to know each other and make Keaton less "skittish." It was almost like a real beginning of a relationship, like actual dating, but they knew the outcome already, or he hoped he did anyway.

Keaton still had his doubts, but he was dealing with them. He truly loved being around Chay, and he really, really liked him. Okay, maybe it was more than like. Which bothered him, because Chay could easily become everything to him. Hell, he was halfway there already, but Keaton was trying not to dwell on it. He was following Chay's example and going with it. He didn't doubt Chay's sincerity so much as he doubted outside factors. One thing he'd learned, Chay was honest to a fault, even when it came to telling him his shoes were ugly—which he did the other day—so if the man said he was sticking around, well, Keaton was pretty sure he meant it.

The puppy gave another sharp tug just as the knock came at the door. "It's open, Chay."

The door opened, and Chay's dark head popped in, looking around. Trying to find the puppy, Keaton presumed.

"He's over here." He pointed at the dog tugging on his jeans.

Chay grinned and stepped through the doorway. "Hi, Bit."

The puppy let go of Keaton's pants, bounced across the floor to Chay, and immediately grabbed the leg of his scrub pants, growling and shaking his head like a possessed demon.

Chay laughed and made his way, with great difficulty—due to the tugging, growling pest at his feet—to Keaton. "Does he have a name yet?" He gave Keaton a quick peck on the lips.

Keaton smiled and kissed back. It still amazed him that Chay felt comfortable with him. Most men would be having a major identity crisis in the same situation, but not Chay. Chay was happy as a pig in shit. The man seemed so comfortable in his own skin it was almost disgusting. "Pita."

Chay blinked. "Peta, as in the 'people for the ethical treatment of animals'?"

"Nope. Pita, as in 'pain in the ass.'"

Chay chuckled and peeked down at Pita, shaking his leg a little, playing tug-of-war. "It fits." Chay pulled out a chair and sat down. "Did he keep you up all night?"

"He would have, but I got smart and put him in bed with me."

"You're brave. He didn't pee in the bed?"

"Nah, we had a nice long talk about what happens to puppies who *go* in the house."

Chay smiled and ducked his head under the table. The growling had stopped. Was that the smell of…? "Are you sure he speaks English? 'Cause he just *went* in the house."

"Oh damn." He'd been taking Pita out every hour. Keaton looked at the clock. Shit, he'd gotten wrapped up in reading the Apache book Chay had given him, and he'd forgotten to take the pest outside. He glanced down at Pita and pointed. "Bad dog." He grabbed the pup by the scruff of his neck, showed him the puddle, said, "No," rather forcefully and took him outside.

Pita had done all his business inside, because once Keaton set him down outside, the little pest took off, pouncing after a grasshopper. Keaton shook his head.

He smelled Chay before he heard the door close. Two hands landed on his shoulders and began kneading. "I cleaned up the puddle."

"Thank you."

"Welcome. We have to go meet with John, my pack leader, in about an hour." Chay bent and kissed the back of his neck, nipping before he straightened.

That was nice. Keaton shivered at the sensation. And damn if his cock didn't stand straight up. Well, not straight up—it was sort of to the side. He had the urge to reach down and adjust. He shifted a little, wiggling side to side. It didn't help.

Chay chuckled. "What are you doing?" He placed another kiss on Keaton's neck.

"Cut that out."

"Why?" Chay breathed the word across the bare skin above his shirt collar.

Not fair. Keaton shivered again. "You're giving me a boner."

Chay squeezed his shoulders, his thumbs digging in. "Is that a bad thing?"

Oh, really, really not fair. He dropped his head forward, relaxing into the massage. "It is when we have an appointment to keep."

"I haven't touched you since the other night."

Was that a pout? Keaton's cock twitched. Damn, Chay was something else. The man sounded disappointed. He smiled, remembering the other night. "Since the 'episode'?"

"Exactly. And stop laughing at my terminology." Chay's fingers dug in harder, reprimanding.

"I'm not." He tilted his head side to side, then glanced up to check on Pita.

"Yes, you are. I can hear it in your voice." He kissed the side of Keaton's neck. "I'd called it a temper tantrum, but you seemed to object to that."

He snorted. "I wasn't throwing a temper tantrum."

"Whatever you say, Bit."

He turned to face Chay, chuckling, making his glasses slide down. "That's right, don't forget that. Whatever I say goes, and we'll get along great."

Chay smiled, his eyes twinkling. He pushed Keaton's glasses back up his nose before settling his hands on Keaton's hips. "You look sexy in glasses."

"I look like the nerd that I am."

"No, you look smart. It's hot." He ran the backs of his fingers down Keaton's cheek. "You only need them for reading?"

"Uh-huh. I'm farsighted." Keaton leaned into the touch.

Chay caressed his neck, staring at Keaton's lips. "No problems seeing in wolf form?"

Keaton shook his head. Damn, the smell of arousal poured off Chay. He knew if he looked down, Chay would be every bit as hard as he was. It made his head swim. He loved how Chay always touched him.

What had Chay asked? Oh yeah. "No, Dr. Winston, I have perfect vision in wolf form."

"Yeah, that makes sense. Lupine eyes and human eyes are different." Chay's head dipped toward his, those brown eyes still zeroed in on his lips.

Keaton rose up on tiptoe, waiting for those sensual lips. A car horn honked in the distance, jerking him out of his daze. They were outside. Geez. This man made him lose his head. Chay might not care what people thought of him, but Keaton did. He did not want Chay to end up being an outcast. He stepped back.

Chay blinked and met his gaze. "Spend the weekend at my house."

Whoa. He should refuse, he knew he should, but he didn't want to. He bit his bottom lip.

"You want to. I can see it in your eyes. Geez, Bit, you're as hard as I am. I can see it, smell it. Just agree." He dragged his thumb over Keaton's bottom lip, freeing it from his teeth.

Chay swore he knew what he was getting into. "I want to. But...."

"But what? You're not still caught up in the whole gay, not-gay thing, are you?"

Not so much, but he feared Chay being ostracized for loving him. Okay, in the back of his mind there was the fear that Chay would wake up one day and decide he didn't want him anymore. "I dated this guy in college. He was straight; well, he claimed to be, anyway. He said it was me, something about me." He shrugged. "I don't know. He was a wolf too. Even though I didn't feel anything, I tried to convince myself he was my mate and that's why he was so drawn to me. After meeting you, I know it was a line of crap. When his friends found out he was seeing me, he tried to deny I was his boyfriend. I found out later that he'd never even broken up with his girlfriend. I was some sort of experiment or some sort of sexual exploration for him. I got tired of it."

Chay kissed him right there out in public, in front of his apartment where anyone could see. It was a soft, gentle kiss, tender.

Keaton sighed into Chay's open mouth. He should pull back... for Chay's sake... but it was too nice. His cock throbbed, getting more and more uncomfortable. He quickly decided to pull back for his *own* sake.

Chay let him. "I'm not like that, Bit. I'm sorry you got hurt, but I'm here for the long haul. You're stuck with me. This isn't some sort of sexual identity crisis for me. You are *my* mate. *Mine.* You belong to me and I belong to you. And quite frankly, even if you didn't, I think I'd want you."

Whoa. Keaton felt like the ground moved out from underneath him. He was speechless, but it was a good speechless. He knew Chay told the truth. It was still hard to believe, but he did believe it. Keaton grinned.

Chay grinned back. "Does that mean you'll spend the weekend with me?"

He nodded. "Yeah, I will. Let me get some clothes and Pita's bowls and dog food. We can go meet your pack leader, and I'm all yours until Sunday night."

"I like the sound of that. But you don't need to get anything for Pita. I bought him stuff for my house too."

Oh boy. That smacked of commitment.

Keaton launched himself at Chay, forcing the man to catch him. He kissed Chay breathless. He didn't even realize Chay held him off the ground until Chay set him on his feet and pulled back.

Chay started laughing and glanced at his feet.

Keaton heard the growling and saw the slight sway Chay made and looked down.

Pita had a hold of Chay's scrub pants again, growling and shaking his head. The pup's tail was going ninety to nothing.

When they drove up to John Carter's house, the place was surrounded by cars. It looked like a pack meeting. That was odd. Chay racked his brain, trying to recall a reason the whole pack would be here but couldn't think of any.

"Hey, isn't that your dad?" Bit started waving to someone.

Sure enough, it was his dad, standing out in the yard with a couple of other pack members. His father waved at them. "Yeah." Chay waved back and parked his truck by the curb several yards from the pack leader's house.

"Uh, Chay?"

"Huh?"

"Why are there so many people here?"

"I have no clue. I thought we were only going to introduce you to John. Normally that's how things work. You meet the pack alpha, then you run with the pack for a couple of full moons, then you're either admitted to the pack or not."

"Yeah, that's how it works in my pack too."

"Well, whatever it is, it's not bad. My dad would've warned me. You ready?"

Bit nodded, scooped Pita up from between them and into his arms. "Yeah, let's go."

They got out of the truck, and his dad met them. "Hey, boys. What have you got there, Keaton?"

Bit smiled and held the puppy up. "This is Pita."

Joe scratched the puppy's head. "Hey there, little fella."

"I can see where Chay got his love of animals." Bit winked at Chay.

Oh man! His Little Bit was flirting with him. Chay grinned, ignored the fluttering in his stomach, and clapped his dad on the shoulder. "What's going on? Why is everyone here?"

Joe looked up from petting Pita. "Well, to welcome Keaton into the pack of course."

What? "But, Dad, Keaton hasn't even met John yet." Chay glanced over at Bit.

Bit shrugged, seeming as puzzled as Chay felt.

Joe took Pita out of Bit's arms and smiled. "John is waiting for the two of you in the kitchen. I'll watch Pita and go out back to grab a hamburger. I'll see the two of you when you're done." He turned and walked off. Immediately several cubs who'd accompanied their fathers to the meeting, rushed at him, wanting to pet the golden retriever.

Okay, something strange was going on. Why would John admit Keaton to the pack without meeting him first? Granted, Chay's father was one of the pack betas, but John had never let someone in without meeting them first. Chay frowned. Unless.... Did they know Keaton was his mate?

"What? You look like something is bothering you." Bit touched his arm.

Chay looked at him and shook his head. "Nothing. Come on, let's go meet John so we can eat. Smells like they're grilling burgers."

Bit raised a brow at him but didn't question him further.

They found John and his wife, Mary, in the kitchen, gathering up condiments, plastic utensils, and paper plates. John came to them as soon as they entered, his brown eyes crinkling at the corners as he smiled. "Chayton."

"John."

The pack alpha's eyes widened when he meet Keaton's gaze.

Keaton immediately turned his head, baring his throat in a show of respect.

John frowned and cocked his head, a lock of his short salt-and-pepper hair falling into his eyes. "Why in the world aren't you leader of your own pack?"

Bit raised his head and met John's gaze. "I've no desire to lead. I'm actually next in line for the position in my birth pack, but I have no intention of taking the job."

Lead? Chay frowned. What had he missed?

John nodded and extended his hand to Bit. "John Carter."

Bit greeted him with a handshake. "Keaton Reynolds. Nice to meet you, sir."

"It's nice to meet you too, Keaton. Joe has had nothing but nice things to say about you. He said you were powerful, but...." He whistled. "You don't want to run your own pack? I don't think I've ever met a wolf who has three forms who wasn't a pack leader."

Three forms? Bit had three forms? Chay stared at Bit like he'd never seen him before. How had he not realized that? It was extremely rare to find a wolf that had three forms. All wolves could shift from human to wolf, but a few could also shift into a half-wolf, half-man form.

John chuckled. "You look shocked, Chayton. Didn't you know? Can't you feel the energy coming off of him?"

Chay shook his head. He was too busy trying to control his errant cock when Keaton was around. The only energy he felt was due to their mate bond.

"Ahh, interesting. Your senses are confused because of who he is to you."

Bit's gaze shot to his.

His shot to Bit.

What did that mean? How did John know Keaton was his mate? Before he could ask, John patted Bit's shoulder and smiled.

"I have to admit, I'm a little leery of your power, but you can sense that already, can't you?"

Keaton nodded. "Yes, sir. I'm used to it."

John smiled, the wrinkles at the corners of his eyes becoming more pronounced. "I bet you are. Because of Chay, I'm going to do something I don't usually do." He extended his hand toward Keaton again. "Welcome to the pack, Keaton."

Keaton shook John's hand again. "Thank you."

"Come, let me introduce you to my wife, Mary, and then I'll take you outside so you can meet the pack. Then we can all eat. It's nice outside. We decided to set up tables out back. I figured this may be the last nice day we have this autumn. Don't you agree, Chay?"

"Yes, sir. It is nice."

John led Keaton over to Mary while Chay stood there, shell-shocked. How had John known about them? Did his dad somehow guess? And how in the hell had he not realized Bit was so powerful? Chay had never met a wolf with all three forms before, but he was sure he'd recognize it if he had. He could tell when a wolf was an alpha wolf or not, and he hadn't even realized Bit was that dominant. It was clear he wasn't an omega wolf, but Chay hadn't thought Bit was even more of an alpha than he and his dad.

"Chay? Would you mind helping me carry this stuff out?"

Chay looked up at Mary and blinked. When had Keaton and John left the room? "Sure, Mary." He grabbed the ice chest she indicated and opened the door, allowing her to pass with the plates and a picnic basket full of condiments.

"I like your friend, Chay. He's very polite. He looks very young, though. Such a pretty boy."

Chay grinned. Yeah, Bit was pretty all right. Prettiest man he'd ever seen, with that smooth pale complexion, those big blue eyes.... Oh damn, his cock stirred. "Yes, he is." He wasn't sure which statement he responded to, but Mary didn't question it, and he didn't bother clarifying.

After helping Mary set up, Chay was bombarded by questions about Keaton from pack members. Everyone wanted to know where he was from and why he wasn't a pack leader. And the most frequent question was about his age. Chay decided not to tell Bit about that, knowing he wouldn't be amused.

"Chay."

Chay turned to find his father, John Carter, and Frank Red Hawk standing behind him. "Yes?"

John motioned him over. "Chay, I talked to Keaton about the shooting the other night, and he seems to agree with Frank that it was poachers. What do you think?"

"Well, we haven't had poachers on pack land or in the reservation in years, but I don't see any evidence that says it's not poachers."

His father nodded. "That's what I said."

John dipped his head. "Given that Keaton's new here and no one has a reason to want him dead, I think that is the most logical conclusion too. We need to keep an eye out, though, just in case. Chay, you let us know if you get any more animals with gunshot wounds."

"Yes, sir. I will."

"And, Frank, you'll keep us updated from your end as well?"

"Sure will."

"Good, good. I'm going to go find my mate." John waved and left, leaving him with his father and Frank.

Frank smiled. "It looks like our little white wolf is grown after all. A college professor, huh? Nice fellow. When John introduced us, I apologized to him for tranqing him."

Chay grinned. Yeah, his mate was a nice fellow when you got to know him. It made Chay feel good that others could see that too. "Yeah, he teaches Ancient Civ. Beware. He has quite an interest in the Apache. He's relentless with his questions."

Frank laughed. "I know. John told him my brother was tribal chief when he introduced us. Bobby came to my rescue. Said they met the other night at a poker game." Frank's stomach growled, making him chuckle. "I guess that's my cue. I'm going to go get myself a burger. Talk to you gentlemen later."

"Later, Frank," his dad called out.

Chay waved.

His dad smiled. "Keaton seems to fit in well. John and I took him around and introduced him to everyone."

Chay nodded. "Where is he?"

"Last I saw, he was eating a burger and talking to Bobby."

"Dad, what's going on? Why did John allow Keaton into the pack so quickly? I'm not complaining, but—"

"Joe." A couple of his dad's friends came up and started talking to him. Chay's presence was soon forgotten.

Chay sighed and shook his head. Oh, well, he'd find out later. It wasn't like he didn't know where to reach his dad. He went in search of food, then Bit. He was walking around, eating a burger and drinking a Coke, when he found his missing mate. He heard Pita before he spotted Bit.

Bit rolled around in the grass playing with Pita and four little boys. It was the cutest thing. The boys, Bit, and the puppy were all in a pile, laughing and tickling one another.

God, the man was sweet. He wondered if Bit had any idea how appealing he was when he laughed. Chay had the urge to go join the fun, but figured people might not appreciate him rolling around on the ground, kissing the life out of Bit with their cubs present.

He'd known Bit didn't feel comfortable among people his age. He should have known Bit would get along well with children.

Pita saw Chay first. The pup bounced over and grabbed Chay's pants, growling and tugging.

Chay laughed, reached down, and petted the pest.

Smiling, Bit caught Chay's gaze, his eyes shining. "Hey." He pushed himself up and jogged over to Chay, leaving the kids playing together behind him. "They rescued me."

"Rescued you?"

Bit leaned in and whispered, "Yeah, look to your left."

Chay looked and noticed three of the pack members' teenage daughters, giggling and staring at Keaton. Chay threw his head back and laughed. Apparently, Bit wasn't comfortable around women either.

Chapter Seven

What a strange evening. Nice, but strange nonetheless.

Keaton adjusted the water temperature in the shower and started undressing. He smelled like a dog from rolling around in the grass. He'd forgotten how much fun it was to play with the cubs. In his birth pack, he'd always gotten along better with the cubs than he had the adults.

Now he was a member of Chay's pack. Unlike his birth pack, everyone had been friendly. He'd actually felt welcome. The big question was would he still feel that way after his new pack found out about his sexual orientation? Strangely, judging from this evening, he thought he might.

He strongly suspected John Carter knew he was Chay's mate. The man never came right out and said anything, but he hinted at it. Keaton had kept quiet; he wasn't about to spill the beans. It was up to Chay when, where, and who to tell about their relationship. Although, if he wasn't mistaken, Joe Winston knew too, but again he wasn't positive.

"Hey, Bit—"

A sharp intake of breath, then the scent of arousal filled the bathroom. He suppressed the urge to smile and finished pulling off his underwear before turning around. "Yes?"

Chay stood there, staring, his mouth ajar. "Damn, just... damn."

The heat in Chay's gaze made Keaton a tad bit self-conscious, but he quickly pushed it aside in favor of checking Chay out. He was shirtless and barefooted, wearing only his blue scrub pants. The man's chest was a work of art. Nicely defined muscles without being bulky. There wasn't a hair in sight on that beautifully tanned chest or those toned abs. *Oh boy.* His very impressive erection was clearly evident in those loose pants. *Wow.* That was for him. It had to be. Keaton's own cock started to fill.

Chay still stood in the doorway, looking him over, his eyes wide, his mouth turned up at the corner in a seductive grin.

Keaton swallowed. How could this beautiful man stand there and stare at him like he was some sort of Adonis or something? He didn't get it. What could Chay possibly see in him? He was... well, scrawny was the best word for it. He didn't have the nice chiseled body Chay had. He was short and thin and....

"Stop that. I can see what you are thinking, and it's not true. You are a fine-looking man, Bit." Chay walked forward and grabbed Keaton's waist. He covered Keaton's lips and pulled his hips against his own, jarring the protest out of Keaton.

Instead he moaned, opening up and letting Chay's tongue inside. Chay's chest felt warm against him, firm. He flattened his palms against Chay's pecs, feeling the accelerated heartbeat and choppy breathing. Damn, Chay knocked him off-balance. If he didn't calm down, he'd be begging the man to fuck him. He pulled back and looked up into amber wolf eyes. "Y-y-you wanted something?"

Chay's smile was downright feral. "Is that a trick question?"

"Huh?"

"Nothing. I actually came to see if I could take a shower with you." Chay didn't wait for an answer. He pressed his cotton-clad erection against Keaton's, moving his hips side to side.

That was nice. Keaton shut his eyes and pressed back. Warm lips closed over his shoulder, followed by the sting of teeth. He loved the dominant side of Chay. The man might not have experience with the same sex, but damn, he was a whirlwind in all things sexual. He certainly knew how to stimulate his partner. Keaton's stomach muscles clenched and every hair on his body stood up as goose bumps covered him from head to toe. *Ooh. Was that a lick?* He tilted his neck to the side, giving Chay better access.

Chay nibbled up his neck, then pulled back. A finger trailed across his nose.

What the...? Why did he stop? He blinked his eyes open to find Chay studying his face, a small serene smile on his lips.

"So pretty." The finger traced the bridge of his nose again, and Chay's gaze followed it. "I love these freckles."

Keaton shook his head. "I'm not pretty."

"Yes, you are. My pretty Little Bit." Chay kissed him on the nose.

He rolled his eyes. *Good Lord.* "You do realize I'm not a woman, right?"

Chay chuckled. "Oh, yeah." He grabbed Keaton's prick. "It's obvious."

Keaton sucked in a breath.

"Obvious in a *big* way." He leaned away, looking down at Keaton's cock. He squeezed and stroked, his eyes glued to the action.

The heat and excitement radiating off Chay made his toes actually curl. "Oh." Fuck, it was sexy to be wanted. His prick twitched in Chay's hand.

"Mmm. You like that, Bit?" His breath feathered across Keaton's cheek.

Keaton shivered and nodded. What was there not to like? *Like* was way too mild of a word. He bucked into Chay's hand, trying to show him how good it felt.

Chay let go abruptly and stepped back. He grinned at Keaton and reached to untie his scrubs.

Keaton whimpered at the loss of contact but quickly recovered when Chay pulled his scrubs and boxer shorts off. Keaton was actually speechless. He'd seen Chay's dick the other night, tasted it even. But now he got a really good look. It was nice and thick, about the size of his own, but darker, redder. There was hardly any hair, just a patch over his cock. Even his legs had very little hair. And, man, were they nice legs. The man looked simply beautiful.

Chay caught his hand and tugged him toward the shower. "Come on, baby. Let's get in." He opened the glass door and pulled Keaton in with him.

Damn, the man had a great ass, with dints in the sides, firmly muscled, rou—*What?* "Baby?"

Chay closed the door and shoved him up against the tiled wall. "Yeah, Bit, *my* baby. My *pretty* baby."

Before Keaton could correct him or complain about the cold tiles, Chay grabbed his ass with both hands and drew him up.

Keaton clutched his shoulders.

Chay took his mouth in a starving kiss.

Keaton's mind blanked out. He couldn't care less about Chay calling him pretty or little or baby. His whole body came alive. His back pressed up against the cool white tile, his front pressed against hot Chay, and the warm water poured down over them as Chay's mouth devoured his.

Chay's cock slid beside his as his hips rocked.

Keaton pushed back, rubbing his prick against Chay's. His dick was so hard, every little sensation was magnified. He gasped into Chay's mouth, his dick throbbing with the pleasure.

Chay broke their kiss, blinking the water out of his eyes. "Fuck, Bit. That feels good." He grabbed his cock and Keaton's in one big hand. Chay stroked as he thrust his hips against Keaton's.

Keaton gasped and held on to Chay's neck, trying to support some of his weight. He moved his hips, helping as best he could.

Chay bit his bottom lip, his canine teeth longer than usual, as he stared into Keaton's eyes. Chay's eyes were amber, the irises bigger than normal. Dark strands of wet shoulder-length hair stuck to the side of his lean face and high cheekbones.

Keaton stared, awed by the sheer beauty of his face, as Chay's eyebrows furrowed and his neck strained. Keaton's orgasm drew so close, he could barely concentrate on moving. His breath came in pants. His fingers and toes clenched, and his back stiffened. His coordination sucked. He was too turned-on—his thought process had taken a hike. All he knew was the need to come.

Fortunately, Chay didn't seem to have the same problem. Chay held them together, his hips and hand moving faster. "Oh yeah, baby, that's it. Come with me." Chay's back arched, and he groaned, his eyes squeezing shut. Then his body tightened, and heat spurted across Keaton's cock and stomach.

The smell of semen and Chay's plea pushed him right over the edge. His balls pulled tight, and the electric feel of orgasm raced up his spine, making him rigid. "Chay!"

He came so hard, it took several minutes for his mind to start working again.

Chay leaned on him, pressing him between his big body and the wall, still pumping their cocks slowly until they were both only semierect.

Chay chuckled against his neck, and a hand came up and caressed his cheek. After a kiss to his neck, Chay stood up straight, still holding on to him. "Can you stand?"

Keaton grinned stupidly. He knew he looked like a goober, but he couldn't help it. Chay had zapped the energy right out of him. He would have asked if *that* was a trick question, but he wasn't sure he remembered how to talk, hence he only nodded.

Chay let go of him long enough to grab the shower gel and the mesh sponge, and then he came back and washed him.

Keaton sighed and closed his eyes, relaxing into Chay's ministrations. He should probably protest, but he didn't feel like it. Chay could do whatever the hell he wanted to him, and he didn't care. He felt too good. Too relaxed.

He was washed and rinsed, and then there were fingers in his hair massaging shampoo into his scalp. "Ahh...." That was nice.

Chay lathered his hair and kissed Keaton's forehead.

He tilted his head up, offering his lips, puckering.

Chay chuckled again, dropped a chaste kiss against his mouth, and moved him up against the tile. *Cold.*

"Think you can stay right here without falling over while I wash?"

Keaton leaned on the wall and nodded.

A pair of lips pressed against his forehead. "Pretty baby."

He opened his eyes, looking into Chay's. Chay's eyes were once again brown, human. Chay smiled and raised an eyebrow. *Dickhead.*

Keaton shrugged and closed his eyes again. Life was good. He'd just had a mind-numbing orgasm. His mate was physically attracted to him, even though he was a guy. He had a new pack and a new puppy. Yup, life was good. Chay could call him whatever he wanted.

Chay idly combed through Keaton's hair. "Keaton?"

The scalp massage felt so good, Keaton was almost asleep, but Chay must have something on his mind if he was calling him *Keaton* instead of *Bit.* "Huh?" Keaton raised his head off Chay's chest and looked at him. "What's up?"

"How come I didn't know you have three forms?"

Uh-oh! Was Chay mad about it? "I'm sorry. I didn't think it was that big a deal. It's not like I actually use my third form."

"Sorry? Why are you sorry?"

"You're upset?"

"What? No, I'm not upset. Just confused. I can't believe I didn't realize how powerful you are. You don't exactly act like some major badass around me. Why do you play it down? Hell, you play it down so damn well, I didn't even realize it."

"I hate fighting. And I'm not a badass."

Chay grinned and shook his head. "You're a lover not a fighter, huh?"

Oh yeah, especially where Chay was concerned. He chuckled. "Something like that."

"You said you were next in line for leader of your birth pack. How'd you end up being next in line anyway? Don't you have to fight for the position?"

Keaton moved to Chay's side, resting his head on his arm so he could see Chay's face more easily. "I sort of did fight, in a roundabout way. When I came out, my older brother and his friends took exception to having a queer in the pack. They jumped me at a pack meeting on one of my breaks from college."

Chay's eyes widened. He turned to his side, facing Keaton, resting his head on his arm too. "Damn. Your own brother?"

"Yeah." It had really hurt at the time, but he'd long since written off his family.

"How old were you?"

"Sixteen."

"How many jumped you?"

"Five, including my brother."

"Holy shit, Keaton. You beat all of them?"

He nodded. "Yup. I took all of them down. After that...." He shrugged. "No one messed with me. The pack realized I was stronger than my brother and sort of assumed I'd be the next pack alpha after my dad."

"Your brother doesn't have three forms?"

Keaton shook his head. "My dad does, though."

"Then why did you leave? It sounds like you had it made. You obviously earned the respect of your pack."

He'd thought so too at the time. He'd even thought his father was proud of him. "My parents thought I was rebelling when I told them I was gay. I graduated high school at fifteen and was going into my first year of college. I guess they thought I'd outgrow it. I didn't. I made the mistake of bringing my college boyfriend home with me the spring break I was studying for my doctorate. My parents freaked. They pretty much disowned me, or would have if I'd stuck around. My father tried to use my trust fund against me. I wadded up the account info from the trust fund that he dangled in front of me and threw it in his face. I left my car there, and my boyfriend and I used what money we had on us to get a bus back to school. I got a job when I got there and took out a student loan, and that was that. I proved I didn't need my parents or their money. The really sad part was, I broke up with my boyfriend three days afterward."

"Oh, baby." Chay hugged him, squeezing him tight.

Damn, that was nice. The memory itself didn't get to him anymore, but Chay's obvious concern for his feelings did. For that he decided he wasn't going to smack Chay for calling him baby. He buried his face in Chay's neck, hugging him. He kissed Chay's chin and met his gaze. "It's all right. I'm over it."

"It doesn't matter. You're mine now, and I'm not giving you back. It's their loss."

Damn. Chay was going to go to his head if he kept talking like that. What in the world had he done to deserve this man? And how in the hell had he even considered giving him up?

A loud panicked whimpering rent the air. Then toenails clicked in a frenzied rush across the room.

Chay chuckled. "Your puppy is awake."

"I noticed." Keaton leaned over the edge of the bed. Pita stood on his hind legs with his front paws on the side of the mattress, hopping up and down, trying to jump onto the bed.

As soon as Pita saw him, the whimpering turned to barks.

Chay threw the covers off and got up. He grabbed a pair of boxers and headed for the door, whistling. "Come on, pest. If you are sleeping in my bed, you're going outside first."

The puppy stopped barking and bounced over to Chay.

Keaton couldn't help but grin as Chay scooped Pita up, receiving puppy kisses on the chin, and left the room, laughing. *What a man.* Keaton couldn't think of any other man who'd get out of bed to take a puppy—that wasn't his—outside. Of course he didn't know any other vets either. God, you just had to love a man who loved animals.

The two of them came back in no time. Chay set Pita on top of the covers and crawled underneath them. He pulled Keaton against his side and kissed the top of his head. "Bit?"

"Yeah?"

"Move in with me."

Keaton should say no. It was way too soon. Chay was going to have to explain their relationship to his family and friends if he moved in. It was a really bad idea. "Okay."

Chay kissed his forehead again. "Thank you for not arguing."

"I should."

"No, you shouldn't. When are you going to learn I know best?"

Keaton snorted. "As soon as you learn my name isn't Bit, Baby, Pretty Baby, or any of the other ridiculous things you call me."

Chay woke up harder than a rock. Which wasn't all that unusual. He'd had morning wood every morning he could remember since he was about fourteen. What *was* unusual was the nice warm body snuggled up against him.

Bit lay on his side facing him. He had one leg thrown over Chay's, and his arms were wrapped around one of Chay's arms. His face was buried against Chay's shoulder. Those pretty blond curls looked pale against Chay's dark skin. Chay turned onto his side and ran his fingers through the soft locks.

Keaton sighed in his sleep, leaning into the touch. Damn, he was cute. His sweet little turned-up nose wrinkled slightly and his eyelashes fluttered, but he didn't wake. Chay couldn't remember ever waking up with such an appealing bed partner. Bit might deny it, but he *was* pretty; prettier than any woman Chay'd ever dated. He had such an angelic look about him. He wasn't feminine exactly, but he wasn't the poster boy for masculinity either, not that Chay'd ever tell Bit that.

He kissed the freckles on the bridge of Bit's nose, and Bit blinked up at him and gave him a lazy grin before closing his eyes again. Taking that as encouragement, Chay slipped his hand down under the covers. He caressed Bit's side and his hip, then slid his hand around looking for.... *Oh yeah, there it is, nice and hard.*

Bit rolled over onto his back, his legs spreading. His eyes remained shut but the grin got bigger.

Chay smiled and took advantage of the opportunity. He pulled the covers back and explored, taking his time to really look at his mate.

Bit's arm muscles were firm, but not distinct. He was slender with a hint of definition in his pecs and a tad more in his abs. Like Chay, Keaton didn't have any excess body hair. His skin was fascinating, different from Chay's own skin color. He was very pale. If he had a tan, Chay couldn't see it. He could even see faint traces of blue veins in places.

Bit's shoulders were slightly wider than his narrow hips. And his hip bones were very prominent. It was sexy actually. Hell, everything about Keaton appealed to him. Chay was completely mesmerized by him. It was kind of strange, really. He had always liked his women more on the voluptuous side. Skinny had never been his thing, but given the choice now, he'd take Bit over anyone, hands down.

The only place on Bit that wasn't slim and small in size was his cock. It was a thing of beauty, thick and hard. Chay still wasn't sure whether that was good or bad, but he needed to know how Bit tasted, how Bit would feel in his mouth... in his ass. And *boy* did he want to feel Keaton's snug hole wrapped around his prick.

Chay's belly clenched at the thought. He couldn't wait to fuck Bit. Bit was so responsive. He'd look absolutely gorgeous riding Chay's cock. He shivered. Just watching the man come was a treat. He'd always liked anal sex. That couldn't be any different with a man than a woman... could it? Well, other than the extra parts he had to be careful of and not squish. Mm-mm.... His dick throbbed at the image of Keaton writhing in pleasure beneath him.

He ran his hand down the inside of Keaton's thigh to his knee, feeling the baby soft skin lightly furred with platinum hairs. Bit spread his legs farther, giving Chay an excellent view of his tightly drawn balls. Chay traced the same path back up and stroked his knuckles over Bit's testicles. They drew up more at the touch and Bit squirmed a tad.

Chay did it again, and again Keaton tried to squirm out of reach. Chay grinned. He'd found a ticklish spot. This was fun. He liked being able to explore without Bit arguing with him, telling him he was straight and shouldn't want to do that. He'd have to do that later, just to watch Bit sputter and look all shocked. He was cute when he got flustered.

Chay scooted down, nudging Bit's legs wider with his shoulders. Since meeting his mate, he'd begun wondering what it felt like to suck dick. He shrugged. Only one way to find out. He leaned forward and ran his tongue up Bit's balls.

Keaton gasped.

He did it again and closed his mouth over them, sucking lightly, because he'd always liked that done to him.

Bit grunted.

Chay licked his way up Bit's shaft and flicked his tongue over and around the head. It was smooth and hot. It felt nice against his lips. He took his time, running his lips up and down, licking, tasting, exploring. Finally he enveloped Bit's prick in his hand and held it up for his mouth. He wrapped his lips around the head, then slid his mouth up. Now that really felt kind of neat on his tongue. He knew how damned good it felt on the receiving end.

"Holy fucking shit!"

He glanced up into big, stunned blue eyes and chuckled, his lips still wrapped around the head of Bit's cock.

Keaton moaned and dropped his head back to the bed. "Oh God."

Chay wet his lips and slid his mouth farther down, sucking on the way up. Bit's thighs tensed, so he did it again. The whole time he watched his mate.

Bit's hands fisted in the sheets, his whole body stiff. If Chay didn't know better, he'd have thought Bit was in pain.

"Chay, you don't have to do—"

Chay went farther down this time, almost all the way. He would have, but his reflexes kicked in and it was either back off or gag, so he pulled back.

"Oh my God. Do that again."

He squelched the urge to laugh and did it again and again and again. He wasn't sure what to do, so he did what he liked done to him. When he had Bit nice and slick with his saliva, he started using his hand too, working it up and down, squeezing a little.

Bit's head started thrashing back and forth on the mattress. His fingers white-knuckled the bottom sheet. He writhed and moaned, making Chay feel like a king.

He could feel every moan Keaton made. Could hear Bit's heartbeat, his rapid breathing. Chay became more and more aroused by the minute. Watching Keaton was such a turn-on, Chay ached. His prick leaked against the bed and he moved his own hips, trying to get relief.

"Chay, I... I... gonna come. I... I...." Keaton's head came off the bed again, his eyes pleading.

Chay didn't relent; he sucked harder. He wanted Bit to come. He needed to know what his mate tasted like.

It didn't take long. Keaton arched his back and a ragged groan tore from his lips as he spilled himself down Chay's throat.

The salty taste washed over Chay's tongue, surprising him. But he didn't stop. He continued to work Bit's prick, taking all he had. He didn't stop until Bit relaxed back onto the bed. By then he was too damned needy. He let go of the still semierect dick in his mouth and crawled up Bit's body, straddling his hips. He grabbed his own cock and pumped. For some strange reason, he had this insatiable need to come on Bit, to mark him as his own. He had no idea where such a primal thought came from, but it made him even hotter.

Keaton's eyes shot open, and he moaned and reached out to Chay.

Chay lost it. His back arched. He managed to stroke himself once more, and then he came. He stared into Bit's eyes. Semen splashed over Chay's hand and Bit's stomach. Chay suppressed the urge to rub it in and dropped forward, one hand still wrapped around his cock, the other supporting himself beside Bit's head. He took a deep breath and closed his eyes. *Fuck.* Waking up with this man in his bed every day was going to kill him.

But what a way to go.

His breath finally evened out. Keaton pulled at him, making him lie down, half on top of Bit, half on the bed.

Bit kissed his jaw.

He wasn't sure, but he thought he heard, "Thank you, Chay." He was about to tell Bit it was his pleasure when....

"Uh, Bit."

"Yeah."

"Your dog is chewing on my big toe."

Chapter Eight

Keaton finished making the bed, turned out the light, and left the bedroom. He didn't mind cleaning. It had never been his favorite thing, but if it kept Chay happy.... Chay was a bit of a neat freak.

Keaton was particular about how his laundry was done, so other than cooking, the living arrangements had been fairly smooth sailing.

He'd moved in a week after Chay asked him. It hadn't been that big a deal because he'd only signed a three-month lease and all the furniture had been rented with the apartment. He wasn't out much money—except for the two months' rent left on the apartment—and moving had been pretty simple.

The bad news was he and Chay both hated to cook. So they ended up waiting around until both of them were starving to death before either would go make something for dinner. So far, dinner consisted of cold cuts, ordering pizza, or eating leftover pizza from the night before.

He was trying to talk Chay into taking a cooking class, because Keaton hated to cook, but thus far Chay was still holding out. The man had put the pizza place on speed dial in response to Keaton's suggestion; he claimed he cooked enough at the firehouse. Keaton wondered how hard it would be to teach the dog to cook. The pup *was* smart; he was housebroken already. If they could just get the beast to sleep in his bed instead of theirs....

Oooh, bed. He liked bedtime. They hadn't actually had intercourse, as in *intercourse*, yet. They kept getting distracted and too aroused to get to that point, but they sure had done a lot of dry humping and jerking off.

Keaton shivered and bent to get a scoop of laundry detergent. Thinking about Chay and sex made him hard. He dumped the cup of detergent into the washing machine and closed the lid. He grinned, wondering where Chay was and how much time they had before they were supposed to leave. Tonight was their first full moon together. Keaton couldn't wait to go hunting with his mate.

A warm set of lips settled on the back of his neck and two arms engulfed him. One wrapped around his chest, pulling him back against a hard muscular chest, and the other hand cupped his balls.

Oh, he'd found Chay. Or had Chay found him? He didn't care which. "I was just wondering where you were." He set the timer on the washing machine and leaned back into his mate.

"Umph." Chay nibbled his way down Keaton's shoulder.

Goose bumps raced up his arms. "Did you finish putting the doggy door in?"

"Ummm...." The hand around his chest slid up under his shirt and pinched his nipple.

Keaton squealed. It was quite undignified, but he couldn't help it. His nipples were sensitive. Chay had found that out by accident the other night and had been playing with them ever since.

The hand fondling his balls slipped up to rub his erection through his jeans, pressing him closer to his lover. His cock got even harder.

Chay's prick was like a brand against the small of his back. God, he loved knowing Chay got hard for him.

Chay's hair fell over Keaton's shoulder as he nuzzled his face into the crook of Keaton's neck, licking and nibbling. It tickled but felt good too. Keaton tried to reach up behind him and wrap his hands around Chay's neck, but Chay drew back, turning him around to face him.

Chay grabbed his ass and pulled Keaton roughly up against him. Yeah, someone was really horny. Keaton's feet left the floor as Chay brought their hips together.

Keaton scrambled to brace his hands behind him on the washer.

"You drive me crazy, baby. I came in here to ask you if you wanted to eat before we go hunting, and I see that tight little ass of yours bent over getting soap. Fuck, you're sexy." Chay's voice sounded deep and sultry as he thrust his hips against Keaton's.

Make that *two* someones who were really horny. That smooth, sexy voice made Keaton's prick jerk and his balls draw tighter. He moved his hips against Chay, staring into his big brown eyes. Fuck, the man was a walking wet dream.

"Pull your shirt up." Chay closed his eyes. When he opened them again, they glowed amber.

"What?"

"Pull your shirt up," he growled.

"I can't; I'll fall."

"No, you won't, I have you. Let go of the washer and grab my neck."

He did as directed, taking hold of Chay's shoulder with one hand and picking his shirt up with the other.

Chay dipped his head and caught Keaton's nipple between his teeth, all the while still moving their dicks together through their pants.

Keaton's whole body jerked and he hissed out a breath at the sting of teeth on his nipple. His cock throbbed inside his jeans, and his body tingled.

Chay moved over to the other nipple, then raised his head. His teeth elongated. Chay's control seemed to wane with the onset of the full moon.

Keaton knew he better do something before he ended up dry humping a wolf on the floor of the laundry room. As sad as it sounded, he was so damned turned-on, he'd do just that. He leaned forward, sank his teeth into Chay's shoulder, and ground his hips harder against Chay's. "Faster, Chay." Chay had to be close, because Keaton was about to lose his damned mind. He felt his eyes blur as they shifted, and closed them.

Finally Chay cried out against him, his hips moving erratically as he came.

Keaton climaxed almost immediately. His body stiffened against his mate. His balls drew tight and emptied into his pants. "Oh fuck. Chayton!"

Chay set Keaton's feet on the floor before their bodies stopped shaking with climax.

Keaton's knees gave out and he slid to the ground.

Chay followed. It took Keaton several seconds to realize Chay was shifting. He lay there and watched as Chay finished shifting into a large, solid black wolf. Damn, the man was even beautiful as a lupine.

Keaton smiled and pulled Chay's shirt off him.

Chay crawled out of his jeans and Keaton divested him of his boxers. The fur on Chay's belly and sides was wet.

Keaton chuckled. "You are going to have dried cum stuck to your fur."

Chay growled, then licked him in the face.

"Okay, okay, I'll wipe you up. As soon as my legs start working again."

Chay lay down beside him, idly licking his chin, his lips, his neck.

He scratched behind Chay's ears and buried his face in the thick black fur while he relaxed, making his eyes shift back. One of them needed thumbs. "I guess this means I'm driving us to the reservation."

Keaton lay there for several minutes, snuggled against Chay's warm furry body. They were both almost asleep when toenails clicked against the linoleum floor of the laundry room. He heard the panting and caught the scent of a stinky—been outside playing—puppy.

Then Chay yelped.

The yelp was followed by a fierce, immature little growl.

Chay yelped again and jumped up.

Keaton opened his eyes in time to see Pita go rolling across the floor, ending up on his back against the dryer. He looked at Chay.

Chay sat up, rubbing his ear with his paw.

Keaton burst out laughing.

Chay glared at him.

The puppy, however, got up and pounced at Chay, his tail wagging. Apparently, Chay being in wolf form didn't bother the pest at all. He wanted to play. This time he got a mouthful of the fur on Chay's chest, growling and shaking his head.

Keaton sat up. He couldn't stop laughing. He wondered if Pita realized it was Chay, and then decided he most likely did, because Chay's scent was the same. Which was probably what made the pup think it was playtime. Chay always lay on the floor to play with him.

Chay growled and gathered the pup in his mouth by the scruff of his neck, then brought him to Keaton. He dropped Pita in Keaton's lap and nipped Keaton's chin.

"Okay, okay. I'm sorry. It wasn't.... Hell, yes, it was funny. Sorry...." He started laughing again.

When he finally got his mirth under control, he got up. He ended up having to lock Pita in the laundry room with the dog gate because he wouldn't quit pouncing on Chay. First it was Chay's ears, then his tail. Chay became seriously agitated, so Keaton had taken pity on him.

He cleaned himself and Chay up, changed clothes, and got Chay some clothes for the morning. Keaton drove them out to pack land in his Impala and parked in a stand of trees next to Joe Winston's car. Chay had told him about the place the other day. It was secluded, and no one ever messed with their cars here. "Well, we're here. Is anyone supposed to meet us?"

Chay shook his head.

"We're on our own?"

Chay nodded.

"Okay, then. Let's get going." He got out and walked around to the passenger side. He opened the door for Chay and tossed his keys and wallet underneath the passenger seat. When Chay exited, Keaton sat in the passenger seat and started taking his shoes and socks off. He looked up and noticed Chay watching him. He smiled, reaching out and petting his mate's head. "Listen, Chay, there is something I forgot to tell you."

Chay cocked his head to the side.

Keaton took a deep breath and pulled his shirt off. He should have brought this up earlier. He hoped like hell it didn't freak Chay out. "In wolf form and in man/wolf form, I can communicate telepathically."

Chay's eyes widened.

"Yeah, sorry. I guess I should have told you sooner. It's just that it's kinda weird. I know not many people can do it, and well... if it freaks you out, I won't talk to you like that."

Chay came forward, put his front feet in the car, and raised his head to lick Keaton across the cheek.

Keaton sighed his relief and hugged his mate's neck. After a moment he stood up and finished undressing. He closed the car door and shifted quickly. Fully changed, he glanced up and saw Chay watching him.

He tilted his head and then realized Chay was expecting for him to "talk" to him. If he could have smiled, he would have. He wagged his tail and walked over to Chay, then ran his head up under Chay's taller wolf's chin.

"Well.... Where to? You know this area better than I do," he sent telepathically to Chay. He held his breath, waiting for Chay's reaction. This wasn't something most wolves could do. He and his father could communicate back and forth, but other wolves without the power could only hear him. His brother had always hated when Keaton spoke to him like this.

Chay, bless him, licked Keaton's muzzle, then nudged him in the shoulder and took off running.

"Hey, wait up."

They played and explored for several hours until they finally caught a rabbit to share. Several times during the night, it felt like someone was following them, but there was no scent. Whoever it was stayed downwind. He asked Chay about it, but Chay couldn't smell anyone either. It was probably some of the younger wolves playing with them.

Finally, around two or three in the morning, Chay led them to a small cave where they curled together and fell asleep.

Chay woke up, still in wolf form, so horny, his hips were practically humping air. He slowly became aware of heat at his back. The scent of his mate teased his nose, making him ache with need. He stood, looking down at the small white wolf.

Bit lay on his stomach, his head resting between his front paws, his hind legs curled under him, and his tail straight out.

Before Chay even realized what he was doing, he was standing over the pale body, his mouth latched on to the back of Bit's neck.

Keaton's ears popped up, but other than that, he didn't move. The slow Southern accent drawled in his head, *"Uh, Chay? I hate to be a party pooper, but we have no thumbs, no lips to speak of, and no lube. Mind if we take this back to the house?"*

Chay blinked and let go of Bit's neck.

Bit rolled over, his big blue wolf eyes peering up at Chay.

Fuck! What was he thinking? They couldn't do that in this form. Well, yeah, they probably could, but not here, not now, and definitely not for their first time. They could shift and....

No, he wasn't parading bare-assed all the way back to the car. He crawled off Bit and nudged him with his nose to get him moving.

Apparently, Keaton got the message. He popped to his feet and licked Chay's muzzle. *"Lead the way."*

Chay didn't waste any time. He climbed out of the cave and trotted back to the car, knowing from the smell of him that Keaton followed. In fact, that's all he could concentrate on. The scent drove him crazy, and if he was any judge, Bit was every bit as horny as he was.

"You know, you really have a nice tail."

Yeah, Bit was as turned-on as he was. He would have laughed if he could have; instead he hurried his pace.

When they got back to the car, several other pack members were there, including his father. At least they'd mistake his arousal for the fact that he'd just awakened. Not that it mattered; they would ignore it. It was bad form to acknowledge another's excitement. He only hoped none of them decided to strike up a conversation. He really wanted to get home.

Bit changed before he did and opened the car door to get their clothes out. He was not going to notice that nice, round, little ass. He wasn't. Oh shit, did he whimper?

"Morning, boys. The two of you have a nice evening?" Joe called out over the hood of his car.

Bit waved and put his briefs on, covering that tempting backside... *thank God.*

"Hi, Joe. We had a nice hunt. How about you? Next time we'll have to go out all together."

His dad walked over as Chay shifted back. Mentally he groaned, but he couldn't very well be rude and rush off. That would draw attention and speculation. Not that he minded everyone knowing, but he didn't feel like explaining it *right now*. He wanted to get Bit home and naked again.

He reached around Bit, grabbed his boxers and jeans off the seat, and quickly donned them. "Hi, Dad."

"Morning, son. You boys want to go get some breakfast?"

Hell no. Not unless Bit is on the menu. "Uh...."

Bit pulled on his shirt and handed Chay his. "Can we take a rain check? We need to get home and let the puppy out. We locked him in last night."

Yes. Thank you, Bit. Chay tugged his shirt down over his head and nodded. "Yeah, Pita is probably crossing his legs."

Joe snickered. "Or flooding the house."

Bit laughed. "I hope not. I think we have him housebroken."

"I'm going to breakfast. You boys change your mind, give me a call." He turned and walked back to his car, then stopped. "By the way, I expect you both for dinner sometime next week. I'll talk to your mother and let you know what night." He waved and got in his car.

Bit looked up from tying his sneakers and raised a brow.

Damn, Bit had sexy eyebrows. Chay groaned. Sexy *eyebrows. Good Lord.* Apparently a significant amount of blood flow had been directed to his dick that would have normally been in his head... either that or he'd lost his damned mind. Good thing his cock was doing all the thinking. Chay shrugged and put his shoes and socks on. "I always have dinner with them once a week. The past two weeks notwithstanding."

"Are you ready?"

"Hell yes." More quietly he added for the benefit of others who might be listening, "We should hurry. Pita is probably hungry too."

Bit winked, climbed into the driver's seat, and started the car. "Chay, get my wallet out from under your seat."

Chay got in, shut the door, and dug under his seat. "Why, does it have a condom in it?"

Keaton snorted. "Not hardly." Wolves didn't catch or transmit diseases.

"Yeah, but if you did and it happened to be prelubricated...."

Bit's eyes widened as he pulled onto the road. "Does this mean we are going—"

"To fuck? Hell yes. I mean if you're okay with that of course."

The car sped up. "I've *been* okay with it. I've been waiting on you."

Chay glanced over, noticing the bulge in Bit's jeans and couldn't help himself. He reached out and grasped it. Hell yes, Keaton was hard. Chay'd known he was, but.... Oh damn. He loved the feel of that hard prick throbbing in his hand. "Fuck, Bit, hurry."

They made it home in record time and barely got the door closed before Bit practically climbed up his body.

He grabbed two handfuls of that sweet ass and drew him up as Bit's mouth latched on to his neck. Those skinny arms wrapped around him. Thighs squeezed his waist. He moved Bit up and down, rubbing their pricks together, his cock already leaking. They were going to have to take the edge off. There was no way he would make it inside that tight little body before he went off like the Fourth of July.

He started down the hall toward the bedroom. "You didn't really lock the dog door did you?"

"Mumph." Bit nipped his skin and drew back, staring at his neck. He shook his head and dove in again, his mouth sucking.

Chay shivered; his Bit was marking him. He made it to the bedroom and dropped Bit on the bed. He took off his shirt as Bit leaned on his elbows, watching. He tackled his shoes next, then stripped out of his jeans, taking his underwear with them.

Bit stared at him, one hand touching himself through his pants. He looked fucking edible. "Jesus, Bit, get naked." He didn't even give the man time to respond. He grabbed both of Keaton's shoes and jerked them off, then attacked the socks and pants. He yanked them and Bit's briefs off. That pretty cock sprang free.

Keaton tugged his shirt up to his armpits, immediately dropping onto his back and stroking himself.

Fuck, if that wasn't the sexiest thing. Chay groaned and climbed onto the bed between Bit's open legs, settling on his knees. He gripped his own prick and pulled in time with Bit's hand.

Bit caught his bottom lip between his teeth and whimpered. He actually whimpered, and then his wide blue eyes peered up at Chay. Bit pumped his hand faster, his eyes now glued to Chay's cock. "God, you look good." The head of Bit's dick glistened with precum.

Chay groaned, his own prick harder than a steel pipe and throbbing in his hand. He reached out with the other hand and cupped Bit's balls, squeezing lightly. "Come for me, pretty baby. Come for me so I can fuck you."

Bit lost it, moaning loudly as his hips rose off the bed. His body stiffened, and he shot on his hand, his stomach.

The glazed look on that beautiful face and the smell of spunk pushed Chay right over. He thrust up into his hand twice and felt his balls pull tighter. He leaned over Keaton and watched the thick white liquid splatter on that pale belly. "Oh. Oh. Biiiit!"

Bit ran his fingers through the spunk on his stomach and brought them to his mouth, then licked them clean. "Mmm...."

Damn. His hips actually snapped forward. Geez. He sat back on his heels, watching his mate.

Keaton's dick was only half-hard when he sat up and pulled his shirt over his head, then tossed it to the floor.

Chay's cock never even lost interest.

"Want you inside me, Chay. You okay with that?"

"Hell yes. Been wanting to fuck you for weeks now."

"Then why haven't you?"

"You wanted to take things slow."

Keaton groaned and grabbed Chay's cock.

He hissed, pushing up into Bit's hand.

"Never listen to anything else, but you listened to that...," Bit grumbled, then bent forward and took him into his mouth.

Chay's whole body trembled. He was already very sensitive. That hot wet mouth was heaven. You'd never know he'd recently come. He ran his fingers through the blond curls, watching that pretty mouth take his dick. Damn, but Bit could suck cock. The man had a natural talent. He could deep throat better than anyone Chay had ever met. "Damn, Bit. This is nice, but...." He pulled away from Keaton and opened the night-stand drawer. God, he hoped he had some lube in there.

Bingo. Lube and condoms. They didn't need the condoms; he'd had them for a contraceptive. Wolves could get women pregnant.

"How do you want me?"

Chay gurgled—he actually freaking gurgled. He grabbed Bit and drew him up the bed, pressing him into the mattress for a kiss. "How do you want it?"

"I... I.... However you want. It's up to you." Bit's gaze darted around before settling on him.

He nipped his mate's lip. "No, it's not up to me. How do you want to be?"

Bit swallowed. "On my back, if it won't bother you."

Chay blinked. "Bother me? Hell no, it won't bother me. Why would it?"

Bit shrugged.

"Oh no. You aren't getting away with that." He seized his cock and tapped Bit's leg with it. "I don't think this is going anywhere soon. I've got time."

Keaton groaned and rolled his eyes. "Never mind."

Chay sat back and shook his head. Something was bothering his mate, and he was going to find out what it was. He just hoped like hell Bit didn't decide to dig his heels in and be the stubborn bastard Chay knew he could be, because he really, really wanted to fuck Bit's pretty little ass... soon.

Keaton sighed. "It's hard to pretend I'm not a guy if—"

"What?"

Bit winced.

Where the hell had that come from? He'd thought they'd gotten past all the gay/straight stuff. He dropped the lube, grasping Bit's legs and pulling them up, making him bend his knees. He stooped over and ran his tongue up Keaton's testicles before sucking on them. Chay pushed Bit's legs closer to Bit's chest, practically bending him in half, and traced his tongue down. He licked Bit's crease and teased his anus.

"Oh my God! Oh my God! Chay!" Keaton squirmed and wiggled. He acted like he couldn't decide if he wanted closer or if he wanted to get away.

It didn't matter—Chay didn't give him the chance to do either. He continued to trace the tight puckered hole with his tongue, then lapped his way back up Keaton's balls. Sometime during his rimming, Keaton's prick had woken up again. Chay took Bit's cock into his mouth and sucked.

"Oh!"

He drew back and caught Keaton's surprised gaze. "You think I try to pretend you're a woman?"

Bit's jaw dropped. He shook his head slowly from side to side.

Chay grinned. "Good. I don't want to hear that again."

Bit nodded, his eyes glazed over.

Chay let go of his legs and retrieved the lube. He slicked up his cock. Keaton's groan of appreciation had him lingering longer, playing it up for his mate. Damn, it felt pretty good too. He could just.... *Bit's tight little ass. Focus, Chay.* He let go of his prick and squeezed some more lube onto his fingers.

Bit grabbed his legs and held them back, his eyes nervous as he watched Chay.

"Shhh... relax, baby. I know damned well who you are. I've never pretended you were anyone else. Not gonna start now." He gripped Bit's foot with his nonslick hand and kissed the arch. "'Sides, no one else gets me as hot as you do." He sucked the big toe into his mouth as his fingers slid over the ring of muscle.

Keaton gasped.

Chay pushed a finger in, and they both groaned.

Damn, it was snug. His cock jerked with anticipation. He pressed another finger inside, watching his mate's face for signs of discomfort.

There weren't any. Bit's cock was rock hard against his stomach again. His eyes closed, a slight smile on his lips. Fuck, Bit was a good-looking man. "Ready for another finger, pretty baby?"

"Ready for your cock."

"You sure?"

"Uh-huh."

Chay slid a third finger in, watching Bit's face closely.

Bit sighed.

He pulled his fingers out and lined the head of his cock up with the ready hole. He pushed, and Keaton's body swallowed him up. "Oh goddamn, you feel good." He pressed forward slowly, his body arguing with him the whole way, telling him to hurry up. He ignored it, taking his time, savoring the feel of his mate's body squeezing him tight.

Bit whimpered. "Move. Please move."

He did, thrusting gently at first. He'd done this before with women, but this was different, better. It was Bit, his mate.

Bit made such sweet sounds: gasps and sighs. Chay felt himself getting close. Smelled the drops of cum seeping from Keaton's prick. He grabbed Keaton's legs under the knees and pulled him up to meet his thrusts, moving faster.

Bit groaned, his eyes going wide.

Chay did it again.

Keaton's whole body tensed, his ass tightening.

Chay groaned too. He sped his pace more and watched the pleasure play over Keaton's face. He smiled and took notice of the angle he was using. He'd forgotten all about that. Hadn't even considered that it was supposed to feel good when you stimulated the prostate. "You like that, baby?"

"God yes! Faster, Chay. Harder."

A tingle raced up Chay's spine. Damn, if that wasn't hot, he didn't know what was. He started snapping his hips faster. "Touch yourself. Jerk yourself off for me, Bit."

Bit grabbed his prick, pulling in time to Chay's strokes. It was the most erotic thing Chay'd ever seen.

Keaton's teeth sank into his bottom lip as he pumped his cock. Within seconds he tightened around Chay, begging.

Chay didn't know what he was saying, didn't understand a word of it, but he knew what Keaton asked for. He fucked Bit fast and hard, driving into him. Within seconds Bit's body shook, his moans growing louder and louder. His muscles clamped tight around Chay and the scent of spunk filled the air.

Keaton was always beautiful, but something about the look on his face when he came undid Chay.

Chay came with a ragged moan, his body spilling into his mate's. He collapsed over Keaton, breathing hard, riding out the aftershocks.

Bit's arms wrapped around him, and he nuzzled his face against Chay's. When he found Chay's lips with his, he brought them together.

He moaned into Bit's mouth, kissing back. God, he loved this man.

Chay was practically floating when the gasp came from the doorway.

"Motherfucker!"

Chapter Nine

Remi stood in the doorway, Pita cradled in his arms. He glared at Keaton and set the dog down. The puppy immediately rushed to the bed and started barking and hopping up and down.

Remi opened his mouth and shut it several times before pointing his finger at Keaton. "You. This is your fault. You've brainwashed him."

"Out!" Chay grabbed the covers, threw them over himself and Keaton, and slid to the side and out of Keaton's body.

Keaton gasped at the pleasure, then snapped his mouth shut.

Surprisingly, Remi turned around and walked out of the room.

Chay sat up and ran his hands through his hair. "Fuck."

"I'm sorry."

"Why?" Chay's brow furrowed.

"Well... that Remi found out."

He shook his head. "No. You don't have anything to be sorry about. It's Remi's fault. He's always walking in. The fucker never has figured out how to knock on a damn door. Doesn't matter; I've been putting it off. This is a good thing." Chay bent, kissed him, and smacked his hip. "Get up and get dressed." He got off the bed, then swooped Pita up in one hand and held him at face level. "And *you*. For the love of God, hush."

Keaton sighed and trudged to the bathroom to wash up. When he came back, Chay was fully dressed, sitting on the edge of the bed waiting for him. Keaton didn't want to do this. Call it a hunch, but it was going to be pretty ugly.

"Bit...."

"Yeah?" He'd never admit he liked Chay calling him that.

Chay stood, wrapped his arms around Keaton's waist, and kissed his forehead. "Thank you." He traced the bridge of Keaton's nose with his thumb. "God, I love these freckles."

Keaton rolled his eyes. "You're insane, you know that?"

Chay nipped his chin. "It's part of my charm. Come on. Let's go talk to Remi. I'd kick his ass out, but he was my best friend for the past twenty years."

"Was?"

Chay raised an eyebrow, then grabbed Keaton's hand and led him to the living room.

Remi sat on the couch. He looked up as they walked in, took in their entwined hands, and glowered at Keaton. "What did you do to him?"

Chay held up a hand. "Remi, don't start. This has nothing to do with Keaton."

"What? Yes, it does," Remi shouted.

Keaton nodded, then realized what he was doing. Good Lord, was he actually agreeing with Remi?

"Listen, Remi, this is none of your business. But you're my friend, and I'm going to explain this to you, this once." Chay let go of Keaton's hand and sat on the couch, turning slightly toward Remi.

Pita pounced over and started pulling on Chay's pant leg, growling. Keaton grinned, picked up the pup, and sat in the chair catty-corner to the couch.

Remi ran his hands down his face. The man really was handsome; too bad he was such an ass. He sat forward and rested his hands on his knees. "Why, Chay? Is this some sort of rebellion or something to piss your mother off? It wasn't bad enough that you brought home a half-white friend, now you have to bring home a white lover? A guy, for crying out loud. You aren't even gay."

Chay sighed. "It has nothing to do with my mother. And can we stop with the whole gay, not-gay thing? It's irrelevant. Keaton is my lover, and I'm keeping him, that's that."

"What, did you all of a sudden decide you didn't like women anymore?"

"I like women. I just like Bi—Keaton more."

Remi glared at Keaton, then turned back to Chay. "This is un-fucking-believable. What does he have on you? Is he black-mailing you or something?"

Chay closed his eyes and pinched the bridge of his nose. Keaton had the sudden urge to take him in his arms and tell him it would be all right, but he knew it wouldn't. Remi was only the first. Lena Winston was going to react ten times as bad.

Chay dropped his hand and looked at his friend. "Remi—"

"Well, hell, Chay, what am I supposed to think? You never liked men that way before."

"I'm going to say this once. You can deal with it, or you can go, it's up to you. I love Keaton and he's staying...."

Keaton gasped, his eyes going wide as he glanced over at Chay. Poor Remi looked like someone had sucker punched him. Wait, no. Not "poor Remi"—the man was an asshole.

Chay kept talking, oblivious to their reactions. "...here. This is his home now. He isn't going anywhere... ever. If you can't be nice to him, then you're no longer welcome here."

"So it's me or him?"

"Not if you can behave and stop insulting him. We've been friends for a long time, but I'm not going to allow you to bad-mouth and torment Keaton."

Remi stood up, outraged. "You would throw our friend-ship away for... for"—he pointed at Keaton—"that... that little faggot."

Chay jumped up, anger radiating off him. "That's it! Get out. Get the fuck out and don't come back until you can be-have."

Remi glared at Keaton one last time and stormed out, slamming the front door behind him.

Keaton closed his eyes and dropped his head back on the chair. *Fuck.* This sucked.

Pita rose up, putting his front paws on his chest, and start-ed licking his chin.

Keaton put him on the floor and looked around for Chay. He stood at the back window, peering out. Keaton didn't know what to say. Should he go and try to comfort Chay? The strangest thing was he had this urge to actually defend Remi. The man had to be in shock.

"Sorry about that, Bit. I know it doesn't excuse his behav-ior, but his dad is a real asshole. He didn't have the easiest time growing up." Chay turned slowly from the window.

"You don't have to apologize to me. You know this is only the beginning, right? It's going to get worse."

Chay nodded.

"Do you really want to be an outcast? Shunned by your friends, your family?"

Chay cocked his head. "Is that what happened to you, Bit? Did your friends all abandon you when you told them you were gay?"

"No. I didn't have any friends."

"Everyone has friends."

Keaton shook his head. "I don't."

"Why?"

"First, I was too rich, my family too snobby. Then I was too smart; I made people uncomfortable. After that, I was way too powerful of a werewolf and made everyone uneasy. Next there was my sexuality." He shrugged. "I'm not a person who inspires close relationships, I guess."

"What about boyfriends?"

"There was only the one. And we were never that close."

Chay raised a brow. "Because he wasn't out?"

"Yeah, he insisted he wasn't gay. Pretty much everyone I've ever cared about has distanced themselves from me, in one form or another."

Chay walked over to him and reached out a hand.

Keaton looked at it, and his eyes followed it up to Chay's face. When he took the offered hand, Chay drew him out of the chair, sat down, and pulled Keaton onto his lap.

Chay kissed his nose and leaned back in the chair, holding him close. "I'm not going anywhere, Bit. You can quit waiting for me to leave. It's not going to happen."

Keaton wished he could believe that wholeheartedly. He did believe it on some level, but there was still a little bit of doubt in the back of his mind. "I can't help it. I feel like I'm destroying your life. I've already lost you a friend. God only knows how your parents are going to react."

Chay placed a hand on the side of Keaton's head, holding him to Chay's chest, and kissed him again. "It's destiny, Bit. If my friends and family desert me, they didn't care that much about me in the first place. It doesn't matter to me that you are a man instead of a woman. And it isn't just sex."

Keaton looked up at Chay, pulling back slightly to see his face. "Are you trying to tell me you love me?" He was shameless, but he couldn't help it. Keaton wanted to hear it again, addressed to him this time instead of in an argument with Remi.

Chay smiled. "Yeah, Bit, I do. But that isn't what I'm trying to say."

"Huh?"

Chay sighed. "I'm trying to tell you that I'm not going to run out on you. I'm not going to split because my family and friends don't like it. You mean more to me than they do. This is something I'm willing to fight for."

Wow. He knew what Chay meant. He'd never felt the connection he had with Chay with anyone else. He knew logically that it was due to their genes, but he couldn't help but think that he'd feel this way even if they weren't mates. He still didn't want to be the reason Chay's life spiraled down the toilet, though. He kissed Chay and smiled. "Okay. I'm here for you, but I'm warning you it's not going to be easy."

Chay chuckled and squeezed him tight, squishing the breath out of him. "I know, I know. Everyone is going to hate me and want nothing to do with me. I got it. You sound like a broken record."

Keaton snorted. "I didn't say *everyone* was going to hate you."

"What about you, Bit? Are you going to hate me?" Chay asked with a glint in his eye and a smug smile on his lips.

Keaton grinned. The man was too smug. "Is this your way of trying to finagle a confession of everlasting love out of me?"

Chay's eyes widened. He tried to look offended, but it wasn't working, with the wicked, knowing gleam in his eye. "Would I do such an underhanded thing?"

Keaton laughed. "You would do whatever it takes to get your way. I have absolutely no doubt about that."

Chay stopped smiling, his eyes suddenly serious. "I love you, Bit. I really do."

Whoa. Keaton couldn't breathe. His heart was about to pound out of his chest. Chay'd said it without Keaton even having to ask. Did he love Chay? He knew Chay expected him to say it back to him, but... could he trust Chay with that vulnerability?

"You don't have to say anything, Keaton. I just thought you should know."

He nodded. In for a penny, in for a pound. It was going to kill him if Chay ever did decide he didn't want him. Telling the man how he felt wasn't going to change that, because he *did* feel it. "I love you too, Chay."

Chay's smile became radiant. "You know, coming from you, that means everything. You stubborn shit."

Keaton's jaw practically hit the floor. "I still hate your damned pheromones, though."

Chay cackled, his eyes tearing up with humor. He grabbed Keaton's head with both hands and kissed him.

The last coherent thought Keaton had was that life with Chay would never be dull.

Chapter Ten

"Did you know there are gay penguins?"

What? Keaton looked up from his book. "Excuse me?"

Chay lay across from him, reading. He nodded and put his magazine—something to do with animals and vets and stuff—on his stomach. "Yeah, there is, really. There are all sorts of homosexual relationships in animal species."

Keaton blinked and pushed his glasses back up his nose.

"There are monkeys and sheep—well, rams actually—and cows and even dolphins. There are even—what? Why are you laughing?"

"I had no idea you were such a nerd."

"What?"

Keaton grinned. Oh Lord, how geeky did a person have to be to know about gay animals? Of course, it could be common vet knowledge, but he doubted it. More than likely it was because Chay watched way too much Discovery Channel. Or maybe it was in the magazine he was reading. "Did you just read that?"

"No. I was reading an article about new egg incubators, and it made me think of the penguins. They actually tried to hatch rocks."

Keaton smiled. This was too good. Mr. Popularity was a geek in disguise. "Chay, who invented the printing press?"

"Huh?"

"Answer the question."

"Uh... Johannes Gutenberg?"

He suppressed a snicker. "Who invented the sleeping railroad car?"

"George Pullman."

Damn, this was getting better and better. Keaton smiled so big, his face hurt. "How about the cotton gin?"

"Eli Whitney. Why are you asking me these stupid questions?"

"How many bones in the human body?"

"Two hundred and six. There are approximately three hundred and twenty in a canine. About two hundred and fifty in felines and two hundred and five in equines."

This was great! No wonder they got along so well. "You, Dr. Winston, are a geek."

Chay rolled his eyes, picked up his magazine, and started reading again. "Takes one to know one," he mumbled under his breath.

Keaton put the bookmark in his Apache history book and set it on the side table. He grinned like a loon, but he couldn't help it. Chay tried hard to hide the fact that he was brainy. Keaton had known he was a smart man, he'd have to be to have gotten into vet school, but he never showed just how smart he was.

Keaton cackled. "I never said I wasn't. Hell, I'm the king of geeks! If I wore shirts with pockets, I'd have a pocket protector."

Chay groaned and put the magazine over his face. "A pocket protector does not a geek make. Nor does tape on the glasses."

"*You* have a pocket protector, don't you?"

"In my lab coat."

Keaton took off his wire-rimmed frames, set them on top of his book, and slinked to the couch. He removed the magazine from Chay's face as he sat next to him.

Chay pulled him forward and kissed his nose. "All right, Goldilocks. Why is it funny that I am not some brainless jock?"

Keaton blinked, opened his mouth, then snapped it shut. He was not going to respond to that nickname. He wasn't. Chay called him by these ridiculous nicknames to get a reaction out of him. If he ignored the name, it would go away. The only ones that stuck were the ones he complained about. But damn, that was a bad one.

"Well, Goldy?"

"No! Absolutely not. No way. You can *not* call me that."

"Or?" Chay had a wicked gleam in his eye.

"Or I'm going to kick your ass." Keaton glared, trying to look fierce.

Chay chuckled. *Damn him.*

Maybe if he started thinking up equally obnoxious nicknames to call Chay, he'd stop? Nah, probably not, the man had a perverse sense of humor; he'd probably like it. Keaton sighed.

Chay dug his fingers into Keaton's ribs, tickling.

Keaton squeaked and halfheartedly fended him off. They fell on the floor in a tangle of arms and legs. He tried to tickle Chay back, but Chay had a longer reach and outweighed him by about fifty or sixty pounds. He ended up on his back with Chay sitting on top of him. They both laughed. It didn't take long before Pita got in on the action. He ran around in circles, barking his fool head off, licking Keaton's face every time he ran by it.

Keaton got a hold of one of Chay's hands, and Pita nipped him on the nose. "Oww!" He stopped struggling against Chay long enough to swat at Pita.

The puppy dropped his chest to the floor, leaving his butt sticking up in the air, tail wagging, and growled at him.

Chay laughed harder. "I guess this means we aren't allowed to play without him."

"I guess not. Little shithead bit my nose. Those puppy teeth hurt."

Chay stopped tickling him and kissed his nose. "Tell me about it. The little brat got my ear the other night, remember?"

Keaton chuckled. "Yup, I remember."

"It wasn't funny."

"Yes, it was. The big bad wolf brought down by a tiny puppy. It was hilarious." He smirked.

"All right, Goldilocks—"

Keaton groaned. "I'll make you a deal. You don't call me Goldilocks anymore, and I won't tell the entire pack you were felled by a seven-week-old puppy."

Chay sighed. "Okay, add in a kiss and it's a deal."

"Oh gee, I don't know." Keaton pretended to think about it.

Chay braced himself on his hands above Keaton. He growled and nipped Keaton's bottom lip. "Behave and kiss me, Bit." His tongue skimmed over the seam of Keaton's lips.

He opened his mouth with a sigh, letting Chay in. The kiss was gentle at first, long languid strokes of tongue and a little nibbling. It wasn't long before he smelled Chay's arousal. It incited his own.

Chay moaned, his hard prick pressed into Keaton's thigh, and the kiss quickly became heated. Chay rolled them over so Keaton was on top. He pulled Keaton's shirt over his head and tossed it on the couch. His mouth closed over Keaton's shoulder and his hands groped everywhere: Keaton's back, his ass, his hair.

Keaton arched into Chay's hands, enjoying the caresses. His hard cock begged for attention. He moved down, dislodging Chay's teeth from his shoulder, and pushed his cock against Chay's.

Chay gasped and rolled them again. He climbed off Keaton and started kissing his way down Keaton's chest. He sat next to Keaton, bending over his body. When Chay got to the waistband of Keaton's gym shorts, he eased them and the briefs off Keaton.

After Keaton's prick came free of the elastic band, Chay engulfed it in his mouth.

Keaton hissed out a breath and fought to keep his hips still as Chay sucked him. "God. Chay come up here." He leaned over and snagged one of Chay's bare feet and pulled, letting Chay know what he wanted.

Chay unfolded his legs and slid his body out beside Keaton, giving him better access.

Keaton turned on his side, matching Chay's movements, and tugged at the drawstring until he got it undone. He pushed the pajama pants off Chay and the thick cock came free with a bounce. Keaton fisted it, guiding it to his mouth.

Chay's tongue trailed across his balls. Keaton groaned around the hot prick in his mouth as Chay sucked lightly and laved his testicles.

Keaton worked Chay's dick between his lips, trying to concentrate on his mate's pleasure instead of his own. The smooth hot length of Chay's dick slid in and out of his mouth with ease as Chay licked up his shaft. His hips pushed forward before he could stop himself. He wanted Chay's mouth around his cock.

Chay didn't disappoint. He sucked Keaton down, taking half his prick in and squeezing the base in his hand.

Keaton moaned and moved faster on Chay's prick, his head bobbing now. He was really getting into it, his hips making short jabs, when Chay pulled his head back, letting Keaton's dick slide all the way out. Keaton continued to suck his mate.

"Uh, Bit."

"Uh," he answered around Chay's prick.

"The dog is staring at me."

Keaton almost choked. He let the cock slip out of his mouth and looked down at his mate.

Chay frowned, staring past Keaton's hip.

"So what? Suck me."

"No, the puppy is watching."

Keaton groaned and got up. He didn't see how that was a problem as long as Pita didn't decide to join in, but Chay obviously wasn't going to continue with their audience. "Bedroom." He offered Chay a hand up and led the way down the hall.

They hit the bed at the same time, regaining their former positions in a hurry.

Chay's mouth wrapped around Keaton's dick, making him gasp. He quickly returned the favor and swallowed Chay's cock down. Inside of seconds, they were both moaning, hips pumping their pricks into the other's mouth.

One of Chay's hands grabbed his ass, urging him to move, and the other hand teased his crease. Oh fuck, the man was something. He might not have been sucking dick long, but damn, he was good at it. He couldn't deep throat like Keaton could, but he made up for it with enthusiasm and inventiveness.

Chay pushed a finger into his mouth beside Keaton's dick as he continued to suck. Keaton's balls drew tighter when he realized Chay's intent. Chay did exactly as anticipated. He removed the finger from his mouth and began teasing Keaton's hole with it.

A shiver raced up his spine as the finger pressed in. He let Chay's cock slip out of his mouth. "Fuck yes."

Chay moved his finger in time with his mouth, fucking and sucking for all he was worth.

Keaton glanced down his body, watching his dick slide in and out of Chay's mouth. It was hotter than hell, seeing his gorgeous mate take his cock. It pushed him right over. Keaton stiffened, his hips pressing forward farther into Chay's mouth and his balls emptying themselves down Chay's throat.

Chay pulled his finger free and laid his head on the bed, panting for air.

Keaton took a few seconds to catch his breath and let his body stop trembling. "Are you okay?" He didn't give Chay time to answer. Instead he grabbed Chay's cock, noticing the drops of semen on the tip, and swallowed it, taking him all the way down.

Chay's hips bucked and he gasped. "Fuck yes. I am now." Within seconds Chay came, filling his mouth with hot, salty spunk.

He lay there sucking lightly on the softening cock for quite some time. He was almost asleep when Chay reached down and dragged him up.

Somehow he managed to get in the bed the right way with Chay spooned around him. Chay kissed his neck and snuggled close, making him feel loved and cherished. *This was the life.* What a great way to spend a chilly Saturday afternoon.

He'd nearly drifted off when Chay's voice pulled him back. "Bit. The dog is staring at me again."

His stomach was eating itself, he was so hungry. Chay groaned and got out of bed, careful not to wake Bit. What a terrible way to ruin a perfectly good day. He hated cooking, and if he remembered correctly, he'd used all the sandwich stuff for breakfast. He'd *had* to use sandwich stuff for breakfast because Bit had fixed the last of the Pop Tarts and Eggos for dinner last night. He was going to have to cook, if they were going to eat. *Damn it.* Maybe he should hire a chef? Hell, he'd settle for a short-order cook at the moment.

Chay went to the living room to find his clothes. He put on his pants and dragged his feet all the way to the kitchen. He took inventory of the pantry and came up with macaroni and cheese. Now if he could find some sort of meat, they'd be set.

He was standing in front of the fridge, staring, when he heard something outside. Probably the neighbor's cat. Oh well, he should check it out. Standing in front of the freezer hadn't magically made food. He shut the door and ambled to the living room.

Pita came down the hall, yawning. The puppy spotted him and wagged his tail.

"Hey, pup. You hungry too?"

Pita bounced over and headbutted Chay's shin, asking to be petted.

He chuckled and scratched behind Pita's ears.

A loud clank had them both jumping and heading to the front door. What had that cat gotten into now?

Chay opened the front door.

A man ran down the driveway. *What the...?* "Hey!"

The stranger looked back, running faster.

Pita growled and charged out the door.

"Shit. Pita!" Chay took off after the puppy. He caught him halfway down the drive. The man, however, was well on his way to a clean escape. Chay sniffed the air. The stranger was a wolf, but the scent wasn't familiar. He thought about chasing him, but to what end? A quick glance around didn't turn up any damage. He'd never had any problems with burglars or vandals and such before. He lived in a relatively nice neighborhood. It was older but still in great shape.

The wind blew, making the leaves swirl around his feet. He shivered. Damn, it was cold out. Fall had definitely arrived. He tucked Pita under his arm and looked around the house in a more thorough inspection. He still didn't see anything. Nothing seemed to be disturbed. He must have scared the man off before he could steal anything. Was he a visiting wolf? Or maybe it was a homeless man, trying to get warm? Not that he'd ever seen any homeless people in his neighborhood before. Just because he was a wolf didn't mean he wasn't a garden-variety criminal too.

To be on the safe side, he checked around his truck and Bit's car. Everything appeared fine. He shrugged and walked back to the house, scratching the puppy's head as he went. "You were going to get him, weren't you, boy?"

"What the hell are you doing outside, barefoot, with no shirt in this weather?" Keaton stood at the door in a pair of sweatpants and a T-shirt. He was rubbing his arms and his hair stuck up every which way. God, he was cute.

"Hey, Bit." He kissed Keaton's forehead on the way into the house and handed him the puppy.

Bit shut the door and locked it. "What were you doing outside?"

"I heard something and came to check it out. Saw a guy running off. Pita charged out the door after him."

Keaton's eyes widened. "Really? Did you catch him?"

He shook his head. "Nope. But Pita sure tried."

Pita squirmed in Bit's arms and Bit put him on the floor. He scampered toward the back of the house. They heard the dog door open and close.

"Is it safe for him to be out there?"

Chay shrugged. "Yeah, we scared the guy off. I couldn't find any evidence that he tampered with anything."

"Hmm...." Bit walked past him, still rubbing his arms. "Did you get a good scent? Was it someone you recognized?"

He followed Bit into the kitchen.

Bit stood at the refrigerator door, leaning on it, looking inside.

"Yeah, I got a good scent. The man was a wolf, but I didn't recognize him."

Bit moved some stuff around in the fridge and stood back up, once again staring into the open refrigerator. "You think maybe we should call the pack? Or maybe the police?"

Chay wondered how long it would take Keaton to realize they needed to go grocery shopping. "And tell them what? If I didn't recognize the scent, he's not from our pack, and there wasn't anything messed with. Besides, I don't think he'll be coming back, knowing that I saw him."

"What did he look like?" Bit started rubbing his arms again.

"I didn't *see* him see him, but I know he was about five-eight with a slim build. He had on a dark green jacket, a red ball cap, and black jeans."

"Hmm. You think it was someone nosing around?"

"More than likely. Probably looking things over, seeing if there was anything easy to steal. I'll call John Carter tomorrow and see if any visiting wolves have checked in with him."

"Yeah, that's probably a good idea. Why don't we lock Pita in for the night, though, just in case."

Right on cue the dog door opened and closed. Pita came bouncing into the kitchen.

"I agree. It's better to be safe than sorry." Chay leaned against the cabinet and watched the puppy go to the fridge, put his front feet on the bottom ledge, and have a look.

Bit shooed him away. After another minute he shut the door and turned toward Chay. "We don't have shit to eat."

Chapter Eleven

Keaton woke to an insistent whining noise. *What the hell?* The whine came again, followed by a constant thud. He blinked his eyes open and looked at the clock—8:00 a.m. Keaton grunted and mumbled, "Fuck."

He reached for Chay and came up empty-handed. Chay's side of the bed was cold. Which would explain the thud. The man was insane for working out at eight on a Sunday morning. And how did he listen to that crappy music?

Pita started whining again.

"Damn it." Keaton sat up and ran his hands down his face. Jesus Christ, he was going to have to work harder at tiring the man out at night. The thought that Chay could still get up at this time of day after the strenuous exercise the night before was a real blow to the ego.

Apparently the puppy had slept through Chay's departure too. Keaton threw his legs over the side of the bed and padded naked down the hall to let the puppy out.

He opened the dog door for Pita and cool air whooshed in, deflating his morning wood. Damn, it was cold outside. He should get some clothes on, but his stomach growling brought him up short. He was already closer to the kitchen. What a dilemma. He shrugged and headed for the kitchen. He'd grab some cold pizza from the night before and take it back to bed and eat. There was bound to be something on TV. Just because Chay was demented and up working out, didn't mean he had to get out of bed yet.

He got into the kitchen and found the pizza box lying open, empty on the table. "Damn it." Chay could have at least saved him a piece. Shit. He wasn't a morning person at the best of times. "Wake up with no one to snuggle with, dog whining, shitty music playing, fucking freezing outside, and now no damned food." He growled.

Pita came in from outside as Keaton left the kitchen. They walked together to the extra bedroom Chay used as a workout room.

He opened the door, and the deafening tones of Gray Mummy or White Zombie or whatever the name of that damned band, assaulted him. Whatever it was, Pita thought it sucked too. He took off back to the bedroom. *Wuss.* Keaton rolled his eyes.

Chay sat on the bench in a pair of black wind shorts and sneakers, doing biceps curls.

Keaton blinked at the flex of sweaty muscles. Ooh, that was a nice sight. His cock appreciated the view too. His stomach, however, couldn't care less; it demanded food. He walked over to the stereo and turned it down.

Chay looked up at him and smiled. "Morning, Bit. I didn't wake you up, did I?"

"Nope, Pita did."

"Oh shit, babe! I was hoping to finish working out and then go get you some donuts. I ate all the pizza."

Wow. How cool was that? Okay, maybe he wouldn't strangle Chay over the pizza. He still had issue with waking up in bed alone and shitty music... well, and the weather too, but he didn't suppose that was Chay's fault, so he'd let it slide this once.

Chay set his dumbbell down and came to him. He bent and brushed his lips over Keaton's.

Keaton considered not responding for about half a second, then decided that would be childish, not to mention cutting his nose off to spite his face. He opened up and kissed Chay back. *Yum, pizza.* His stomach growled again.

Chay pulled back, smiling. "Want me to throw on some clothes and go get you some donuts?"

God, he loved this man. He decided that the shitty music was forgiven too. "Nah. I'll go get dressed and get some. I'll even get you some too, if you promise to eat them in bed with me."

Chay grabbed Keaton's semierect cock and squeezed. "You forgive me for not waking you up properly?"

Keaton shivered, his cock taking interest. It looked like he was going to have to forgive that too. He bucked into his mate's hand, hardening fully.

The gleam in Chay's eye was positively wicked as he jerked Keaton's prick. "If I eat donuts in bed with you, are we gonna play ring toss?"

He snorted. "Not with my donuts. I'm starving. You can do what you want with your own. But I'm warning you right now. I get sprinkles in my ass, and I'm moving into the guest room."

Chay laughed and pumped Keaton's dick faster.

Keaton closed his eyes and went with it. Chay was well on the way to being forgiven for things he hadn't even done yet. Damn, it felt good.

Teeth nibbled at his jaw and the fist around his prick got tighter, moved faster. He was so close, he felt as though his knees were going to give out. He surged up into Chay's hand twice before he gasped for air and spurted all over the place.

Chay kissed him once more and let go of him. Keaton staggered a little and braced himself on the doorframe. Damn. It was like he'd been hit by a Mack truck.

Chay came back with a towel and cleaned Keaton, the floor, and his own hand. He tossed the towel over his shoulder. "You know, speaking of the guest room, I've been thinking about that. Since I use this room as my weight room, why don't you take the other spare bedroom and do something with it? You can turn it into an office or maybe a library."

Keaton blinked. *Huh?* What the hell was Chay talking about? It was obvious that one of them *hadn't* come. Keaton finally focused on what Chay had said and shrugged. It was a thought. Maybe he would... after Chay told everyone they were mates. "I'll think about it." He looked down at the tented material of Chay's shorts. "You want me to take care of that for you?" Keaton's belly rumbled.

"Nah, I'm good. It will keep until you get back. Go get you something to eat."

He started to argue, but his gut decided to protest by cramping. "Okay. You convinced me. I'm starving." He kissed Chay on the chin and turned to leave.

Chay swatted his butt as he left.

Wow. What a morning. And to think he'd thought it was going to suck.

Keaton searched for his car keys before he went to change. One of the things that had sold him on the silver Chevy Impala was that it had an automatic start. He could turn it on with the remote, and it'd be all nice and warm by the time he got in it.

Technology... you had to love it. Well, it wasn't the only reason. It was a cool-looking car and fast too.

He found his keys on the table in the entry hall, started the car, and headed back down the hall to get dressed.

He threw on a sweat suit and shoes, grabbed his wallet, and ran out to the car. Damn, it was cold. He hated winter. Well, technically it was autumn, but... cold sucked. Fortunately, his car was nice and warm inside. The drive to the donut shop was pretty quiet. All the sane people were still in bed. Which is where he'd be if he could cook. He was going to have to consider trying to cook if he couldn't talk Chay into it. There were too many other things he could be doing if he wasn't always going to get food. It was a sad state of affairs when everyone at the local burger place knew him on sight. And the pizza place staff actually knew him by name.

He pulled up to the donut shop and noticed his brakes were a little squishy. Hmmm, that wasn't good; he needed to have someone look at them. The pedal shouldn't go that far down. He shrugged, maybe it was air in the brake line? He left the car running and locked it with the remote. He ordered a dozen chocolate-covered, a dozen glazed, and two-dozen donut holes. He figured if he got enough, maybe they'd have some left for tomorrow morning, or knowing Chay, they'd only make it until lunch. Chay could eat his weight in donuts. The man had a sweet tooth that put Keaton's mother to shame.

On the way back, Keaton ate donut holes and flipped radio channels. Why was it they all played commercials at the same time? Up the road, there was a kid on a red bike, riding on the sidewalk. Keaton wasn't sure why, but he had the feeling the kid was going to dart out in front of him. He stepped on the brakes to slow, just in case his intuition was correct. Nothing happened. *What the...?* He pumped the pedal. The car slowed, but not enough. *Shit!* His brakes were out. He reached for the emergency brake release and put his foot over the brake at the exact same time the kid rode his bike into the street.

Keaton didn't have enough time to stop, so he swerved to the left. A huge oak tree stopped his forward progress.

"Are you Chayton Winston?"

Chay looked up to find a small Native American woman in a pair of dark green scrubs standing before him. He nodded and stood. "Yes, ma'am."

"Come right this way. He's been asking for you." She hit a button on the wall and led him through a set of double doors. "The doctor is going to want to talk to you before we release him. He'll give you a list of instructions. Oh, and the sheriff is waiting too, but I thought I'd take you in to see Keaton first." She stopped before an open doorway and turned toward him. "He's a little groggy and not making a lot of sense. That's because of the concussion. The doctor ordered a CAT scan when he was brought in, and it looked fine. In a couple of hours, he ought to be more like himself."

Chay nodded. He wanted to see his mate. As soon as he stepped inside the room, Bit smiled.

"Hi, Chay. You aren't hurt, are you?" Keaton had a bandage on his forehead and seemed a little paler than normal, or was that the harsh lighting? He looked very small lying there, his big blue eyes blinking sleepily at Chay.

"What?" Chay walked over to the bed and grabbed his hand, brushing a kiss across his brow where he was uninjured. "I'm fine, Bit."

"Okay. I was worried you'd gotten hurt too."

"I wasn't with you, babe. You were by yourself. You went to go get donuts."

Bit's grin faded. He appeared a little green around the gills, putting his hand over his stomach. "Yeah, I don't think I want to eat the donuts right now. You go ahead, though."

Bit really was out of it. Chay wondered if he even knew what happened. He smiled reassuringly and kissed his mate again. "The donuts are gone, Bit. Don't worry about it. Just rest. We'll get you home as soon as they say."

"Okay—hi, Joe!" Bit's free hand shot up in the air and started waving.

Chay thought Bit was hallucinating until he heard his dad's voice.

"Hi, son. How are you?" Joe walked around to Keaton's other side and patted his hand, once he snagged it from midair.

Bit turned his head toward Joe and yawned. "My car's dead, but Chay's all right. I think I ate too many donuts."

His dad shot Chay a startled glance.

Yeah, he knew the feeling. He didn't like seeing Keaton this way either, but he at least realized why Bit was acting goofy. "He'll be okay. He's a little out of it. From what I've been able to gather, he actually lost consciousness on impact. According to the nurse, they did a CAT scan when they brought him in and didn't find any hemorrhaging. What are you doing here, Dad?"

Joe frowned. "My son's mate was in a car accident."

Chay gasped.

Keaton giggled. "Oh, hey, that's cool. He knows." He tugged on Chay's hand. When Chay looked down at Keaton, he smiled. "You don't have to tell him now. He knows. And I don't think he's mad either. He doesn't sound mad." Keaton yawned and turned his head toward Joe. "Are you mad?"

"No, Keaton, I'm not mad." He gently ruffled Bit's hair, then looked back up at Chay. "I haven't told your mother yet. I admit, I'm a coward. You know how she is."

Bit started snoring softly.

Chay brushed a lock of hair off Bit's forehead. "Yeah, I do. She's not going to take it well."

Joe shook his head. "No, she's not. But she can't change it, so she'll have to get over it and deal with it. It's not like we choose our mates. How are you? Are you okay with it? You seem to be, but...."

"Yeah. I'm cool with it. I freaked out a little at first, but now...." He tilted his head. "Now it doesn't matter. He's mine, you know?" With his eyes he pleaded for his dad to understand.

His dad smiled. "Yeah, son, I know. I'm happy for you. I know how bad you've always wanted a mate. And I admit, I'm a little disappointed I'm not going to be getting grandkids to spoil. But I like Keaton. It will be nice having another son. And besides, that puppy is pretty darned cute. I supposed he'll make a decent grandpuppy." He winked.

Chay blinked away tears. He hated to admit it, even to himself, but he'd been half afraid his dad would turn his back on him.

Joe walked around the bed and pulled him into a hug. "You could have told me."

He nodded and hugged his dad with his free arm. "I was scared to, I guess. Remi knows. He... we aren't friends anymore."

Joe leaned back and sighed. "Give it some time. You've known Remi for ages. You know how he is. Let it soak in. He'll come around."

Chay shrugged. "Doesn't matter. I'm not giving Keaton up. Not for Remi's friendship, not for Mom's peace of mind, not for any reason."

"That's how it should be, son."

"How'd you know?"

Joe smiled fondly. "Because I know you, son. I knew when you called after Keaton was brought in to you. I could tell by the tone of your voice."

"You told John Carter."

It wasn't a question, but Joe answered anyway. "Yes."

Suddenly, Keaton gasped, his eyes fluttered open. "Omigod!" He tugged on Chay's hand. "Where's Pita?"

He rubbed the top of Bit's hand. "He's at home, Bit."

"Oh, okay. I was worried." He looked around, then blinked up at Chay. "Where are we, Chay?"

"Hospital, Bit."

"Why?"

"You wrecked your car."

"I did?"

"Yeah, you did."

Joe cleared his throat. "Chay, is this normal?" He sounded scared.

Chay glanced up, saw the concern in his dad's eyes, and tried to reassure him. "Yes, Dad. He has a grade three concuss—"

"Hi, Joe."

His dad's eyes widened, and then he peered down at Bit. "Hi, Keaton."

Chay bent and kissed Bit's forehead again. "Shhh.... You're scaring Dad."

Keaton yawned. "I'm sorry."

"Mr. Winston?" The sheriff walked in and looked at them.

"Yes?" Joe answered.

Chay cleared his throat. "Dad, I think he's talking to me." To the sheriff, he held out his hand. "I'm Chay Winston."

Dad frowned and mumbled under his breath, "He said *Mr.* Winston." Chay couldn't quite hold back his grin. Calling him Mr. instead of Dr. was always a sore spot with his dad. His dad was proud of him and liked to let everyone know his son was a doctor, not a mere mister.

"I'm Sheriff Benson. The nurse said you're with Mr. Reynolds?"

"Dr. Reynolds," Joe corrected.

Chay smiled and elbowed his dad in the ribs. "Yes, sir. I am. Keaton's my... partner."

The sheriff shot a startled glance toward Joe, then back to Chay before quickly composing himself. "Would you step outside with me? I'd like to talk to you."

"Sure." He looked back at Bit and noticed he was asleep again. "Dad, you coming with us or are you going to stay with Bit?"

Joe extended his hand toward the sheriff. "I'm Chay's father, Joe Winston."

The sheriff nodded. "Mr. Winston, you're welcome to come too."

"That's all right. I'll let Chay talk to you. I'll stay here in case my other boy needs something."

Chay blinked and dipped his head at his father. "I'll be right back. Don't let him freak you out. If he wakes up again, reassure him. And come get me if the doctor comes in, okay?"

"Got it." Joe pulled a chair closer to Bit's bed and sat down.

Chay walked back into the little room in the ER in a daze. His chest actually hurt. He wanted to run to Bit and hold him and never let go.

"Son, what's wrong? You look like you've seen a ghost." Joe stood and crossed the room to him.

"Someone cut the brake line on his car. It wasn't an accident."

Joe gasped.

Chay strode right past his dad and over to Keaton's side. He stared at the battered and bruised face and felt his heart sink. He'd just found his mate, and now someone was trying to take him away. *Someone was trying to kill his Bit.*

Chapter Twelve

Several hours after being released from the hospital and a number of catnaps later, Keaton lounged on the couch. Chay used the arm of the couch to prop himself up, and Keaton used Chay as a backrest. Chay had been all over him since they'd left the hospital. Not that he was complaining. "Come on, Bit, think."

Keaton covered his face with his hands and groaned. He rested the back of his head on Chay's chest. He was dizzy. "I *am* thinking. And I have no idea. I can't imagine anyone wanting to kill me. I'm not important enough to kill."

The arms around his waist tightened and Chay's chin settled on his shoulder. "Come on, babe. How can you not know if you have enemies? How about students? Have you failed anyone recently?"

He shook his head and wished he hadn't when the room started spinning. "No."

"Okay, let's go about this another way. Do you think you getting shot is related? If that's the case, it's got to be someone who knows you're a wolf."

"I don't think so, Chay. I mean, how could they be related? I haven't lived here long enough. You were the first person I met who realized I was a wolf. Well, you and the game warden, but I didn't actually meet him until after I met you."

Chay got quiet and still for several minutes but didn't relax his hold. His lips teased Keaton's ear, and then he moved away.

"Okay, the other night, the night of the full moon, there was someone following us...."

"Yeah?"

"Yeah, and you got shot, and now someone cut your brakes. Do you really think those are all coincidences?"

"Actually, yes. I think the gunshot was poachers. I think it was probably another wolf following us, maybe even your dad, keeping an eye on us. And the car... well, the brake line.... That sucks, but it still could be an accident, couldn't it?" Man, he was getting sleepy again. He yawned and snuggled back into Chay, making himself more comfortable.

"The sheriff didn't seem to think so. And how do you explain the guy I chased off last night?"

"Okay, let's say it was cut. I don't have any ideas who did it. The only one here who can't stand me is Remi, and I don't think he dislikes me enough to kill me. He may be an asshole, but he's not stupid. He wouldn't want to go to jail for the likes of me."

"I agree Remi didn't do it. But I don't agree that these incidents are unrelated. Poachers don't generally leave their kill. And it wasn't my father who followed us the night of the full moon—I asked him at the hospital. So think." Chay smoothed the hair off Keaton's forehead.

He jumped when Chay brushed his cut. "Oww. I am thinking."

Chay kissed his ear. "Sorry. And you aren't thinking hard enough. This is serious shit, Keaton." He sighed. "Okay, if I'm correct and these things are related, then it's someone who knows you are a wolf. You already said you didn't meet anyone here who knows that, until after the gunshot. That means it's someone from Georgia. The man I chased off was a wolf. Do you have any former pack members who want you dead? What about your brother?"

Keaton thought about it for a minute. His brother was a dick, and there was no doubt he didn't like Keaton. He shook his head, then yawned. "No, no pack members. And my brother has no motive. I'm nothing to him. I was disowned. He now has everything he wanted without having to chance getting caught killing me. My brother shares my DNA, after all. Like Remi, he's an asshole, but he isn't stupid. A bit of an idiot maybe, but not stupid."

Chay growled and ran his hands through his hair. He was getting aggravated, but Keaton was having a hard time staying awake, much less trying to figure out why someone would cut his brakes. He grabbed Chay's arms and wrapped them back around him. The action was as much for Chay as for himself.

"We need to clean the garage out, so we can both fit our vehicles in there."

"What vehicle? Mine is toast, remember?"

"Yeah, I remember." Chay tilted Keaton's face up and back, kissing him. Chay rested his forehead against Keaton's. "We need to figure this out. It's not like we can tell the sheriff, 'Oh yeah, there are these other weird coincidences too, only Bit was a wolf when those happened.'" Chay leaned back.

A chuckle escaped. "Yeah, that would go over well. He'd likely arrest you if you told him that." Keaton yawned again. "Look on the bright side. Being a wolf, I'm not as easy to kill as a normal human."

"Yeah, that's not very reassuring. I'd just as soon you not be hurt."

"Me too. I'm sleepy."

After that he must have dozed, because the next thing he knew, Chay's hands rubbed up and down his chest and arms. He could hear the TV in the background.

Chay must have sensed he was awake because he began placing nibbling kisses on Keaton's neck.

"That's nice. How long did I sleep?" He tilted his head to the side, giving Chay easier access.

"Only about twenty minutes." His mouth latched on to Keaton's neck, sucking.

"Mmm...." Keaton's cock started filling.

Chay let go of his neck. "How do you feel?"

He grabbed Chay's hand and placed it on his growing prick.

Chay chuckled and squeezed. "That's not exactly what I was asking, but I guess this means you're feeling better."

"Uh-huh." Turning his head, Keaton searched for his mate's mouth. He was nice and cozy and more alert than he'd been in several hours. Keaton didn't want to think about brakes and people following him. He wanted his mate.

Chay's hand moved off Keaton's prick and slid under his waistband, holding him with nothing between them, as he slanted his mouth over Keaton's. Chay's tongue stroked his, slow and easy, matching the rhythm of his hand.

Keaton sighed into his mouth and lifted his hips, urging on Chay's actions. He relaxed and let his mate explore his body and his mouth. Why was it that Chay's hand on his cock felt better than his own hand?

"Oh...." A loud clank came from near the front door, and Pita started barking, his toenails clicking rapidly against the wood floor.

Chay's mouth left his, and his head jerked toward the commotion.

Keaton blinked, trying to make heads or tails of the situation. Maybe he was still a little groggy, because he hadn't heard the front door open. Then again, maybe it was just Chay who had him off-kilter. He followed Chay's gaze to find Lena Winston standing in the open front door, her keys on the floor and her mouth hanging open. *Uh-oh.*

"Mom, shut the door before the puppy gets out." Chay extracted his hand from Keaton's pants. Not that it mattered. Keaton's prick had quickly deflated anyway.

Lena picked up her keys and turned. For a brief second, Keaton thought she was going to leave. But she shut the door and turned back to them. "How could you? Your father tells me when I get home from shopping that Keaton got hurt. I come over here to see if either of you need anything, and this is the thanks I get?"

Chay exhaled behind him, and Keaton realized Pita was still running around barking. He dropped his hand beside the couch and snapped his fingers.

Pita came rushing to him, shutting up as Keaton picked him up and settled him in his lap.

Keaton smelled Chay's agitation. It had an underlying scent of fear. His heart went out to his mate. Chay had told him earlier that Joe had come to the hospital to check on him.

While he was there, he'd told Chay he knew about them and was happy for them. Keaton vaguely remembered seeing Joe.

He had known Lena would be the problem. Deep down, he suspected Chay did too. He patted Chay's leg in support.

"Chayton Montgomery Winston. You answer me right now. Explain yourself."

Chay grabbed his hand and squeezed. He slid out from behind Keaton and looked down at him. "You all right?"

He nodded. He wondered what bothered Lena more—his sex or his skin tone.

Chay turned back to his mother. "Mom. We are not going to stand here and have a screaming match. If you want to sit down and talk, that's fine, but I'm not going to have you yelling."

Lena flinched.

Keaton felt bad for her. She didn't know what to do. She was definitely mad, but she was hurt too. After a long, tense moment, Lena crossed her arms over her chest. "Does your father know about this?"

"Yes, Mom. He knows that Keaton is my mate."

Oh shit. Keaton suppressed the urge to groan. Now Joe was going to get bitched at too. He liked Joe. He hated being the cause of not only Chay's grief, but Joe's too. Heck, he might not care too much for Lena, but he didn't like hurting her either. She obviously loved her son. She was just... intolerant.

"What?" Lena jabbed a finger in Keaton's direction. "*He* is *not* your mate. That's an abomination. You are doing this to hurt me."

Chay sighed. It sounded sad, depleted. "Mom, why would I want to hurt you?"

"You've always liked your father better." Tears streaked down her cheeks, and her voice cracked.

"Ah, Mom, that's not true. How could you say that?" Chay walked to her, holding his arms out.

She stepped away. "Don't touch me! You don't touch me until you can act right. This is wrong, Chay, wrong. You need to kick him out—"

Chay shook his head, still talking calmly. His voice was almost a whisper. "No, Mom. It's not happening. You are going to have to get used to him. He isn't going anywhere. He's my mate, and I love him."

Lena glared at Keaton. "I hope you're happy." She looked back at Chay and spoke as quietly as Chay. "I can't do this. I can't watch you throw your life away like this." Without another word, she turned around and walked out.

Chay stood there for the longest time, staring at the closed door.

It nearly broke Keaton's heart. He set Pita on the floor and slowly got to his feet. He was still a little dizzy, but his mate needed him. He hugged Chay from behind, resting his cheek against Chay's back.

Chay turned in his arms and hugged him too. "What are you doing, Bit? You shouldn't be up moving around." He blinked away tears and hustled Keaton toward the couch.

Keaton wasn't going to let it go. He knew how bad it hurt. He caught the strong, tanned jaw in his hand and pulled Chay down to kiss him. "I'm sorry, Chay."

"Hey, at least my dad is cool, right?"

Sitting sideways beside Chay on the couch with his feet tucked up under him, Keaton ran his fingers through Chay's dark hair. *Yeah, but he's getting the ass chewing of his life right about now.* "Your dad is a pretty neat guy. You okay, Chay?"

Chay glanced over at him, leaning into the caress. "I should be asking you that. How are you feeling, Bit? Does your head hurt?"

"No. I'm good. Still a little dizzy, but not too bad."

"Are you hungry yet?"

Keaton shook his head. He was a little, but he didn't want to get up.

Chay bent his head and kissed him. "Thank you, Bit. You feel like crap, and you're consoling me. That's not right."

Keaton ran a finger down Chay's lips, trying to ease the frown. "That's what mates do." He shrugged. "My parents may not have liked me, but they loved each other. I, at least, had a good example in how to deal with one's mate."

Chay traced Keaton's cheek with a finger. "I don't know how anyone could not like you. There is something seriously wrong with your family, Remi, and my mother."

He grinned, the compliment going right through him. He no longer doubted Chay's sincerity in wanting to keep him. "You are a little partial, I think."

"Maybe a little. But I'm always right, so... there is something wrong with them."

"That is warped reasoning." He chuckled, then something occurred to him and he sobered. "Seriously, Chay, there *is* something wrong with them, not you. If they can't accept you, then—"

Chay leaned forward and kissed him, then pulled Keaton with him and lay back on the couch with Keaton on top of him. "I know that, Bit. They'll either come around or they won't. It's not my problem; it's theirs. Logically I know that, but it still hurts."

Keaton pushed himself up to straddle his mate.

Chay gave him a reassuring smile, but he knew how Chay felt.

"Doesn't help knowing that, though, does it?"

"No, it doesn't. But I'll get over it. I have you."

"Is that enough?"

"Hell yeah."

Chapter Thirteen

Chay was having the shittiest day imaginable. When he'd walked into work this morning, he'd had three patients waiting for him, and there had been a steady stream since then. He was worried about Keaton. His receptionist kept giving him dirty looks. Tina, his assistant, kept wandering room to room like she was lost. He caught Tommy, his other vet assistant, studying him more than once.

After lunch when it finally slowed down, he went to his office and called to check on Bit. He'd convinced Bit to call in sick, but damn it, he was still at home alone, and someone was out there trying to kill him. Chay pushed the last button. It took four rings for Keaton to pick up.

"Hello?" Bit gasped.

Chay frowned. "Why are you out of breath? What are you doing? You are supposed to be resting, not playing with the dog or cleaning the damned house or whatever the fuck it is you're doing."

There was complete silence on the other end of the line.

"Well?"

"I'm trying to decide whether to hang up on you or ask you what has you in such a mood. Right now I'm leaning toward hanging up."

"Uh-huh. You're guilty. What are you doing?"

Bit chuckled. "If you start bitching at me, I'm hanging up on you. I'm cleaning out the garage."

He sighed and pinched the bridge of his nose. Damn, his head hurt. He took a deep breath and let it out. It did absolutely nothing for his mood, so he tried it again.

"What are *you* doing?"

"Trying to decide whether to let you hang up on me or to calm down and ask you how you're feeling."

Bit chuckled again. "Well, do you want me to hang up or do you want to know that I feel fine?"

"Why are you cleaning out the garage?"

"You said yourself that we needed to clean out the garage, so I'm doing it."

Chay felt like banging his head on the desk. "'We' means me too, Bit. 'We' is more than one person."

"Pita is helping. That's more than one person."

Chay smiled. His Bit did sound like he felt okay. In fact, it sounded like Keaton was in a great mood. He wished he were there with Bit instead of at the office being scrutinized by his employees and patients. Well, not his actual patients, the animals didn't seem to have an issue, but their owners. "Pita is a dog. He's not a person."

Keaton snorted. "Tell him that. He's actually been a lot of help. I give something to him that he's big enough to carry and he carries it out to the trash can."

He blinked. "You have the puppy throwing things in the trash?"

"No, he can't actually reach the trash. He's making a pile beside the trash."

"You're kidding."

"Nope."

Chay chuckled. "I'll be damned. I'm impressed."

"Don't be. I have to play tug-of-war with everything I give him before he'll let go of it and put it in the pile."

Chay laughed at the image and relaxed. He felt better than he had all day. Leave it to Bit to cheer him up. "How are you feeling, babe?"

"I'm fine. A little bit of a headache when I woke up, but I took something for it, and now I'm fine. Just bored. I'm cleaning out the garage. That way I can park my new car in here. Speaking of which... after you pick me up from work tomorrow—"

Chay groaned. *Damn.* That meant Bit was going back to work tomorrow. "You won't take another day off?"

"Nope. I don't need another day off. It's not like my job is strenuous or anything. Anyway, will you take me car shopping?"

"Yeah, I'll take you car shopping. You know what you want?"

"Not a clue. If you're really nice to me, I'll let you help me pick."

He smiled. He could almost picture those light brown lashes batting, trying to look all sweet and innocent. "You're being careful, right? You are paying attention to things? You have the garage door open, right?"

"Yup. I do. And yes, I'm paying attention. My nose, eyes, and ears are on full alert."

"Good. Don't kill yourself trying to clean."

"I won't. I'm expecting help any minute."

"Help?"

"Yep. Your dad is coming to help me."

Chay's chest swelled with pride. "He is?"

"Yup. He's on vacation this week. He offered to take me car shopping today, but I wanted you to take me. That way we can pick together."

Chay closed his eyes. Damn, he loved this man.

Tina poked her head around his doorframe, looked left, then right. She caught his gaze, started, and her head popped back out.

Chay groaned. He was tired of this. He was going to have it out with his staff once and for all. "Okay, babe, I gotta run. Be careful and I'll see you tonight."

"Okeydokey. Later, Chay."

Chay hung up the phone and leaned back in his chair. He put his feet up on his desk. "Tina. Tommy. Cheryl. Come in here, please."

Tina came in first and cocked her head.

"Have a seat." Chay pointed to an empty chair.

Tommy came in next. His red hair appeared before he did. He seemed... nervous.

Chay pointed to the seat next to Tina. "Sit."

Cheryl came in the door, openly glaring at him. "Yes?"

Chay glanced around his office, looking at all three of them. "Do we have a problem? All three of you have been act-ing strange all morning."

Cheryl put a hand on her hip. "You tell me, Dr. Winston. Do we have a problem? There are all sorts of rumors going around."

Chay raised a brow at her. "Rumors?"

"Yes. They are saying you're gay." She glowered.

"Why is it any of your business?"

"Are you saying it's true?"

"Technically, I'd be considered bisexual, but yes, I'm with a man."

Cheryl coughed and sputtered. Judging by her reaction, she'd expected him to refute the accusation. "I quit. I refuse to work for a—"

Chay smiled. "Get the fuck out. I don't want to hear anything else you have to say."

Cheryl huffed, turned on her heel, and marched right out of the office. After banging stuff around for several minutes getting her things, she stormed out of the clinic, slamming the door behind her.

Tina blinked and her eyes widened. "Holy cow! I knew she was a bitch, but...." She shrugged. "She's only pissed because now she doesn't stand a chance nabbing you for herself."

Chay frowned. Tina didn't seem bothered by his announcement. So why had she been acting strange? "What do you have to say? What's with the looking from room to room?"

Tina's eyes shot wide, and she put a hand to her chest. "Me?"

"Yes, you."

She ducked her head and blushed. "You thought it was because of you? I mean, well, I was curious, but that wasn't.... I was looking for Pita. Where is he?"

Chay chuckled. "You mean all this time you've been trying to find Pita?"

Tina nodded. "I mean, I *am* surprised. I always thought you only liked women. But hell, Chay, my older brother is gay. I couldn't care less if you are or not. You know?"

Chay blinked. "Jake is gay?" He'd known Jake for years. Jake was a pack member. He was a little older than Chay, and they'd never been the best of friends, but they *were* friends.

"Well, yeah. Has been since longer than I can remember."

"Hmm."

Tommy smiled.

Chay frowned. "What?"

"I have the sudden urge to jump up and dance around the clinic and sing, 'Ding-dong the witch is dead.' Man, I'm glad you fired Cheryl."

"She quit."

Tommy shrugged. "Who cares; she's gone." Holding up his hand, he gave Tina a high five.

Wow, Chay hadn't thought Cheryl was that bad. And apparently Tommy was okay with his sexual orientation too.

Tommy looked back at him and grinned, obviously reading the confusion on Chay's face. "I'm shocked, Chay. But I don't give a damn. Your private life is your own." He shook his head. "Man, you got chicks all over you, and you.... Never mind. It's your life. If you're happy, I'm happy."

After that his day got progressively better. He was about to call Keaton again to check up on him, but then Tina came back into his office. "So... is Pita going to be back tomorrow?"

"Probably."

"Cool, I've gotten used to the little fur ball. When do we get to meet Keaton?"

Chay's eyebrows shot to his hairline. "You want to meet Keaton?"

Tommy popped his head around the corner. "'Course we do. Gotta see if he's good enough for you, Doc."

Tina chuckled. "Yeah, that too. But I figured I'm in love with the man's dog, I should at least get to meet him, right?"

Chay was astounded. He shook his head and burst out laughing. He looked at Tommy.

Tommy shrugged. "I was just thinking, though, we are going to need a new receptionist. My sis needs a job."

"Yeah, okay. Give her a call and see if she's interested."

"Thanks, Doc."

"Welcome."

Tommy and Tina disappeared after that. Chay smiled. It would seem that not everyone was going to abandon him as Bit had predicted. Somehow it made him feel a little better. It wasn't his mom, but well... maybe she'd come around too.

Chapter Fourteen

As Wednesdays went, this was a good one; he had the urge to whistle. It was sickening really. A grown man shouldn't go around this happy. Especially considering all the crap going on in his life recently, but somehow with Chay by his side, it seemed manageable. Scary, but not the end of the world.

Keaton threw an apple into the air and caught it as he shrugged his backpack farther up his arm. One of these days, he was going to have to get an attaché case, but darn it, that just seemed... nerdy. Yeah, he was a nerd, but he didn't have to advertise. Of course, dressed as he was and carrying a backpack, he usually got mistaken for a student. He wasn't sure what was worse, nerd or kid.

Chay was parked by the admin building. As Keaton approached, Chay smiled and pulled his sunglasses down with his finger.

Keaton opened the door, tossed his backpack into the back seat, and slid in next to Chay.

"What are you smiling at?" Chay leaned over and kissed him.

"Mmm." He kissed back, nipping his mate's bottom lip as he did so. "Just thinking how good you'd look in a red sports car."

Chay pushed his glasses back in place and sat up. "Oh? You want a sports car?"

"It's a thought. Let's go." He shut the door and put his seat belt on.

"Yes, sir." Chay drove out of the parking lot.

Keaton took a bite of apple, then offered it to Chay.

He shook his head. "No, thanks. Tina, Tommy, and I had a huge lunch. Tommy's sister started work today and brought us all tamales."

"Ahh...." Keaton smiled at the mention of Tina and looked around. Chay was still in scrubs, but Pita was nowhere in sight. He sniffed. Nope, Pita wasn't in the truck. Pita had gone back to work with Chay today. Chay claimed Tina threatened to beat him if he didn't bring the pup.

"You went home before you came to get me?"

"No, I came right from the office. Why?"

"Where's the dog?"

Chay chuckled. "Tina is puppysitting. I'm going to go get him on the way home."

Keaton took another bite of apple. "Uh. Okay." Maybe he'd get to finally meet Tina. Anybody who adored his dog as much as Tina did had to be pretty cool.

Keaton finished his apple as Chay parked the truck in the dealership parking lot.

Chay smiled. "Come on, let's go find you a new car."

Keaton smiled back and got out of the car. Taking the apple core with him, he tossed it in a trash can by the building. Chay grabbed his hand, and they wandered from car to car. It felt like the most natural thing in the world to stroll hand in hand with his mate, but about ten minutes into the strolling, it occurred to Keaton that people were gawking at them.

"Chay? People are staring." Keaton gazed around the car lot, watching people quickly turn away when he spotted them.

"So?" Chay tugged his hand as he bent forward, looking in the window of a blue car. "What do you think of this one, Bit?"

Keaton glanced back at their entwined hands.

"What?" Chay peered up at him.

"Doesn't that bother you?"

"No. Does it bother you?"

Did it? He thought about it for a minute. He wasn't used to the scrutiny. Jonathon wouldn't so much as accidentally brush against him in public. He actually liked holding Chay's hand. He squeezed Chay's hand and shrugged. If people didn't like it, that was their problem. "Not really."

Chay rolled his eyes and pulled on Keaton's hand. "Then quit giving me shit and look at this car."

Keaton looked. He wasn't impressed. Finding the perfect car was proving more difficult than he'd thought. It appeared it was going to take more than one day of shopping. They had similar tastes. However, all the cars he picked didn't have enough legroom for Chay, and Chay seemed to find the biggest damned cars on the lot. Which made Keaton feel like a twelve-year-old stealing his parents' car for a joyride. The sports cars sat way too low for Chay. He couldn't stand feeling like he was sitting on the ground. When Keaton complained that the luxury cars were too "suburban housewifeish" for him, Chay laughed so hard he scared the salesman off.

He was about to tell Chay he didn't like this car either, but then an "Ahem" came from behind them.

Keaton turned, letting go of Chay's hand.

A man in a gray suit stood there smiling at them. "Can I help you, gentlemen?"

"I'm looking for a new car. Something that isn't too big and something that isn't too small. Something sporty and American."

"Good. Let me see if I can help you with that." The man extended his hand. "Brad White."

"Keaton Reynolds." He shook the man's hand.

The man sized Chay up, extending his hand.

Chay shook it. "Chayton Winston."

Brad nodded and looked back to Keaton. "Is this your first car?"

Keaton barely suppressed the urge to roll his eyes.

Chay, the fiend, started cackling. "No wonder people are looking at us funny, Bit. They think I'm some perv who's robbing the cradle."

Keaton sighed and shook his head. He beamed at a very startled Brad. "Just ignore him. He has a warped sense of humor. No, this isn't my first car."

Brad gave him a wobbly smile and flicked a glance at Chay. "Okay. You want something sporty, American, not too big."

"Right. It needs to have legroom for him and not make me look like a kid who stole my parents' car."

Brad chuckled and led them to the other side of the lot.

Keaton ended up with a red Dodge Charger. It had been a contest between the silver and the red, but the final selling point had been how good Chay looked behind the wheel of the red one. He signed all the papers, and now he was waiting on them to bring the car around. Chay had just left to get Pita and some food. They were going to meet back at the house.

Then again, maybe he'd skip dinner and go to bed. He didn't feel too good. His stomach cramped.

The man drove up with his car, and he climbed behind the wheel. He thanked the man and left the lot. Damn, his eyes were blurry. He blinked, trying to focus. Fortunately, he wasn't too far away from home. Damn. Could his eyes be shifting? He blinked again—everything was still in color. How odd. Halfway home, the stomach cramps became more intrusive. He felt so terrible he didn't even get a chance to enjoy his new car.

By the time he pulled into the garage and got out, he was so dizzy he had to lean on the car before shutting the garage door.

The smell of food assaulted him as he opened the kitchen door. Pita came running toward him.

Chay stood at the counter unpacking hamburgers. Without looking up he asked, "How'd it drive?" He turned, holding out a plate with burger, fries, and ketchup. He frowned. "Babe, you look terrible. What's wrong?"

Keaton reached for Chay but missed due to the lack of clarity. He would have fallen but Chay grabbed him.

He clutched his stomach as another more violent cramp hit him. "Bathroom now," he managed to wheeze out.

Chay set the food on the counter, swooped Bit up in his arms, and ran for the bathroom. They made it just in time.

Chay ran his hand over Bit's hair again as the phone began to ring. He didn't like this. Not at all. He'd tried to heal his mate immediately by cutting his finger and making Bit ingest the blood. It was a known fact that werewolf blood could help heal their mate, but Keaton had thrown that up too.

"Hello?"

Chay started at the pack doctor's voice. He'd forgotten he was calling him. "Doc Baker. This is Chayton Winston."

"Hi, Chay. How are you?"

Keaton heaved again. Nothing came up. *Poor baby.*

Chay stroked his back. "Not good, Doc. I think my mate's been poisoned."

"The nice young man your father and John introduced us to? What are his symptoms?"

"He's vomiting. He says his vision is blurred, and he seems like he's wheezing to me."

"Did you give him blood?" Rustling sounded in the background.

"I did and he couldn't keep it down."

"Hmmm...." There was a slam and the start of a car engine. "I'm on my way over. Try giving him more blood. I'll be there in a minute."

"Thanks, Doc." After hanging up the phone, Chay set it on the vanity. "Bit?"

"Uh?" Keaton wheezed.

"Fuck, baby. Hold on. We're going to try more blood."

"It isn't going to work."

"Why not? If we can get it down you, it might."

Bit started coughing.

Hoping to get more air into his lungs and eliminate the wheezing, Chay hefted him upright. He was burning up. "Fuck." Chay ran into the living room where he'd left his medical bag. He brought it back and sat behind Keaton. "Hang on, babe. It's gonna work."

"It's not gonna work. I'm not human." He dry heaved again.

Taking out a scalpel, Chay cut his hand. He stuck it in front of Keaton's face. "Here, hurry before it heals."

Bit shook his head, but did as he was told, sucking the blood from Chay's hand. Shivering, he leaned back against Chay. He stopped sucking. "Damn, it's cold in here."

Chay shook his hand in front of his mate's mouth. "Suck."

"The cut is already closed," Bit whispered. "It healed."

Pulling his hand back, Chay rubbed Keaton's arms, trying to warm him.

Keaton rested against him for several minutes before the doorbell rang.

"Gotta get up, babe. I have to let the doc in. You'll be okay for a minute?"

Nodding, Keaton leaned forward.

As Chay opened the front door, he heard Keaton vomiting again. *Damn, damn, damn.* Grabbing Dr. Baker's arm, Chay shut the door and dragged him to the bathroom. "Hurry, doc. The blood I just gave him came right back up."

"I was afraid of this. I didn't know if it would work or not, Chay. Usually our mates are human. I'm not sure giving another werewolf blood will do anything. He's already a wolf, and he already has the unique healing abilities that the rest of us do."

Chay sighed. "Yeah, that was Keaton's theory too." And goddamn it, it made sense. What now?

Keaton lay on the floor, one arm across his chest the other flung to the side, unconscious.

The air left Chay's lungs as he raced forward. "Oh God no." He grabbed Keaton and hauled him into his lap. Everything seemed to slow down. He barely registered Doc Baker rushing forward. He felt for Keaton's pulse. It was weak, but there. Chay had to do something. This was suddenly way more serious than just letting the poison wear off. It was killing Bit.

Tears streaked down Chay's face as he cradled Bit to him. He racked his brain. What antidotes did he have? Was there anything that would counteract poison instantly? What the fuck kind of poison was it? Did he have time to get Bit to the emergency room?

"Chay, we are going to try getting your blood into him intravenously."

"Huh?"

"I have a line used for person-to-person transfusions."

Doc Baker dug through his bag. He pulled out some tubing with needles attached at the ends. "I'm not sure it will work, but we don't have anything to lose." He snagged Chay's arm and tied it off with an elastic band he got from his bag. "Fist."

Chay complied and Doc stuck him.

"Stand up, get above him, so gravity can do its work." Doc stuck Keaton with the other needle.

Chay reluctantly extracted himself from Keaton and stood, realizing what the doc was thinking. He untied the elastic from his arm and stared down at his mate. Was Keaton breathing better? It had only been about thirty seconds, but it appeared to be working.

Doc found his stethoscope and listened to Keaton's chest. He smiled up at Chay and nodded.

The lump in Chay's stomach slowly dissolved. It was going to work.

He brushed the sweaty blond curls off Bit's forehead and stared. His eyes caressed those fine features, the round little angelic face, the arched brows, the freckles he loved so much. Chay sighed and forced himself to relax. Bit would make it. It had been close, but Chay's blood had saved him. He woke earlier, long enough to rinse his mouth and let Chay undress him and carry him to the bed, but he'd quickly succumbed to sleep again.

Now Chay sat in bed with Bit's head in his lap. He tried to relax and just be happy Bit was alive. He was happy—extremely—but he was scared too. More scared than he'd ever been. Someone tried to kill Bit again, and they damned near succeeded this time.

How could he combat an unknown force? He had to find out where Bit had gotten that apple—that had been the last thing Keaton had eaten. The doc had told him that the only poison that worked on werewolves was sodium fluoroacetate. Further confirmation that the perpetrator was a wolf. True, a high enough dosage could kill any species, including humans, but it took a very miniscule amount to kill a wolf. He knew that from vet school. It was once used to control predators. What he hadn't realized was that a werewolf's regenerative properties couldn't heal them from a dose of it. According to Doc Baker, it was the one toxin their bodies couldn't drive out. And it was odorless, so even their keen sense of smell couldn't pick it up.

Chay exhaled and dropped his head against the headboard with a thud. This was some really scary shit they were dealing with. He didn't know what to do. He couldn't keep Bit locked up and they couldn't move. Whoever it was would follow them. He was certain of it. In fact, he was positive that whoever it was *had* followed Bit to New Mexico. He was going to have to ask Bit again when he woke up. He needed to know everyone in Keaton's past who might have cause to kill him.

Bit's eyes blinked open. The scent of arousal overwhelmed Chay almost immediately. Bit blinked again, and his eyes changed to their lupine equivalent. He opened his mouth, presumably to say something, and his canines lengthened, making not only Chay, but himself gasp. Sitting up, he turned toward Chay, a questioning look on his face. He gazed at Chay's lips for a mere second, then grabbed Chay's face and sealed their mouths together. He crawled out from the covers and straddled Chay's hips, his cock pressing hard and insistent against Chay's belly.

Chay tried to pull back, but Bit wouldn't let him. He growled—actually growled—at Chay. Chay finally managed to grab Bit's head and push him back. It wasn't that he minded the mauling, but damn, he'd at least like to know Keaton was okay. "Geez, Bit."

Keaton gasped and clutched his head. Ears appeared on the top of his head and his face began to elongate.

Chay stared, fixated.

Bit pulled his hands up and watched as long talons pushed out the ends of his fingers. That was weird. They should have fused into paws.

Chay's jaw dropped open. Keaton had just, for the first time in front of Chay, changed into his third form, half-wolf/half-man. His face was wolf, as was the tail Chay could see waving behind him. He had a fine covering of platinum fur all over, and in some places, like on the head and back, the hair was longer. His torso was still clearly human, but his hands and legs were something in between. His cock... still very human and still very hard.

"What happened?" Bit asked in a voice not his own. It was hoarse, low, growly, with a lisp to it.

"You were poisoned. We gave you blood. Don't you remember?"

The pale wolf head shook back and forth. Keaton took several deep breaths and closed his eyes. Slowly his face morphed back to human, followed by the rest of his body, but his fangs peeked out from under his top lip and when he opened his eyes, they were still lupine too. Keaton reached for him again, bringing Chay to his knees and tight against him. "I need, Chay. Bad."

Keaton's hips surged up against him, and he whimpered. "Please."

Chay nodded, not really understanding the arousal, but he'd do anything for his mate. He grabbed Bit's cock and

Keaton's head dropped to his shoulder, nestled into Chay's neck.

Bit let out a low growl. It wasn't fierce or angry, more of a rumbly, purring sound, the equivalent of a moan since his teeth were still shifted. It wasn't long before Bit's hips snapped into his hand.

Chay looked down, watching the slim hips rock forward and back, the thick cock slide in his palm. His own cock jerked, surprising him. He'd been too busy trying to please his mate to worry about himself. It hadn't started out as sex, but it was certainly about sex now.

He squeezed a little harder and let go. This time Bit's growl sounded fierce and Chay felt the fangs against his neck. Smiling, Chay enfolded his fist around his prick too. He wrapped both his hands around their cocks and stroked them together. It wasn't long before both their hips were moving.

Bit's forearms rested on Chay's shoulders and his cold nose tickled the side of Chay's neck. Then his tongue snaked out, licking.

Chay let his head loll back. His eyes closed and he concentrated on the feel of his hands sliding over his cock, mashing and rubbing Bit's shaft against his. The heat of Bit's throbbing dick felt good against him.

Keaton's breathing sped up in time with the thrust of his hips. He bit down on Chay's shoulder, hard.

Blood dripped down Chay's chest and back, and like that, he came. He hollered, actually fucking yelled, and shot so hard he felt like he would pass out. Cum splashed up his arm, his belly, his thighs, everywhere. There was too much to be all his.

Keaton let go of his neck and let out a growl that rivaled Chay's, his hips snapping against Chay's and the growl became a hoarse yell before Keaton fell to the bed on his back.

Chay followed him down, landing right beside him. They both lay panting, covered in semen.

After several minutes, Chay's brain woke up. *What the fuck was that?* It had to be some sort of pheromone thing or something. He'd never come so hard in his life. He damned near forgot his own name. He wasn't sure if that was something he wanted to try again or mark down on his list of stay-the-hell-away-from-permanently. Shit, he wasn't even sure Bit survived it. He turned his head to check.

The expression on Keaton's face almost made Chay laugh. Poor Bit's eyes were so wide, they looked like they were about to pop out of his head, but they were back to human. He stared at the ceiling, blinking periodically. His mouth opened, then snapped right back shut, like he wanted to say something but just couldn't form the words, though his canines had receded. He gasped like a fish trying to get air.

Finally Chay decided to help him out. "You okay?"

"I think so." He grabbed Chay's hand, entwining it with his. "Good Lord."

Chay nodded. "You can say that again."

"Is your shoulder okay?"

Chay glanced down at it. It was already healed, the wound closed, the blood starting to dry. "Yeah."

"What the hell was that?"

"A side effect from giving you my blood?"

"Yeah, probably. Don't do that anymore. I don't like not having control of myself. I lost it. I freaking bit you. I can't believe I did that. That's scary."

He reached over with his other hand and caressed the smooth, beloved cheek. "Not as scary as almost losing you."

Chapter Fifteen

Keaton glared down at his phone, then checked the clock behind him. This was getting ridiculous. Chay called him every fifteen minutes. He held up a finger to his class and pulled his phone off his belt. "Excuse me. I have to take this." He punched the Call button and put his back to the podium. "Chay, not now. I'm still alive. I'm just finishing up my lecture. I'll call you back," he whispered into the phone.

"Okay, just checking. Love you."

"Love you too," he mumbled, and hit End. He turned back to his class and smiled. "Sorry about that. Are there any questions?"

No one raised their hand.

"Okay, class dismissed. See y'all next Tuesday. Have a good weekend." He certainly would, and his weekend started today since he didn't have to work on Fridays.

They filed out as Keaton gathered his things. He didn't pay too much attention until he smelled another wolf. He hadn't had a wolf in his class before. He glanced up as the last student left the room and noticed a man standing beside the door.

Tall, with impossibly wide shoulders, he made Chay seem small. He was Native American, in his midthirties or thereabouts, and had short black hair. He wasn't classically handsome, though he was appealing, in a rough, masculine sort of way. He looked dangerous, and he was most definitely a wolf.

Keaton cleared his throat. He wasn't going to cower, even if he was a tad on the worried side. He was stronger than this wolf, but he hated to fight. The sudden urge to call Chay back overwhelmed him.

"Dr. Reynolds?" The wolf stepped into the room.

"Yes?" Keaton stood up straighter. He couldn't sense any malice, but if the guy was psycho enough to want to kill him, he wouldn't. Would he?

The man extended his hand and bared his throat. "I'm Jacob Romero. John Carter sent me."

John Carter? Chay's—his new alpha? Keaton looked at the man's hand and stepped back. "I don't understand."

Jacob gave him a sheepish grin and dropped his hand. "He asked me to keep an eye on you. His beta, Joe Winston, was very concerned about you and asked that you be assigned a bodyguard."

Wow. Joe got him a bodyguard? "I see." He pulled his phone off his belt. "If you'll excuse me for a moment?"

Jacob nodded. "Of course. Do you need the alpha's number or are you calling Joe?"

"Joe." Keaton backpedaled, keeping his eye on the other wolf. He felt like the man was telling the truth, but he wasn't going to take any chances. He'd promised Chay he wouldn't. He found the Winstons' home number and nearly pushed it. Then he thought better of it. Lena would probably be home. He quickly found Joe's cell number and dialed.

"Hey, Keaton, what's up? Everything okay?"

Keaton almost smirked. Chay hated it when Joe read the caller ID and immediately addressed whoever called. "Yeah, Joe, everything is fine. Listen, do you know a Jacob Romero?"

"Dad," Joe corrected.

"What?" Keaton frowned.

Jacob raised a brow.

Joe chuckled. "You are supposed to be calling me Dad, and yes, I know Jake. I guess this means you didn't get the message I left you on your voicemail?"

He hadn't checked his messages today because he assumed they were all Chay, fretting over him. Keaton smiled. "No, I didn't. And sorry, I forgot... Dad. He says he's here as my bodyguard."

"He is. John and I discussed it last night after we found out about you being poisoned."

Keaton nodded. "Okay, just checking."

"No problem, son. If you need anything else, holler. I'd talk to you, but I have to run. Lena has me up on the roof fixing the antenna."

"Be careful. I'll talk to you later."

"Later, son."

Keaton pushed End and replaced the phone at his waist. "Well, Jacob—"

"Jake please."

"All right, Jake. Have you eaten lunch?"

Jake shook his head. "No, I've been trying to stay downwind of you all morning."

Keaton laughed. "You did a damn good job. I had no idea until right before you walked in here. What made you decide to introduce yourself?" He slung his backpack over his shoulder and motioned for Jake to precede him out the door.

Jake stepped outside and turned to face him. "My curiosity got the better of me."

"Yeah, how so?"

"My sister has been bragging about you for weeks. Well, not *you* exactly... your dog. I had to meet the man who owns 'the absolute epitome of puppyhood.'" Jake smiled. "My younger sister, Tina, works for Chay."

Keaton laughed quietly. He had to meet Tina. It would seem the woman had designs on his dog.

They were sitting in the diner across from the campus when Keaton's phone rang again. He smiled and shook his head.

Jake chuckled. "Chay?"

"Every fifteen minutes." He hit the Call button and put the phone to his ear. "Still alive."

Chay's rich laughter echoed over the phone. "I'm glad to hear it. What are you doing?"

"I'm eating lunch."

"You didn't call me back."

"I got sidetracked. I sort of ran into my bodyguard."

"Your what?"

Keaton flinched. Apparently Chay didn't know either. "It appears that your dad and John decided I needed another wolf to keep an eye out for me."

"Damn, that's awesome. And a great idea. My dad freakin' rocks. Who is your bodyguard?"

Keaton looked up at Jake. "Let's put it this way. You better tell your VA I'm onto her. And she's not getting my dog."

"Huh?"

Keaton winked at Jake, knowing he could hear everything Chay said. "Jake Romero."

"Oh hey, Tina's brother. Good, you're in fine hands. Jake's a great guy. I've known him since I was a kid. Tell him I said hello. And don't believe anything he tells you about me. I didn't do any of that stuff, I swear." He could hear the good humor in Chay's voice.

Keaton shared a look with Jake and raised a brow.

"I'll fill you in after you hang up."

Keaton chuckled some more. "Good. I want all the gory details."

"Hey, I heard that," Chay grumbled good-naturedly. "Behave yourself."

"Yes, dear."

Chay groaned. "Okay, I guess since you have a bodyguard, I'll leave you alone and let you eat. I want details when you get home. I wanna know how often Jake is going to be with you. Tell Jake I'm going to pay him for whatever work he misses, no arguments. Tell him thank you."

"Anything else?" Keaton grinned. Chay was too cute when he worried.

"Uh, not that I can think of. Don't eat stuff someone leaves on your desk. Oh, and have Jake check your car before you drive it."

"Yes, dear." Like he'd eat another apple left on his desk. What did Chay think? He couldn't check his car himself? What was he helpless? Keaton rolled his eyes.

Jake chuckled and held out his hand.

Keaton handed him the phone.

"Chay?" Jake's eyes twinkled at him across the table.

Keaton heard Chay's voice, quieter but still easily discernable. "Hey, hi, Jake."

"I got it covered. I won't let anything happen to him. I promise."

"Thanks, Jake."

"You're welcome." He handed the phone back to Keaton.

"Okay, I'm back. Anything else?" Keaton waited for the barrage of "be careful" and "pay attention" and all that. It didn't come. Chay seemed to have relaxed with Jake's assurance.

"No. It's cool. I'll see you around five."

"All right. See you at home. Love you."

A soft, happy sigh drifted over the phone. "Love you too, Bit."

Keaton smiled and hung up.

After that, he and Jake ate their lunch and talked. Jake told him about Chay as a young wolf and all the trouble he'd gotten into. He talked about how friendly everyone in their pack was and his job as a private detective. Jake was down-to-earth, easy-going, and very nonjudgmental. He was a hell of a nice guy, and he brightened up Keaton's day. His company was a welcome distraction. Keaton decided he had found himself a new friend.

Jake spent the remainder of his guard duty with Keaton being fully aware of his presence. He even sat inside the lecture halls with Keaton. Keaton couldn't see any reason for the man to sit around outside the door, although Jake did go check the halls periodically.

They left class together, and Jake walked him to his car. After Jake looked it over, he handed Keaton a card. "Take this. It has my cell number, my office number, and my house number. You can always reach me at one of these numbers. Call if you need me. I'm going to follow you home. Then I'm off duty until

Monday. In fact, if you want, I can pick you up and bring you to work." He offered his hand, and Keaton shook it.

"Thank you, Jake. I... can I pick you up? I got the new car, and...."

Jake chuckled. "And you'd like to drive it. Okay, I tell you what. I'll meet you at your house Monday, and you can drive us. Deal?"

"Deal." Suddenly a thought occurred to Keaton. This man had no issue with his and Chay's relationship. "Hey, Jake. What are you doing tomorrow evening? You wanna bring your sister and come have dinner at the house with Chay and me? I've been wanting to meet Tina."

Jake smiled, appearing truly delighted. "I'd love to. Let me see what Tina is doing, and I'll give you a call. What time?"

Keaton shrugged. He better make it kinda late, considering his and Chay's culinary skills... or lack thereof. "Seven thirty?"

Jake nodded. "Okay, works for me. You need Tina or me to bring anything?"

"Nah. Just yourselves. If Chay screws dinner up too bad, we'll order pizza."

Pita ran around in circles barking. It was cute but annoying as hell. Chay wasn't a decent chef at the best of times, and the pup wasn't helping him concentrate on reading the recipe with all that yapping. Keaton had called earlier to inform him that he'd invited Jake and Tina to dinner tomorrow night. Chay was delighted Bit was making friends. He was relieved to find out Jake was acting as Bit's bodyguard. That had made the tension he'd been feeling ease some. But no way in hell was he going to get stuck cooking for company. Fair was fair. He was going to play the "but I cooked last night" card, and he was going to play it to the hilt.

He'd run into the kitchen and pulled out the cookbook while still on the phone with Bit. Fifteen minutes later, he was off the phone and he'd made no progress. Every time he settled on a recipe and took out ingredients, he realized he lacked a key item that made up the dish. He shook his head, picked up all the ingredients from the last no-go, stepped over Pita and put them back. They needed to go shopping. They were, apparently, out of everything.

Chay grabbed the cookbook and strolled to the pantry for one last check.

Pita bit the leg of his scrubs and started tugging.

Maybe he could order takeout, toss the containers, and pretend to have made it. It was a thought. Chay jerked his leg back up next to his other one. "Give it a rest, pup." The question was, could he pull it off without actually lying to Bit? Nah, probably not. Chay sighed and flipped through the book again.

It appeared as though he had everything for the recipe on the second-to-last page. He couldn't pronounce it, but it looked edible. He reached for the flour when the sound of a car brought him up short. "Crap." Out of time. Chay was anxious to see his mate. He swooped the growling puppy up and went to the garage to open the door for Bit. He should buy an automatic garage-door opener. A trip to Sears was definitely in order.

He lifted the door open with one hand, and... no Bit. He could have sworn he heard an engine. Glancing over in front of the house by the curb, he saw John and Mary Carter getting out of their car.

"Hi, Chay." Mary waved and rushed forward.

John followed her, carrying a big box. "Hey, Chayton."

"Hey, guys." Chay motioned to them to come on through the garage. "I thought you were Keaton. What brings the two of you out this way?"

Mary hugged him. "We brought you and Keaton some things," she said, petting Pita's head. Beating Chay to death with his tail, the mutt ate the attention up.

Chay's eyebrow shot up as he set Pita down, then closed the garage door. "What kind of things?"

They trailed behind him into the kitchen, almost tripping over the excited puppy.

Mary smiled and patted his arm. "We wanted to do something nice. You being newly mated and all."

John set the box on the kitchen table.

Apparently, he wasn't going to have to tell anyone about him and Bit. It would seem his dad had taken care of it.

Mary dug into the box, pulled out a smaller white box, and set it on the table. "I brought you guys a cake, and some towels, and a fruit basket."

John shook his head, smiling, as Mary continued to pull things out of the box. "We figured there wasn't likely to be a wedding. And all new couples deserve gifts, so we brought a few things. I tried to talk her out of the fruit basket."

Mary snorted. "Yes, he did. He said I should get a meat tray."

Oh wow. How cool was that? Chay chuckled. "Mary, we *are* wolves," he joked. "Thanks, guys. I can't believe you did this."

John slapped him on the shoulder. "Your father is one of my oldest friends and my beta. You didn't think we'd just ignore the fact that you finally found your mate, did you?"

Chay shrugged. "Well, considering.... Yeah, I guessed it would pretty much go unnoticed or unacknowledged, anyway."

"Nonsense." Kissing his cheek, Mary continued, "Everyone who knows you knows you've always wanted a mate. So what if your mate's not quite what we all expected? He seems like a nice young man, and you are obviously happy, so we are too."

Man. Hugging Mary back, Chay grinned. "Thank you."

"You're welcome," they chorused.

John leaned against the table, suddenly looking serious. "I'm sorry your mother isn't taking it well. Rest assured you'll get no grief from the pack. This isn't unheard of. I know of two other similar cases. A friend of mine in Texas is mated to another wolf. He's actually married, and he, his mate, and his wife are all quite happy together. They have four kids between them, and when I talked to Emilio last, he and Michael had two grandsons and another grandchild on the way."

Chay cleared his throat. "Yeah, well, I doubt seriously Bit, er, Keaton is going to let me have a wife." He chuckled nervously. "I hope you aren't expecting kids or anything. I mean—"

John laughed. "No, no, not at all. I was only pointing out that there are other wolves who have male mates. That happens to be how Emilio and Michael deal with it. They've been together for over forty-some-odd years. Since they were children. Sarah has been with them for over thirty."

Feeling better, Chay nodded. It was nice to know they weren't expecting him to chase after women even though he was mated. Because it wasn't happening. He wasn't sharing his Bit, and he knew darn well how Bit would feel about sharing him. "Would the two of you like something to drink?"

Mary made swishing motions with her hands. "Oh no, we aren't staying long. We're on our way to a dinner party. We just wanted to congratulate you and throw in our support."

Chay smiled. "It means a lot to me, thank you."

Grabbing Mary's hand, John pulled her to his side. "You let me know if you find out anything else about who is trying to hurt Keaton. I have Jake Romero looking into it and watching Keaton while he's at work."

"I appreciate that. Keaton met Jake today. He invited him to dinner tomorrow evening, so I'm going to go over some things with him and see if between the two of us we can't get Keaton thinking. He has to know who's doing this. I'm betting it's someone from his old pack."

John nodded. "I'm betting you're right. Is he okay? Doc Baker called us last night to let us know what was going on. I'd already decided to assign Jake to watch his back when your dad called and asked me to make the arrangements."

"I appreciate it, John."

"We take care of our own, Chay. You know that. I expect to be kept up-to-date, and if you need anything, I expect to know about it." He offered his hand, and Chay shook it.

"Yes, sir. Thank you again. For everything."

He saw them to the door. John stopped him again, waving Mary on to the car. Waiting till she was out of hearing, he took an envelope from his pocket and tucked it into Chay's hand.

"Sorry about the girly towels and stuff. Here's a gift certificate to the mall. You boys go get something you want, something fun." He winked and strolled to the car to open his mate's door.

Well, son of a gun. Didn't that beat all? Chay stood there flabbergasted as John and Mary both waved and pulled away from the curb. Chay smiled and shut the door.

He glanced at the clock on his way to the phone. *Where was Bit?* He wasn't too late, but Chay was already paranoid with the recent attempts on his life. He'd driven Keaton up the wall with his phone calls today, but that was tough. He wasn't going to stop worrying until they found out who wanted to kill Bit. He picked up the phone and began dialing Keaton's cell number when someone knocked on the door.

Chay frowned and sniffed the air as he headed to the door. Whoever it was, was a wolf and didn't smell familiar.

Pita ran through the doggy door, barking, and beat Chay to the front. He immediately started growling.

Chay blinked. Pita growled a lot, but it was usually the "hey, play with me, aren't I cute" growl. This growl was mean, cute—because Pita was too little to be vicious—but mean. Chay picked him up and peeked out the peephole. "Shh. Quit growling, pest."

Chay didn't recognize the man, but he looked harmless enough. He looked like.... Chay opened the door. "Hello?"

"Hi, is Keaton here?"

Chapter Sixteen

"Wilma! I'm home!" Keaton giggled as he set the bags of food on the counter. *Ha.* Chay hadn't gotten dinner. Which meant tomorrow was Chay's turn. *Yes.* Keaton grinned. Why hadn't Chay and Pita come to greet him at the back door like they usually did? Surely they'd heard his car pulling up and him opening and shutting the garage door.

Ooh, what's that? There was a box on the table. He breathed in. A cake? He strolled over and started going through the brown box. Inside was a smaller white one—definitely a cake box—he inhaled again. Chocolate. And some towels and fruit and.... Had Chay gone shopping?

"Bit, we have company."

Keaton turned as Chay came into the kitchen carrying Pita. He was frowning. *Uh-oh.* Keaton walked up to him, rose up on tiptoe, and kissed his chin. He scratched Pita's head and got puppy kisses on the hand. "Who is it?" He sniffed.

His eyes widened. What the hell was *he* doing here?

Chay wrapped an arm around him and hugged him, dropping a quick kiss on his lips. "I'll put the food in the microwave so it will stay warm."

"Yeah. I'll go and see...." Keaton rubbed his sweaty palms on his slacks. "What does he want?"

"Says he came to see you."

Why? In a daze, Keaton went into the living room. He stopped in the doorway.

Aubrey wandered around the living room, his back to Keaton. He looked a little broader through the shoulders, and his golden hair was longer than the last time Keaton had seen him. Sensing his presence, Aubrey turned. One side of his mouth lifted up in a half smile. "Hello, little brother. Looks like you've done okay for yourself. I have to admit, when you wadded up your trust fund statement and threw it in Dad's face, I really expected you to come running back in a matter of weeks. But it looks like I was wrong."

"How did you find me, and what the hell do you want?"

Aubrey's blue eyes widened a bit, and then he smiled, showing straight white teeth. "Is that any way to greet your older brother?"

Keaton squelched the urge to scream and pull at his hair. He wasn't going to let Aubrey get to him. It had been almost two years since Keaton had left Georgia for good, and in that time no one in his family had made an effort to contact him. Of course, he hadn't exactly told them where he was going. "I seem to remember you telling me I was dead to you. Therefore I have no brother. What do you want, Mr. Reynolds?" Yeah, it was juvenile, but what the hell? He'd just as soon make this short if not sweet and leave no room for doubt in Aubrey's mind that Keaton didn't want anything to do with him.

Aubrey chuckled. "Still have an attitude problem, I see." He walked back to the couch and sat down. "Well, apparently you aren't in a forgiving mood, so I'll get right to the point. Mom and Dad want you to come home."

"Excuse me?" Keaton raised a brow, going for the "superior" look that Aubrey always hated.

Aubrey's gaze darted over his shoulder as Chay came to stand behind Keaton.

Chay's hand settled on the small of Keaton's back. Pita growled.

Keaton kept his attention on his brother but took comfort in the solid presence of his mate. "Why would Mom and Dad want me to come home? They disowned me."

Aubrey gritted his teeth and rolled his eyes. "Not exactly."

Interesting. "Not exactly?"

"They hired a private detective to find you. They want you to come home. It's a long story, but no one expected you to take off and—"

"I'm not coming home. If they want to see me so bad, they can come to me."

Chay rubbed between his shoulder blades and leaned in close. Pita licked Keaton's ear.

Keaton sighed and stepped out of reach of the puppy's tongue. Yes, he knew he was being a dick, but that was just too bad. Damn, he was getting a headache. Keaton pinched the bridge of his nose. "Is that all you want, Aubrey?"

"I came to offer to take you back."

"Ah, how sweet.... But no, thank you. *If* I decide to go back, it will be on my own terms. Now, if that's all you wanted... piss off."

Glaring, Aubrey stood up. "You know you ought to follow your boyfriend's example. He's much more polite than you are."

Keaton stalked over to the door and jerked it open. "Yes, well, we can't all be perfect. But he is my mate, and I love him anyway."

Aubrey snorted and walked out. Turning back, he looked past Keaton to Chay. "It was nice meeti—"

Keaton slammed the door shut, strolled up to Chay, and took Pita. "Come on, pup. I brought you some french fries." His food was getting cold. Arguing with Aubrey wasn't worth eating cold hamburgers for.

Chay bit his bottom lip to keep from laughing. *Holy shit!* He'd forgotten how cold Bit could be. Damn, his mate had a temper.

He'd been surprised to see how much Aubrey looked like Keaton. He had the same platinum curls, the same pretty blue eyes. His face was shaped the same, but he had a different nose, not near as nice as Bit's cute little upturned one.

Chay walked into the kitchen to find Bit at the table with a hamburger in one hand, feeding Pita fries with the other.

Bit held the burger up. "Sorry. I just.... Sorry, I should have waited for you to come eat. I poured you some tea."

Chay sat across from Bit and took a swig of his tea. "No problem. Thanks for picking up food. Everything I tried to cook, we didn't have. We are going to have to go to the grocery store tomorrow." He pointed at his mate and glared. "Speaking of which, you cheated. You brought food so I'd have to cook tomorrow."

Keaton grinned, his eyes twinkling, and ate another bite of his burger.

Chay chuckled and unwrapped his own burger. He grabbed the ketchup and put some on the wrapper for his fries.

He too had tried to cheat and make dinner, but he wasn't going to point that out. "I'll make you a deal. How about we both cook tomorrow?"

"We could do takeout."

Chay shrugged. "Yeah, I guess we could. But one of these days we are going to have to start cooking."

"Nah, we should just hire a cook and be done with it."

Wouldn't that be the life? Chay drank some tea and watched Bit frown at his burger.

Pita barked, wanting another fry.

Chay rolled his eyes when Bit tossed Pita several. It was an ongoing argument. He told Bit over and over not to feed Pita from the table. The dog was going to think it was okay to beg when they ate. But he valued his life too much to correct Bit tonight.

"What do they want, Chay?"

He wished he knew. It was anyone's guess as to what Bit's family wanted. "Don't know, Bit. Why don't you call them and see?"

Keaton shook his head. "I don't get it. I mean, what makes them think they can pop back into my life after turning their backs on me?"

"Maybe they're sorry for the way they treated you. Maybe they've realized what a big mistake they made. What if they want to make amends?"

Bit looked up at him, his blue eyes troubled. "You think I should forgive them?"

"I don't know, Bit. It's not up to me. I'm not sure what I'd do in your position. I'd like to think I'd at least call and see what they wanted, but I didn't go through what you did. I know I'm still hoping my mom will tell me she's sorry, but she didn't exactly abandon me. She got pissed and yelled. She never actually disowned me or anything."

Keaton nodded. "Yeah, you're right. I should at least call and see what they want. But not now. I think I need to go for a run. You wanna shift and go with me, after we eat?"

"Sure, we can drive down to the rez. It'll be good to get away for a few hours." There was nothing quite like running in wolf form to help clear your head.

Returning from their nice hour-long run, they pulled up in the drive. The headlights of Chay's truck illuminated Remi's motorcycle parked close to the garage door. Keaton looked around but didn't see Remi anywhere. "Okay, where is he? That *is* Remi's bike, isn't it?"

Chay frowned. "Yeah." He put the truck in Park. "He has a key to the back door—I forgot to ask for it back—maybe he's inside."

Keaton snorted and made a mental note to buy a lock for the back gate and a new lock for the back door. "What does he want?"

Chay shrugged. "Only one way to find out. Come on."

As soon as Chay opened his door, the coppery smell of blood hit them. Chay's eyes widened. "Fuck."

That pretty much summed it up. Keaton hoped it wasn't Remi's blood he detected. He might not like the guy, but he didn't want him dead. Whoever the blood belonged to, it would be a miracle if they were still alive. Keaton could tell by the strength of the scent that it was a large quantity of blood. He reached for his own door, but Chay's hand stopped him. He turned, peering into those deep brown eyes. Chay didn't say anything. He didn't have to. The look in Chay's eyes said it all. *I'm scared. I love you. Be careful.*

Which virtually mirrored Keaton's feelings. He leaned forward, brushing his lips across Chay's, then got out of the truck. He shut his door quietly, looked around, and inhaled deeply. The shiver that trickled through him wasn't due to the nip in the autumn air. The porch light cast shadows across the yard, and the quiet made it that much more ominous. He smelled a wolf somewhere near the house. There was also a lingering scent of at least one other wolf, maybe more. It was hard to tell because the scent of blood overpowered everything else. Keaton shoved his hands into the pockets of his jacket and shuddered again.

Just as Keaton realized the strongest wolf scent belonged to Jake, the man himself called out to them, "Keaton. Chay. Back here. Hurry!"

They rushed to the back fence. Keaton hesitated a brief second, wondering if somehow Jake was who'd been trying to kill him all along, then brushed the ridiculous idea aside.

Chay pushed open the six-foot-tall wood privacy gate first. "What's going on?"

It was dark, but Keaton had no problem seeing Jake. He was on the back patio, naked, covered in blood, with Remi cradled in his arms. "Come on! There's no time. We have to get him inside. He's dying."

Chay's steps stuttered when he spotted Remi.

Remi's clothes and leather jacket were torn to shreds, and he was bleeding badly. He was also unconscious and very pale. He'd obviously been attacked by a werewolf. Keaton took a deep breath, scenting the air, as Chay fumbled with the back door keys. He groaned. The smell of blood made it difficult to smell anything else. He wasn't even positive if there was more than one wolf.

Chay shoved the door open for his friend and tried to take him from Jake. "What?"

Keaton sniffed again. "I think I smell Aubrey." Was his brother trying to kill him?

Jake jerked Remi out of Chay's reach and growled, surprising both Chay and Keaton.

What the fuck?

Chapter Seventeen

Keaton grabbed Chay's arm and pulled him back out of the way. He held up a hand in an I'm-no-threat gesture to Jake.

Jake looked up at him, and for the first time, Keaton realized Jake's eyes and teeth had changed to their lupine equivalent.

Chay gasped.

Jake stood, supporting Remi's weight easily. "Hurry up," Jake growled as he carried Remi's limp body past them.

Chay took off down the hall, turning on lights as he went.

Jake's lupine eyes seemed haunted as he laid his burden on the couch. "Who is he?"

"Chay's friend. His name is Remi."

Jake nodded, brushing a strand of dark hair off Remi's face.

Chay came running back into the room with his medical bag. "Jake, you're gonna have to let me in here."

Jake hesitated for a second, then stepped aside.

"Bit, get over here and help me." Chay leaned down over Remi, using his stethoscope on him. "Find something to prop his feet up, Bit."

Keaton gathered all the pillows he could find and stuffed them under Remi's feet. Pita barked his fool little head off from the laundry room where they'd left him.

Chay shook his head. He looked up at Keaton, tears in his eyes.

Keaton closed his eyes and took a deep breath. He didn't like Remi, but he didn't want the man to die either. The pain etched on Chay's face at his friend's fate brought tears to

191

Keaton's eyes as well. "Can we try to change him?" He was willing to do whatever was necessary to erase the hurt his brother had caused, though not all humans could be changed into wolves, and it was something they rarely tried. Pack alphas generally frowned upon it, though there was no actual rule against it.

"It's the only way he's going to make it. He's barely hanging on. I want to, but we aren't supposed to change someone against their will."

"Fuck that!" Jake pushed Chay out of the way, knocking him on his ass. He bit into his own arm, ripping the skin open. Blood poured out. It must have hurt like hell, but Jake never even winced. He bent over Remi, dripping blood into his open wounds.

Keaton and Chay blinked at each other. Keaton jumped up. "You heard the man." He reached around Jake's bare thigh and worked his fingers into the largest laceration on Remi's chest. He pulled the cut apart, allowing Jake to get more blood in. The smell of Chay's blood tickled his nose, making his eyes shift.

Chay's bleeding arm came around the other side of Jake, hovering over another wound on Remi's chest.

Keaton hurried to spread that gash too. He wasn't sure if it would work or not. Werewolf blood would turn a nonwolf male into one, but Remi was pretty far gone. A werewolf's blood could heal his human female mate without turning them into a wolf. Keaton wondered.... It didn't matter; they didn't have time to chance it.

The combined strength of Jake's and Chay's blood sped up the process. Remi's wounds were healing before their eyes, so it must be working.

The tear on Jake's arm healed and Jake brought it back up to his mouth, intent on ripping it open again.

Chay grabbed his arm. "No. It's working, there's no need."

Jake snarled, jerking his arm from Chay's grip, and prepared to attack.

Keaton tensed, his hands shifting to claws. He moved between Chay and Jake, instinctively protecting his mate. He growled and felt his teeth sting his gums.

Chay pulled Keaton back with him, moving away from Jake.

Jake blinked, flinching like someone slapped him. He held his hands up. "I'm sorry."

Keaton relaxed, letting his hands shift back to normal. His teeth receded, and with the smell of Chay's blood no longer fresh, his eyes changed as well. "I'm sorry too. You all right?"

Jake took a deep breath. "Yeah." He ran his bloody hands down his face. He looked up. His eyes were still lupine, but his teeth shrank back to human.

Chay cleared his throat. "Why don't you go take a shower, Jake? I'll go find you some of my sweats to wear."

"I...." Jake glanced down at Remi, then at his own naked, bloodstained body. "Yeah, okay. I'll go clean up, then fill you both in on what happened. You think he'll be okay?"

Chay nodded. "I think so. Keaton and I will clean him up while you're in the shower. When he wakes up, we are all going to have some explaining to do."

Keaton snorted. "No shit. Somehow I never imagined my-self explaining the existence of werewolves to Remi. Someone should call and tell John Carter too." It was protocol, after all, to tell the alpha of new wolves in his territory.

Chay ushered Jake into the bathroom while Keaton peeled the remaining, mangled, bloody clothes from Remi's body. It was a shame the man had a personality defect, because he was gorgeous. He was damned near as handsome as Chay.

The shower started, and Chay came back with some clothes. "Okay, Bit, I got a bucket of soapy water and a wash-cloth. How are his wounds healing?"

"Good. They're closed. Still red and a little puffy, they're starting to scab over. Damn, that works fast."

Chay set the bucket down and pulled Keaton into his arms, kissing him soundly. "Yeah. I've never actually seen anyone changed. I had no idea it would work so quickly. How long do you think he'll be out of it?"

"I don't know. This is a first for me too. I'm so sorry, Chay." Keaton caressed his mate's cheek. "It was my brother. I'm sure of it. It's just too big of a coincidence not to be."

Chay nodded. "I think so too." He hugged Keaton, holding him for several seconds. "We need to get Remi cleaned up."

"Yeah." They pulled apart and got to work. There would be plenty of time to talk later. They needed to know what Jake knew and what Remi remembered when he woke.

Chay rolled Remi onto his side. "Grab the rag and wash off his back."

He got the rag, wrung it out, and leaned over the uncon-scious man.

"Are there any scratches there?" Chay asked.

"Jesus Christ." There were crisscrossing scars all up and down Remi's back, like he'd been whipped.

"Guess they didn't heal, huh?"

Keaton looked up at Chay as he ran the washcloth over Remi's back and shook his head. "No."

"I didn't think they would, but I've never known anyone who was turned, so...." Chay shrugged.

"What the hell happened?" Keaton dipped the rag again, rinsing the blood out. He washed Remi's buttocks and thighs, noticing similar scars, but not as many as on his back.

"He and our friend Billy were walking back from the movie theater and some guys jumped them. Remi ended up in the hospital in ICU. Billy died."

Keaton gasped, caught off guard. That didn't seem right. The scars were consistent with a whip or a belt. *Why would someone...?* "Did they know the assailants?"

Chay gently laid Remi down, meeting Keaton's gaze. "No. Remi never could identify them."

"Chay, these were done by a belt." He picked up the shirt Chay had brought and worked it carefully over Remi's head. He put Remi's arms through and pulled the shirt down.

"Yeah. Simon, Bobby, and I always figured it was Remi's dad, but we never could get Remi to say so. And Remi's dad didn't have a reason to kill Billy. It wasn't like it was a big secret that Remi's dad was abusive. We all knew it. My dad even tried to get Remi away from his dad, but Remi never would cooperate when CPS questioned him. He didn't want to leave his mom and Sterling." Chay tossed Keaton the boxers he'd brought for Remi to wear.

"Sterling?" He helped Chay lift Remi to put boxer shorts on him.

"Remi's younger brother. He was an infant when Remi was almost killed. Sterling's a great kid."

Keaton shook his head. He'd have never thought Remi the type to sacrifice himself for another, like he obviously had for his younger sibling. He was about to ask where Sterling was now, but then Jake came into the living room.

Jake wore a pair of Chay's sweats and a T-shirt. Damn, Jake was a big man. Chay's sweats looked like tights on him. Jake sat in a chair across from the couch, his eyes back to human. "He looks better."

Keaton glanced down at Remi, now clothed. He did look better. His tanned skin wasn't quite normal yet, but it was close. His breathing was regular.

Chay nodded. "Yeah. I need to dump this water out." He took the bucket of water to the kitchen.

"You want something to drink?" Keaton asked.

Jake stared at Remi for several seconds, then smiled sadly. "He's my mate."

Shit, shit, shit. Keaton ran his hand down his face. "I was afraid of that."

After cleaning up, Chay grabbed three beers and settled in the living room with Bit and Jake. The three of them sat quietly drinking their beers and watching Remi.

Chay sniffed. "He smells like a wolf now."

Keaton's hand landed on his shoulder. "Yeah, I noticed that too."

Jake signaled his agreement by dipping his head. "I'm not surprised. I've never heard of a case where a man was given blood and not been changed."

"What happened, Jake?" Chay asked.

"When I followed Keaton home, I saw a car parked at the curb. I thought it looked suspicious, so I waited."

Keaton sighed. "My brother."

Jake nodded, absorbing that information. "After he left here, I followed him to that little wooded area a few miles away, the one that backs up to your subdivision. He got out and shifted. I parked farther away, staying downwind. Figured I should shift and follow him. By the time I caught up to him, he was already here. I saw the motorcycle and smelled the blood. When I jumped the fence, he was standing over Remi. I ran him off. From a distance, I thought he... Remi, was you, Chay. Until I got close to him."

Keaton squeezed Chay's shoulder. "Which explains a lot. I can see how someone would mistake Remi for Chay. They look similar from a distance."

Chay cocked his head. "But Aubrey is a wolf. He was even in wolf form. How could he not smell the difference? He'd just met me."

Keaton sighed. "My brother is an idiot. He's never been one to trust his senses. He probably didn't even try to differentiate scent."

Jake set his beer down on the table next to him and idly scratched Pita's head. "I guess this gives us a good place to start looking for your attacker. Why would your brother want to kill you?"

Chay turned his head to look at Bit.

Keaton shrugged. "That's it. I have no idea. He has no motive, whatsoever. I'm out of his life."

Chay frowned. "How about your parents?"

Keaton shook his head, bewildered. "I... I don't know. I don't think so. The same thing applies; there isn't a reason."

Chay patted Bit's leg. "Jake, can you look into it?"

"You betcha. Keaton, if you can give me names and addresses and that sort of thing, it'll go quicker. What exactly did your brother—"

Remi groaned and squirmed.

Pita, noticing him for the first time, barked, making them all jump.

Remi's green eyes blinked open, and his hand flew to his head. "Fuckin' A, my head hurts." He focused on Chay. "What the hell happened? I came over here to tell you I was sorry, and this dog—or actually it looked more like a wolf—attacked me. Don't tell me I passed out like some freaking pansy."

Keaton gasped. "You came to apologize?"

Remi pushed himself to a sitting position, wincing. "Yeah. I... uh, yeah. I'm sorry. Chay has been my friend for a long time, and if he chooses you, well, then—" Remi's eyebrows pulled together, his eyes narrowing. "Who are you?"

Jake stood, depositing Pita in Keaton's lap on his way to the couch. "I'm Jake Romero. I'm Keaton's bodyguard." He held out his hand to Remi.

The faint scent of fear permeated the air. Remi scooted back on the couch a little, staring at Jake's hand. He checked

Jake out from head to toe, and the smell of lust filled the room. His body was probably reacting to the scent of blood in the air, but Chay didn't relish telling Remi that.

Remi shifted side to side, trying to hide his growing erection, then drew his knees up. He finally lifted his hand and shook Jake's. "Remington Lassiter. Nice to meet you."

Dipping his head, Jake smiled and let go of Remi's hand. "Likewise."

Remi's nose twitched, and he frowned. "I feel really weir—" His eyes widened, and he glanced down at himself. He grabbed a pillow, placing it in his lap. "What happened to my clothes?" His brow furrowed. "Chay?"

Keaton nudged Chay's shoulder, and Jake cleared his throat. *Great.* Of course they were going to make him break the news.

Chay got up and went to sit on the couch beside Remi as Jake sat on Remi's other side.

Remi looked at Chay expectantly. "I passed out and peed my pants or something, didn't I?"

Chay smirked. "Er, no. I mean, you didn't pee yourself."

"Well, thank God for that. It's bad enough that I fainted." Remi rolled his eyes.

"Listen, Remi. What I have to tell you is going to be a little shocking. I... we... hell. The wolf attacked you and almost killed you, and the only way we could save you was to make you a werewolf."

Remi blinked three times, then after several silent seconds, threw his head back and laughed.

Bit shook his head. "Oh good Lord, Chay."

Jake stared at Chay like he'd grown two heads, his mouth hanging open.

Chay shrugged. "What? There isn't an easy way to tell someone that. Besides, I didn't see either of you offering up explanations."

They both groaned.

Finally, Remi's guffaws turned into chuckles. After a few more seconds, he stopped, wiped the tears out of the corners of his eyes. "Okay, I deserve that for being an ass. I'm sorry I was such a dick to Keaton. I actually heard about the cut brakes from Bobby and came to make sure everything was okay. So, what really happened to my clothes?"

Chay knew it wasn't going to be easy, but... *well, hell!* What was he supposed to do?

"Okay, I'm not shifting. He already thinks I'm an abomination. Let him hate one of you for being a werewolf. I'll stick to being hated for being gay. Someone else is going to have to show him." Bit tucked his feet underneath him and sat up straighter. Damn him, he almost looked amused.

Chay gave him the evil eye.

Bit smiled. "What? I'm just saying...."

"Yeah, whatever." He rolled his eyes. "Jake?"

Remi tilted his head to the side. "Joke's gone far enough, Chay. I said I was sorry, all right?"

Jake stood and started stripping off his clothes.

Remi looked at him and jerked back. His hands came up. "Whoa, hey!"

Jake ignored him and continued to strip. When he was naked, he moved back. "Ready?" he asked Chay.

He nodded.

Remi started to get up. "Okay, this is going too far, I mean rea—"

Chay grabbed his arm to keep him from leaving.

He glared at Chay, then turned back to Jake. Remi's eyes widened. All the blood fled from his face, and he let out a strangled gasp.

Chay followed his gaze to the large black wolf as Keaton pointed at Remi and yelled, "Chay!"

Chay turned just in time to catch Remi as he fainted.

Chapter Eighteen

Keaton sighed, sitting down hard on the edge of his and Chay's bed. Damn, Remi being Jake's mate sucked. Jake was a nice guy; he deserved better.

"What's that for? Did you and Jake get Remi settled?" Chay came out of the bathroom with only a towel wrapped around his waist. The man was fine, all that smooth tan skin and lean muscles. It was enough to distract a man out of his doom-and-gloom ponderings.

"Yeah. Remi is still out of it. Jake carried him to the guest room. He's going to sleep on the floor in case Remi wakes up, and John has been notified about Remi being turned. What was what for?"

"You sighed. Been a fucked-up day, eh?" Chay sat next to him, running his hand through Keaton's hair. "I love your hair."

Keaton smiled and tangled his fingers in Chay's hair, tugging him forward. He leaned his forehead against his mate's. "Yeah, really, really fucked-up. My parents may or may not be plotting my death. My brother definitely is. Remi got attacked and changed into a wolf, and Jake told me earlier that Remi is his mate."

"Holy shit." Chay's eyes widened, and his mouth gaped. "Guess that explains the boner, huh?"

Keaton nodded. "Tell me about it. Poor guy. And you aren't supposed to notice things like that."

"How could I not? It was pretty obvious. I thought it was due to bloodlust." Chay shrugged and kissed Keaton's nose. "Don't write it off yet. Remi's a wolf now too. Likely the same pheromones that are screaming at Jake will start yelling at him too."

Those dratted pheromones. "Yeah, like I said, poor Jake. I don't know what's worse. Having a mate who is a homophobic asshole and wants nothing to do with you or having a mate who is a homophobic asshole and can't keep his hands off you. How the hell does that work? He hates you for fucking him?" God, that was just beyond ridiculous. Did that fly out of his mouth? Keaton laughed and fell back on the bed. "I'm losing my damned mind. That's not even funny."

Chay flopped back on the bed beside him and wrinkled his brow. "You okay?"

Keaton shook his head. "Nope. How do you feel about Hawaii? Surely they need vets and teachers in Hawaii."

"Never been to Hawaii, but we aren't moving. We are going to figure this out and make a life for ourselves here."

Keaton snorted.

"At least we have an idea where to look now. We have a clue where the threat is coming from." Chay's fingers twined with his, squeezing.

He squeezed back. "Yeah. Why doesn't that make me feel better?"

Chay sat up and pulled his towel off, baring his gorgeous body. "Maybe this will help." He straddled Keaton's hips and leaned down to kiss him. It began as a gentle press of lips, but in no time Chay's tongue caressed his. Chay pinned Keaton's wrists, keeping them over his head. His hard cock mashed into Keaton's belly above the flannel PJs he had on.

Keaton's cock filled instantly, and he was pretty sure it was him moaning. He bucked his hips up, trying to get more pressure on his prick.

Chay grinned against his mouth. "Want you."

He nodded. "Want you too."

Chay slid off him, keeping hold of his wrists. He maneuvered Keaton to a sitting position and up off the bed. When Keaton stood, Chay dropped to his knees and slipped Keaton's pajama pants down over his hips, kissing the bare skin he exposed. "I love your body." He kissed one hipbone, then the other. "Love this ivory skin." He pulled the waistband out and over Keaton's dick and placed a kiss on the head.

Keaton moaned, tangling his fingers in his lover's thick black hair. "You're nuts. I'm scrawny and pale. You're the one who has a beautiful body and gorgeous coloring."

Tugging the pants past Keaton's thighs, Chay ran his hand along the insides. His tongue soon followed. "Mmm, then I guess I have a thing for scrawny and pale." He pushed Keaton's pants the rest of the way off and stood. "Bed, pretty baby." He kissed Keaton's nose, then went to shut off the overhead light. Chay sat on the edge of the bed and flipped on the bedside lamp as Keaton got into bed.

Keaton crawled under the covers, and Chay threw them off.

"I want to see you, Bit." He propped himself on his elbow and ran his other hand down Keaton's stomach. "Look how different."

Keaton glanced down at the dark hand covering his abdomen. Chay was as dark as he was light. The contrast was surprisingly sexy. He'd never thought about it before. As he watched, Chay's hand continued down and grabbed Keaton's cock. It felt like Keaton's whole body contracted when Chay squeezed.

He thrust up into Chay's hand. "Chay...."

"Hmm...." Chay moved his hand, dragging it up and down his shaft.

Keaton's toes scrunched. He was whimpering, but he didn't care. The more noise he made, the more turned-on Chay got. It was a win-win situation. He rolled to his side and reached for his mate. He kissed up Chay's jaw, nibbling as he went, and tugged Chay over on top of him.

Chay straddled him and sat up, still stroking Keaton's cock. "It amazes me how such a dominant wolf can be such a submissive man. Do you know how fucking sexy that is, Bit?"

Keaton shook his head. "I'm... I'm... not... I'm not submissive." He might have always taken a bottom role with Jonathon, but he never let Jonathon actually have any control over him. Jonathon's preoccupation with Keaton's family's money had allowed Keaton to manipulate the man easily.

"That's what makes it so damned hot. You aren't like this with anyone else but me. You weren't even like this with your ex, were you?"

"No. Only you." Keaton didn't trust anyone enough to give up control... anyone but Chay. With Chay it was a yearning. Chay needed to take care of him, and he needed to let him. Chay instinctively seemed to know what he needed. Keaton didn't have to pretend with Chay and put up barriers to protect himself. Furthermore, Chay wouldn't let him. It made him feel loved, special.

Chay smiled, kissed him, and rolled them over, pulling Keaton on top. "You are going to fuck me tonight, baby."

"But...."

Chay shook his head and put his finger to Keaton's lips. "I want this, Bit."

"You've never done this."

"Neither have you. It will be a first for both of us. Besides, I've initiated enough virgins; I know what I'm doing." Chay waggled his eyebrows.

Somehow Keaton didn't doubt that. The man was as charming as they came—he could very likely talk a nun into not just sex but anal sex and maybe even a blowjob too. "I hated my first time."

Chay raised a brow.

He shrugged. "Well, not hated. Hate might be too strong of a word. But it hurt, and it was uncomfortable, and I kept feeling like I had to go to the bathroom. And I was terrified of getting caught by my roommate. I couldn't even get a hard-on."

Chay reached between them, squeezed their pricks together, and winked. "I've already got one."

"It won't last."

"Wanna bet?"

Keaton chuckled. God, he loved this man. "Okay, you win."

"I always do, Bit."

Groaning, Keaton sat up. He leaned over and fished through the nightstand until he came up with the lube. He laid the bottle on Chay's stomach, making him squeak.

"Jesus, that bottle is cold."

Keaton giggled. "Does this mean you're going to complain if I don't warm the lube up in my hands first? I hate getting lube all over my hands—it's sticky."

"You never say anything about cum, but you're going to bitch about a little lube?"

"It's different." Moving the bottle from Chay's stomach, Keaton slid off of Chay to his side. Chay turned with him, meshing their bodies perfectly. Kissing and panting, they rubbed their erections against each other.

Chay worked his hand between them, wrapping their pricks together and stroking.

Keaton's cock was already slick with precum, and he smelled Chay's as well. He stared down at his mate's body, freeing himself from Chay's grasp. He gently pushed Chay to his back and positioned himself between Chay's thighs.

Chay, bless him, opened right up, spreading his legs wider. He even handed Keaton the lube.

Applying lube to his fingertips, Keaton pulled his knees under him and leaned over Chay. He licked a long line up Chay's shaft while circling Chay's hole.

Chay tensed for a split second, then relaxed.

Keaton continued to tease with his finger, never quite entering, and put his mouth to good use. He loved the musky scent of Chay, loved the feel of cock against his cheek. He dragged his face down Chay's cock and nuzzled his balls. Glancing up Chay's body, he buried his nose in the warm soft sac and inhaled deeply. A tingle shot through him. His mate's pheromones were so strong here. His cock jerked, leaking. He licked and sucked, then took one testicle into his mouth.

Chay's head shot off the bed, staring down at him. His face flushed with lust. "Mmm, my, Bit."

Keaton took the other testicle into his mouth, sucking lightly. He used his unoccupied hand to lift them and licked under them, all the way to Chay's opening.

Chay bucked against him, spreading his legs wider. "More, babe."

Keaton closed his eyes and worked his finger in. He got to the second knuckle before Chay moaned.

"Oh God." Chay dropped his head back on the bed.

Oh God was right. He was so fucking tight. "Oh my God, good? Oh my God, bad?"

"Different. Stings a little. Kind of burns." Chay pushed out and Keaton slid his finger farther in.

Chay gasped.

It sounded like a good gasp, so Keaton inched his finger out and pressed back in. He got another gasp in return. He grabbed Chay's cock and brought it to his lips, licking up one side and down the other before taking it into his mouth.

Chay groaned, his cock jerking in Keaton's mouth.

Keaton took it as a good sign and decided to add another finger.

Chay fidgeted a little, but other than that he didn't seem to mind. He was too busy alternately fucking Keaton's face and shoving down on his fingers.

He angled his fingers up, searching for....

"Holy fucking shit. Do that again."

Found it! Keaton smiled around Chay's dick.

Chay started making breathy moans. They were sexy as hell. Keaton added another finger and deep throated Chay at the same time.

"Oh, ow. Oh, God. Ow. Ow. Ooh...."

He stopped, keeping his fingers perfectly still, staring up at Chay. He was trying to decide whether it was an "omigod stop you're freaking killing me" ow or a "give me a minute to adjust" ow, when Chay pushed toward his fingers.

Keaton curled his fingers up again, hitting that sweet spot, and swallowed around Chay's cock.

"Stop!"

Keaton froze. He didn't want to, his cock was throbbing something fierce. He was dying to get the show on the road, but he'd rather cut off his arm than hurt Chay.

Chay's head popped up, and he reached down, cupping Keaton's cheek. "If you keep doing that, I'm going to come. Get up here."

He nodded and let Chay's dick pop out of his mouth. "You should turn over. It will be easier."

"No. Like this. Wanna watch you, Bit."

"You're sure?"

"I'm positive." Chay grinned, his eyes twinkling.

Keaton groaned at the trust and love he read on Chay's face. He grabbed the lube and slicked himself and Chay up. He went a little crazy with the stuff, but too much was better than not enough. After tossing the bottle onto the nightstand, he positioned his cock against his mate.

Chay pulled his legs up, holding them behind the knees. The pink opening begged for Keaton's attention.

Keaton pressed a finger in.

Chay moaned and moved toward him.

He didn't waste any more time. His cock wasn't much wider than three of his fingers. He lined his cock up to that snug little hole and pushed steadily in, watching Chay's face the whole time.

Chay hissed out a breath, his face pinched up a tad, but he started shaking his head. "Don't stop."

God, if only he could. He'd never felt anything quite so intense. This felt better than anything he could imagine. *Fuck.* That tight channel squeezed him, holding him like nothing ever had. He gritted his teeth in an attempt to go slow. Sweat beaded on his forehead and dripped down his temples. Abruptly, Keaton felt Chay push out. Keaton focused on Chay's face as it relaxed into a stunned, blissful expression. And what a great expression it was too. It meant not only did he not have to stop, but that Chay was not in any pain.

When Chay's ass finally rested against Keaton's thighs, Chay pulled Keaton's head down, kissing him soundly. His tongue darted in, then back out just as fast. "Bit, you should see your face." His voice was husky, deeper than usual.

Keaton giggled, but it came out as more of a squeak, and squeezed his eyes shut. He didn't have to see his face. He could imagine. It felt tight, all scrunched up. He was so close to blowing, his balls felt like they were practically in his throat. Taking a deep breath, he relaxed and looked at Chay. "Are you okay?"

"I'm fine, pretty baby. Feels weird. Full, a little uncomfortable, but not bad."

Keaton pulled back, his cock slipping almost out.

"Ahh...."

Oh yeah, he could relate. It was a contest sometimes as to what felt better, out or in. Personally he liked out, but well, yeah, it was a contest. He angled Chay's hips up, and pushed back in. Damn, that was just... damn. He locked gazes with his mate and started fucking him slowly.

After about the third thrust, those brown eyes widened, and Chay came unglued. "Fuck yes."

Keaton was actually shaking with the effort not to come. He untangled Chay's hand from the sheet and led it to his hard cock.

Chay grabbed it, his eyes never leaving Keaton's, and pumped.

Keaton picked up his pace, matching Chay's hand. The whole time they stared into the other's eyes. They were both sweating. Chay whispered encouragement to him. It was gibberish, but it only added to his arousal. His fingers dug into Chay's hips, and he slammed into him harder. "Chay, hurry."

Chay nodded, still working his cock. "Yeah, yeah, Bit, now."

Keaton came. Just let go. It was almost painful to hold back, so he went with it, filling his mate up. Lightning arced up his spine, pulling a hoarse yell from his throat.

Chay came seconds later, his eyes wide, still watching Keaton. Spunk sprayed over his hand, on his chest, even on Keaton's stomach.

Keaton's whole body protested. His muscles yelled, "fuck it," and collapsed in on him. His cheek landed on Chay's chest with a thud. It was probably the most ungraceful, unromantic thing he'd ever done. He giggled.

Chay chuckled. "Muscles give out?"

"Yep. That was... wow. Why didn't anyone tell me that felt like that?"

Chay wrapped his arms and legs around Keaton and squeezed. "I did one better. I showed you."

"I love you, Chay."

"Love you too, Little Bit."

Finally managing to get his body to cooperate, Keaton pulled his slowly dwindling erection out of his mate and rolled to Chay's side. Or rather tried to. Chay stopped him, settling Keaton on his chest, holding him close. Chay pushed up, his cock still hard against Keaton's belly.

Good Lord, how could Chay still be hard? More to the point, why was Chay still awake? Why was *he*?

Fingernails scraped up his spine, almost tickling. "Psst... Bit, I didn't lose my erection."

Keaton half chuckled, half groaned, hoping like hell Chay didn't expect him to do anything about it, then fell into a peaceful sleep, right on top of his mate.

Chay flopped down on the couch, watching Bit, who paced back and forth in front of the coffee table, dialing the portable phone. He and Keaton had decided upon waking that Bit should call his parents. If for no other reason than to see if they were home and get an idea on their location if they weren't. Bit acted like it wasn't a big deal, but Chay knew it was. He could sense the tension even though Bit tried hard to hide it.

Jake must have sensed it too, because he went after donuts, coffee, and a change of clothes. He didn't want to leave Remi—or Keaton, for that matter—for too long. The man took his job seriously, and last night he decided his job description entailed twenty-four-hour surveillance. It irked Chay a little that Jake thought he needed help protecting his mate, but he wasn't about to turn down the offer. He was a lot of things, but he wasn't stupid. In his opinion it was better to err on the side of overprotective when it came to his mate's safety. He even insisted on paying Jake for the extra time.

Bit stopped pacing right next to him. "Martha? This is Keaton."

A high-pitched squealing sound came over the phone, making Bit wince and jerk the phone from his ear.

Chay grabbed Bit's hand and pulled him between his legs.

The squeal dissolved into feminine babbling.

"Yes, it's really me. I'm fine." Bit got a goofy expression on his face.

Tugging Bit around to face him, Chay enticed him onto his lap.

"I've missed you too, Martha."

Chay gripped a handful of ass and squeezed, settling Bit a little closer.

Bit kissed his nose, listening to this Martha person on the other end of the phone.

Chay leaned back, concentrating on Bit's conversation. One nice thing about being a wolf was he could easily listen to a phone conversation and get both sides without a speakerphone. Martha was going on about how proud she was that Keaton had finished his doctorate. The woman sounded genuinely pleased to be talking to Keaton. Chay decided he liked her after hearing the affection in her voice for his Bit. He heard a yip and looked around Bit's shoulder.

Remi came yawning into the living room, carrying Pita. His hair stuck out at all different angles, and marks from the sheet marred his cheek. He appeared half-asleep, but no worse for wear. His eyes met Chay's, looking a little unsure and nervous.

Last night after Chay had given Remi a sedative, they'd talked and explained things to him. There was still a lot to go over, but Remi had eventually calmed down and listened. He seemed to finally accept it. Well, as best he could anyway. It had to be a surreal feeling, suddenly finding out that something you thought fiction was true to life. Chay related it to himself suddenly finding out there were unicorns, fairies, and leprechauns.

They had yet to tell him about Jake being his mate. Let the poor man get adjusted.

Remi set Pita on the floor and cautiously took a seat at the end of the couch. Remi looked at Bit, his eyes zeroing in on Chay's hands still on Bit's ass, and he blushed.

Chay ignored his friend's discomfort. If Remi was going to accept them, then he was going to accept all of them. He raised a brow at him. "You okay?" he asked quietly.

Remi nodded and whispered, "A little freaked-out. How long have you been a... a...."

"A wolf? All my life."

"How could I not know something like this?" Remi seemed a little hurt and a lot disbelieving.

"Would you have believed it?"

Remi snorted. "Well, yeah, if you showed me. Kinda hard not to believe it when it's right there in your face." He glanced around. "Where's...?"

"Jake?"

"Yeah. He's not dangerous, is he?"

Chay grinned. "Not to us, but he's not a man I'd want to cross. He went to go get coffee and donuts. We're out of everything, and a certain someone refuses to cook for me."

Bit pinched his shoulder and continued his conversation.

Remi's lips quirked as he shook his head. "He's so fucking pretty, he could be a woman."

Bit's hand shot up, flipping Remi the bird.

Yeah, and real ladylike too. Chay groaned and pulled Bit's hand down.

Remi chuckled. "He's one too, huh?"

"Yes. He's my mate."

Remi's eyebrows furrowed, his head cocking to the side a little.

"I'll explain later."

Remi looked like he wanted to press, but he finally nodded. "Who is he talking to?"

"He's supposed to be talking to his parents." He patted Bit's ass to get his attention. "Bit, who are you talking to?"

"Housekeeper."

Chay's eyebrows shot to his hairline. "Housekeeper?" His gaze flew to Remi.

Remi's mouth dropped open. "His family has a fucking housekeeper?"

Chay shrugged. "Apparently." Geez, he sort of gathered Bit had money, but a housekeeper?

Bit laughed, bringing Chay's and Remi's focus back to him. Absently, he ran his hand down Chay's chest. "Thanks, Martha."

There was a brief pause, and then Chay heard a man's voice. "Keaton?"

Bit's eyes twinkled, making him appear even younger than he usually did. "Hi, Thompson."

Thompson? Who the hell was he talking to now?

Keaton must have read his mind. He covered the phone and whispered, "He's sort of like a butler. He's Martha's husband."

Chay and Remi both blinked, eyes widening. *A housekeeper and a butler?* How rich were Keaton's parents? Good Lord, they could hire a professional hitman to kill Bit. Why would they bother sending their oldest son to sully his hands with the task?

After a short conversation, a new feminine voice replaced Thompson's. "Keaton? Son, is that you?"

Bit fidgeted. "Yeah, Mom, it's me."

"Oh my God. Howard. It's him! It's Keaton."

"Son?" a man—not Thompson—asked. They must have picked up separate lines.

"Yeah, Dad." Keaton frowned, directing a questioning look at Chay.

Chay knew exactly what he was thinking. They did not sound like two people plotting their son's demise.

"Oh, honey. We've been looking for you. We're sorry," Bit's mom said.

"We hired a detective to find you, but from the report Aubrey got last week, there was still no news. Where are you, son?" Howard, Bit's dad, inquired.

"I'm in New Mexico. What do you mean there was no word? Aubrey is here. He is the one who told me you were looking for me."

"What?" both parents asked.

"What do you mean Aubrey is there?" Keaton's dad wanted to know.

"He's here, in New Mexico. He came to my house last night."

"Your house? You have a house, honey?" His mother seemed surprised, but... proud?

"Son, I don't like this. Aubrey called us just last week and told us that the detective still hadn't found you. Why would he do that?" His dad sounded worried and confused all at once.

"Chay?" Keaton looked like he didn't know what to do. He started trembling.

Chay took the phone and pulled Bit to his chest, making him rest his head on Chay's shoulder. "Mr. and Mrs. Reynolds?"

"Who is this?" Howard demanded.

"Chayton Winston, sir. I'm Bi—Keaton's mate."

Bit's mother gasped.

"Well. I... uh, hello, Mr. Winston. I'm Howard Reynolds, Keaton's father."

"Hello, Mr. Reynolds. Listen, we are having some issues here. There have been three attempts made on Keaton's life."

"What?" Howard thundered.

"My God! Is he all right? Keaton?" Bit's mother's voice trembled.

Chay frowned. These honestly did not sound like two people who wanted their son dead. But they had kicked Keaton out of their lives for being gay. *What the fuck?* "Keaton's fine. Listen, Mr. and Mrs. Reynolds. The reason we called is... well...." *Shit.* How did he put this? "I thought you kicked Keaton out? I thought you disowned him?"

"We did not," Mrs. Reynolds shouted.

"Keaton is the one who left." Keaton's dad sounded offended. "We had a slight misunderstanding, but we never disowned him. I admit, we were not happy with some of the choices he made, but Keaton is the one who disappeared out of our lives. We thought he needed time to think, so we let him be. When he up and took off after graduation, that is when we realized he was more than just mad. I assure you, Mr. Winston—"

Keaton rolled his eyes, his shoulders slumping.

"Whoa. Say no more. I know Bit... er, Keaton quite well. I know what a temper he has. I understand." Or at least he thought he did. He wasn't sure why Bit's parents hadn't gone after him, when after several months he hadn't contacted them, but he did know how hardheaded Keaton could be. "And please call me Chay."

Chay talked to Bit's parents for several more minutes, and then Keaton talked to them some more. By the time the conversation ended, Chay felt fairly certain Aubrey hadn't acted on the consent of his parents. But he had to have the help of another wolf, the one who cut Keaton's brake line.

Keaton said goodbye to his parents and hung up the phone. Sitting back with a sigh, he looked Chay right in the eyes. "Looks like we are going to Georgia."

Chapter Nineteen

Keaton was in their room, packing. His and Chay's phone conversation with his parents kept playing over and over in his head.

His parents had insisted he come home so they could get to the bottom of things. After explaining the entire situation to them, they even suspected Aubrey. Keaton was just plain stunned. He'd gone from being disowned to fawned over and chastised for disappearing. And damned if his parents and Chay hadn't all three turned the incident into a lesson, admonishing Keaton for his temper and his "too independent" nature.

Pushing Pita out of the way for the fiftieth time, Keaton closed the lid on his suitcase.

Chay came in with Remi on his heels. "You damned sure are coming with us." Chay tossed a smaller empty bag, to be filled with toiletries, on the mattress. "You need to make arrangements. I've already called Dr. Jensen to cover for me at the clinic, and Keaton got the next week off work."

"Why do I have to come?" Remi sat on the bed. Immediately, Pita pounced over to him.

Digging through the nightstand, Chay heaved the "we've been over this already" sigh. "Because you don't have enough control to be on your own yet. What happens if you get ticked off at someone and turn into a wolf?"

Remi blinked, looking startled. "Seriously?"

Keaton nodded. "Seriously. You've already had your eyes shift twice over breakfast. What if we weren't there to talk you through it?"

"I'd have continued to shift?" Absently, Remi petted Pita.

Opening the toiletries case, Chay dropped in four bottles of lube. "Exactly." He stalked to the adjoining bathroom.

Keaton frowned and took out three bottles of lube, putting them back in the nightstand drawer. He headed for the dresser for Chay's underwear and socks. "We aren't trying to be assholes and run your life. We just don't want you to get yourself in a situation. All new wolves have to learn control. Most of us learn before we are even able to shift. But since you were made this way rather than born, you have to learn now." After placing Chay's boxers and socks in Chay's suitcase, Keaton went to Chay's closet.

Remi sighed and flopped back on the bed. "I haven't even changed yet. Shouldn't you have me change so I can see what it's like? Won't that help me learn faster?"

"Yes and no." Keaton folded and packed Chay's pants. "You will get to shift, before we go." Gathering several shirts, Keaton returned to the bed. "But we don't want you changing from lack of control. We want to walk you through it and have you change because you are trying to change, not accidentally. Changing accidentally is liable to make you panic, and that will be counterproductive."

Pita bounded over, tugging on a pair of Chay's jeans. Pushing the puppy away, Keaton repacked the jeans. "Cut it out, pest."

Chay came in with more essentials, dropping them all in the small case. He frowned and turned back to the nightstand. "Besides, we could use your help." He put something else in the bag and left.

Catching Pita as he pounced, Keaton rescued the clothing again.

Remi snagged Pita. "Well, why didn't you just say you wanted my help in the first place?" he called after Chay.

Keaton looked into the toiletries bag to make sure Chay had gotten his glasses and rolled his eyes. Chay had put the three extra bottles of lube back in. Keaton put them in the nightstand. Zipping up Chay's suitcase, he set it beside his. "Your help would be appreciated. But if you go, I promise to work with you on your control too. Maybe by the time we get home you will have learned enough to go back to work and out in public unsupervised."

Chay brought more stuff for the toiletry bag.

Setting Pita on the floor, Remi let out a frustrated sigh. "Okay."

Keaton smiled. "Good. Then it's settled?"

"Yeah, it's settled. I'll call work, and we can go to my place and pack."

Staring into the bag, Chay groaned and put his hands on his hips.

Keaton went to get a bag for their shoes. "Chay, don't forget my glasses and go get a bag and pack a couple books to read on the way. I want the two you bought me on Apache and Sioux culture and history. Oh, and go get my laptop." He got their dress shoes, figuring they'd wear their sneakers and jeans on the plane. Or maybe.... "Do you want your boots?"

Grunting in response, Chay started digging through the nightstand again.

"My glasses are in the living room. Do you want your boots or not?" Keaton waited for Chay to answer.

Chay tossed the three bottles of lube back into the bag. "No, my tennis shoes are fine."

Remi's brow scrunched up. "What the fuck are you planning on doing that you need four things of lube for?"

Chay shrugged. "I like being prepared."

"For what? A freakin' orgy?" Remi asked.

Keaton laughed. He had been wondering the same thing.

They had an hour and a half before they had to be at the airport. Jake lay on the floor, playing with Pita. Remi sat on the couch, frowning at Jake and trying to get his eyes to shift back to normal. And Keaton was getting more and more annoyed at Remi for not listening to his instruction on how to get Remi's eyes back to normal. Watching the whole process, Chay tried to hide his smile. He wondered how long it would take Bit to lose his temper entirely and start smacking Remi around.

Keaton growled, stomped his feet a few times, and yelled, "Pay attention."

His teeth dropping down, Remi sighed and glared up at Keaton.

Jake chuckled and grinned at Chay. "How long do you give them until they start throwing punches?"

Chay laughed. "Not long. Bit has a hell of a temper. It might actually do Remi good to realize that Keaton can kick his ass."

Jake raised a brow. "You sure about that?"

"Yup. Unless Keaton refuses to use his wolf abilities, and I somehow doubt that."

Squeezing his eyes closed, Remi rubbed them with the heels of his hands.

Keaton threw his arms up dramatically and stomped into the kitchen. A cabinet door slammed and the water turned on and off.

Uh-oh. Something told Chay the fight was about to begin. He stood up and waited. Sure enough, Bit came back into the living room with a glass of water.

Chay lunged at him just as he threw the water in Remi's face. Chay wrapped his arms around Bit as Remi started sputtering.

He had to give Bit credit, the cold water made Remi's eyes change to normal... for a second anyway, until the shock wore off.

Remi's eyes and teeth shifted, and he charged Bit.

Bit's face and hands changed instantly, and he caught Remi by the throat, holding him up over Bit's head.

Jake jumped up.

Letting go of Bit, Chay grabbed Jake and struggled to hold the big guy. "Keaton! Damn it. Stop."

Remi whimpered and morphed into a black wolf as Bit dropped him to the floor.

Jake stopped struggling to get to Remi and stared, but Chay didn't let him go entirely.

Rolling over, Remi bared his throat and stomach to Keaton.

Keaton stood over Remi for several seconds before his face and hands shifted back to normal. "I didn't want to do this, but you just had to force the issue." He bent down and lifted Remi's lupine chin to look at him. "I'm stronger than you. I know more than you, and I can teach you. If you will just listen. Do you understand?"

Remi nodded, still in a tangle of clothes.

"Holy shit," Jake whispered.

Chay agreed, that was a pretty impressive show of power. He'd never seen anyone shift that fast, and Bit had only changed a few body parts. And that wasn't even mentioning little ole Keaton picking Remi up with one arm, over his head, leaving the bigger man's feet dangling. Chay sure hoped to God Bit never got pissed off at him.

Keaton sat on the floor in front of Remi cross-legged.

Pita slinked over, not quite sure what was going on, and rolled to his back, baring his underside to Bit.

Keaton chuckled, rubbed his belly, then picked him up and settled him in his lap before turning his attention to Remi. "Close your eyes and take deep, even breaths. I'm going to pull these clothes off of you. Then I'm going to walk you through shifting back." He set Pita aside and divested Remi of his clothes. When Remi was sans clothing, Bit settled against the sofa, once again pulling Pita into his lap.

Bit's cool, calm demeanor after such a display of power was hot. Damn if Chay's cock didn't stand up and wave hi.

Keaton sniffed the air, his head snapping around to Chay. Raising an eyebrow, he grinned.

Chay raised one as well. Bit could smell his arousal. Good. They still had an hour and a half. He waggled his eyebrows, urging Keaton to finish helping Remi, and realized everyone was staring at him.

Jake shoved him away and went to sit next to Remi.

Keaton chuckled and patted the sofa.

Blushing, Chay made his way to the couch and sat next to Bit.

It took several minutes for Keaton to talk Remi back into human form. During that time, Chay's cock decided to behave and go to sleep. Which was probably for the best. They didn't have time for what he had in mind. Chay was amazed at what a good coach Keaton was. Once Bit got over his display of temper, he was actually very patient.

Remi was getting dressed, a little leery of Bit but with no apparent hard feelings, when someone knocked on the front door.

Chay sniffed. *His parents?* What were they doing here?

Jake opened the door, and sure enough, there stood not just Joe, but Lena Winston as well.

"Dad? Mom?" Chay frowned.

"Hey, son, Keaton, Remi, Jake." Joe came in carrying a suitcase.

"Hey, Dad. What's up?" Keaton hopped up and greeted Chay's father, slapping him on the back. "You going somewhere?" He extended his hand to Lena. "Hello, Mrs. Winston."

To Chay's surprise, his mother took Bit's hand and hesitantly pulled Keaton into a hug.

Keaton wavered for a brief second, then hugged her.

She leaned back and smiled, looking unsure. "Please forgive me, Keaton. You are now a part of our family, and I'm afraid

I've given you a horrible reception. I'd like very much to start over. You aren't anything like what I hoped for my son, but he obviously loves you, and that is all that matters. As Joseph pointed out to me, you were not given a choice of mate any more than Chay was."

Keaton nodded and leaned into Lena. "For what it's worth, Lena, Chay got the raw end of the deal. I made out like a bandit."

Lena chuckled and hugged Bit again. "Oh, Keaton, I thought that too, but now I'm not so sure that both of you didn't get a very good deal."

Chay had expected her to come around, but she'd surprised even him. He had no idea it would be this soon. He was grinning like an idiot, but he didn't care.

His father caught his gaze and winked at him, then set his suitcase down.

Chay winked back, so happy he felt he'd bust.

Lena let go of Keaton and grabbed Chay. "I'm sorry, son. Please forgive me?"

Chay nodded, fighting back tears as he hugged his mother. "There's nothing to forgive, Mom. You had a shock. You're over it now."

Smiling, she pulled back, tears in her eyes, and patted his cheek. "You are such a good boy, Chayton. I love you."

"Love you too, Mom." Chay tugged her over to the couch and sat down.

Joe clapped Keaton on the back. "You didn't think I was going to let my boys go off and fight a big bad wolf on their own, did you? I'm going with you."

Chay sputtered. How had his dad even known they were going?

"Cool. How about you, Lena, are you going with us?"

She shook her head. "No, Keaton. Joseph would be afraid for my safety. Besides, someone is going to need to puppysit, yes?"

"Yes, ma'am. I'll get Pita's food, bowls, and bed." Bit bounded out of the room, a smile on his face.

Pita took off after him, toenails sliding on the wood floor.

Chay watched them leave and turned back to his dad. "What are you two doing here?"

"Doc Baker called me about Remi...." He looked over at Remi. "How are you, Remi?"

"I've been better, Joe. I'm a little freaked, but I guess being a—werewolf?—is better than the alternative. Chay saved me."

Jake cleared his throat, bringing Remi's attention to him.

Remi looked at Jake, blinking rapidly to keep his eyes from changing, Chay supposed. "Chay, Jake, and—" Keaton walked back into the room, bowls in one hand and a bag of food under his arm, Pita bouncing along behind him. Bit set the bowls and food down, and Remi's eyes twinkled. "—and Little Bit saved me."

Keaton slapped Remi on the head on his way past and disappeared down the hall.

Chay laughed. *Oh Lord.* He supposed at least Remi wasn't terrified of Bit. That was a good thing, right? Which was hilarious in itself. Bit was tiny in comparison. Okay, yes, Keaton was the more powerful wolf, but to someone without werewolf senses.... "Dad, how did you even know we were going?"

"Don't look so stunned, Chay. Keaton and I talk quite frequently. We've become friends." Dad looked past his shoulder. "Right, son?"

"Right, Dad." Keaton came back in carrying the puppy's bed. Setting it on the floor, he winked at Chay. "I called him when you were in the shower this morning."

Chapter Twenty

"Keaton!"

Keaton looked up as his mother ran toward him, her arms out. He caught her, staggered backward, and almost fell into the luggage carousel. Fortunately, Chay stopped his momentum. "Uh, hi, Mom."

She started kissing his jaw, his cheeks, his forehead. Finally, she pulled back, holding him at arm's length, looking him over, her pale blue eyes taking in everything. Her golden blond hair had a few more gray strands, but other than that, she was the same petite little whirlwind she'd always been. "Oh, honey, look at you. So handsome." She plucked at his hair. "Your hair is longer than it was at graduation."

What? How would she know? "Mom, you didn't see me at graduation."

She frowned. "Of course I did. You didn't think we'd miss you getting your doctorate, did you?"

"I didn't see you."

"No, you didn't. Your father insisted that we leave you be and stay downwind of you. I have pictures, though. We were very proud of you."

"Joanna, for crying out loud, let the boy get his luggage." His dad strolled up, towering over Keaton and his mom, pulled Keaton from his mother, and gave him a hug.

"Hey, Dad."

"Hey, son. Glad you're home." His big brown eyes stared over his shoulder to Chay, who still had his hand in the middle

230

of Keaton's back. He smiled, bobbing his gray head, and extended his hand. "You must be Chayton."

"Chay, please. Nice to meet you, Mr. Reynolds." Chay shook his hand and tipped his head slightly, showing his respect, but not making it obvious because they were in public. Then he turned, indicating the rest of their entourage. "This is my father, Joseph Winston. And these are our friends, Remington Lassiter and Jacob Romero."

"Howard Reynolds," Keaton's father said as he shook hands with everyone. "This is my wife, Joanna."

"Hello," Joanna said.

They got their luggage and walked out of the terminal. Somehow Keaton ended up with nothing to carry. He tried to take a bag from Chay, but Chay wouldn't let him. "No. Visit with your parents. I've got this."

Keaton nodded and halfheartedly listened to his mother chatter away about how she'd missed him.

His father and Chay's father were having a conversation as well, and Remi hung back with Jake.

When they got to the curb and spotted the limo, Keaton thought Chay's eyes were going to pop out of his head.

Keaton patted his arm. "It's okay. We don't always ride around in limos. I guess they wanted to make sure we'd all fit."

Chay snorted and handed their luggage to the chauffeur.

Keaton grabbed Chay's hand, pulling him in beside him.

Keaton's father stared at their intertwined hands but didn't say anything. After they were all settled in the car and on their way to Reynolds Hall, Howard cleared his throat, getting their attention. "So, Chay, what do you do for a living?"

Chay looked at Keaton, then Howard, a pleasant smile on his face. "I'm a vet, sir."

"What branch? Army, Navy...?"

Keaton chuckled. "No, Dad, he's a doctor. An animal doctor."

"Oh." Joanna practically cooed. "Wow, a doctor. That's wonderful. Now, if you were only a woman, you'd be perfect." She gasped and slapped her hand to her mouth. "My word. I'm sorry, it slipped out."

Keaton frowned at her.

Joe, Remi, Jake, and Chay chuckled.

"Don't mind her, Chay. We are pleased to meet you. We would have preferred it if you'd been a woman, but... you're Keaton's mate. Actually, to be honest, I'm rather glad to see that you are a man. It makes more sense to me now. I was rather shocked when Keaton told us he was gay."

Keaton rolled his eyes. He opened his mouth to let his dad have a piece of his mind, but Chay squeezed his hand, giving him a warning look. He snapped his mouth closed.

Joanna clapped her hands. "I do like you, Chay. I don't think I've ever seen anyone be able to hush him up once he gets a bee in his bonnet."

Keaton glared at her too.

Chay squeezed his hand again. *Damn it.* Now they were all gonna think he was domesticated or something.

Chay grinned. "Well, Mr. and Mrs. Reynolds, since we are being open and honest, I was pretty surprised to find out my mate was a man too. But I love your son, and I'm not going anywhere, so I suppose we will all have to get used to the idea."

Howard smiled and leaned forward, slapping Chay on the arm. "Welcome to our family, Chay."

"Thank you, sir. And in case it crossed your mind... I refuse to have a sex change."

The entire car erupted in laughter.

"Would you cut it out?" Chay grabbed Bit's hand and removed it from his cock for the third time in the last two minutes. There was no way he was having sex in Keaton's parents' home. It was bad enough they lived in a huge fucking colonial mansion with an oak-lined drive, big white marble columns, and a name—the fucking house had a *name*, for crying out loud—but Bit's parents were just down the hall. Heck, for that matter, his own father was in the bedroom right next door. Geez, he felt way out of his element.

Bit groaned and crawled onto him, straddling his hips. "You are the one who insisted on bringing all that lube." He frowned, but his eyes twinkled with mirth.

"Shh.... That was when I thought we'd be staying in a hotel." Bit grabbed his prick again.

Chay batted his hand away. "You could have told me you were heir to a goddamned fortune and from one of the oldest moneyed families in all of freaking Georgia."

Bit leaned down, kissing Chay's chin. "Technically, I'm the spare and Aubrey is the heir. And anyway, I was disowned."

"No, you weren't. You let that king-sized temper of yours take over and you ran away. You and your ego, I swear to God....

And besides that, Aubrey is a psychopath who is trying to kill you. I somehow doubt your parents are going to leave him everything."

Bit nipped his chin. "Your ego is every bit as big. And I didn't exactly run away. It was as much their fault as it was mine. A misunderstanding. Do we have to talk about this? I'm really tired of talking about this." He reached between them, grabbing Chay again.

Chay sighed. His stupid cock didn't seem to care that they were in the house with other werewolves who could hear them having sex; *it* was hard. In fact, the stupid thing got harder every time Bit touched it. "Bit, what if someone hears?"

"They will be good little werewolves and pretend they didn't."

"That isn't reassuring." Chay bucked up into Bit's hand, hissing when it slid down his shaft.

Bit licked across Chay's lips. "We'll be quiet."

"You, be quiet?"

Bit pulled back, frowning. "I'm always quiet."

Chay hugged him, nuzzling his face next to Bit's. "*You* are never quiet." Chay slid one hand to that luscious ass and the other down to the thick cock pressed against his belly.

Keaton surged into his hand, letting out a little whimper.

The bed squeaked.

Chay froze.

"Unh." Keaton bucked again and pulled on Chay's cock. Again making the bed squeak.

"Shh...."

"I didn't say anything."

Chay moved experimentally, making the bed screech. Nope, that wasn't going to work. Heck, the headboard would probably start banging against the wall by the time they got into it. He threw the covers off and patted Bit's butt. "Come on."

Keaton sat up, head cocked. "Where are we going?"

"Chair. Go get the bag with the lube and meet me over there. And keep your voice down."

Bit let out a long-suffering sigh, but did as instructed. He came back and set the bag at Chay's feet.

Chay motioned toward the chair. It was big and sturdy, dark wood with a wide cloth upholstered seat and back.

Keaton raised a brow, but sat down—sprawled, actually. Everything was at the end of the seat, easily accessible. And boy, that thick prick was still hard.

Chay sat on his heels between Keaton's splayed legs as he reached for the bag. His mouth closed over Bit's balls as his fingers found the bottle of lube.

"God yes." Bit grabbed Chay's face in both hands.

Jesus, he was loud. Chay pulled back. "Shh...."

"Yeah, yeah." Bit dismissed the protest and pulled him forward again, practically mashing his face in Keaton's testicles.

Chay licked a line down his balls to the area behind. God, he loved how Bit smelled, all nice and musky and manly. He circled Bit's hole with his tongue.

"Oh!"

"Shh...."

He batted the hands away from his face and pushed Keaton's legs farther apart. He inhaled deeply, then sat back. Ummm.... Who would have ever thought that would be an arousing smell?

He got the bottle of lube open and squirted some on his fingers.

Bit was all spread out for him, balls drawn taut, pink hole beckoning. Chay pressed two slick fingers into Bit's ass.

Bit gasped and squirmed, his prick swaying back and forth. He closed his eyes and relaxed back with a sigh.

Chay came up on his knees, grabbing that pretty cock with his free hand and holding it for his mouth. When he took the tip in, Bit bucked, moaning loud.

"Shh...." Chay pushed his fingers deep into Bit's body, searching for that sweet spot. He used his other hand to hold and squeeze Bit's dick while he sucked and licked.

Bit went nuts. Those soft vocal little noises accompanied the trembling in Keaton's thighs. His eyes flew open, locking with Chay's.

Chay steadily fucked Keaton with his fingers, hitting Bit's gland every time he pushed in. It wasn't long before Keaton wiggled around, trying to push Chay's fingers deeper and trying to push his cock farther into Chay's mouth. He worked Keaton harder, taking his prick deeper with his hand, pumping hard, using the saliva to his advantage. He ran his fingers over Bit's balls on every downstroke.

Keaton tensed, his hole squeezing Chay's fingers, his cock jerking in Chay's mouth.

Chay moved quick, wanting to be inside his mate when he came. He dropped Bit's prick, removed his fingers and picked Keaton up, all in one smooth motion. He sat in the chair and had Keaton straddling him and his cock pressing into Bit's hot, sweet hole before Keaton could even form a protest.

Bit sank down on Chay's cock and let out a moan. His back arched, his muscles contracting around Chay. His eyes snapped to Chay's and he came, hard. Spunk shot everywhere, all over Chay's belly and chest, even on his chin.

The sight of that thick throbbing cock spewing for him almost had Chay coming too. *Fuck.* He hadn't even had to touch Bit's dick when he came. He gave his mate a few minutes for the aftershocks to wear off and tugged on Keaton's hips. "Ride me," he whispered.

Keaton's eyes glazed over. He started moving, raising himself up and down on Chay. His prick never even softened. He dragged his fingers through the semen on Chay's belly and brought them to Chay's lips.

He opened his mouth and sucked those digits in, tasting salty cum.

Bit gathered more of the milky essence on his fingers and stuck them in his own mouth.

"Fuck, you're hot. Love you, Bit."

Keaton smiled at him, a wicked gleam in his eyes, and squeezed his muscles.

Chay felt it all the way to his toes. He gasped, his legs tensing. The familiar tingling raced up his spine.

Grabbing his own dick, Bit stroked it as his muscles contracted and released around Chay's dick.

Chay's whole body spasmed. He came, shooting into his mate's ass, staring into those pale sky-blue eyes. He clamped a hand over his own mouth to keep from crying out.

Keaton was seconds behind him, climaxing again, spilling himself on Chay's stomach. He dropped forward, nuzzling Chay's neck, and whispered, "Love you too."

After a few minutes, Bit got up, letting Chay's dick slip from him. Chay was almost asleep, but the action still managed to make him shiver.

The next thing he knew, Bit was wiping him down with a warm, wet rag. Then he crawled back onto Chay's lap, snuggling in close.

When Chay woke a few minutes later to Bit snoring in his ear, he had a crick in his neck. He jostled Keaton. "Bit, wake up. We're still in the chair, let's go to bed."

Keaton's only response was a grunt.

Chay picked him up and started walking across the room. He kicked the toiletry case Bit left on the floor and tripped. "Umph." Fortunately, he was close enough to the bed that he tossed Bit onto it in order to keep them both from getting hurt.

The floor came up fast. Chay caught himself on his hands and knees with a big thud. It smarted a little, but other than that no real damage had been done.

A loud thump sounded on the other side of the bed, followed by a barrage of muffled giggles.

Chay dipped his head to peer under the bed.

Keaton lay on the other side, on his back, hands over his face, laughing like a fiend.

"What are you doing on the floor?"

Bit turned his head, looking at Chay. "I hit the bed and just kept rolling. I couldn't stop." He was so cute, his face all red from laughter.

"Are you okay?"

Bit nodded, still giggling. "Are you?"

"Ye—"

There was a knock on the wall, followed by Joe's amused voice. "Would you boys go to sleep, for crying out loud."

Oh God. Heat suffused Chay's face. He'd never be able to face his father again.

Bit, the jerk, laughed so hard, he started wheezing.

Chapter Twenty-One

"Grrr... Bit." Chay threw his hands in the air, letting the bow tie drop to his shoulders, and turned away from the mirror. He put his hands on his hips and glared at Keaton. Even irritated, he made quite a fetching picture in a tux. "I can't believe we have to wear tuxes to draw your brother out."

Keaton wiped the last of the shaving cream off his face and walked over to his mate. He reached up and grabbed Chay's tie. "We are wearing tuxes for the party, not for Aubrey's benefit. And you agreed that a party to celebrate our mating would be a good idea." He tied the tie, kissed Chay's chin, and went to find his cuff links.

"Yeah, but I didn't think it was going to be this huge shindig."

"This isn't huge, trust me. You haven't seen huge. This is tiny, miniscule, itty-bitty for my mother. That woman was born to throw dinner parties, and this one is, in her words, 'cramping her style.' It was all my dad could do to keep her to a guest list of thirty. It's basically only pack and friends of the pack."

"But tuxes? Was it necessary to wear tuxedos?"

Keaton chuckled, digging through another drawer. Where had he put the studs to his tuxedo shirt? "You don't know my mother. Party and formal wear are synonyms."

"I can't believe you made me buy this tux, and you wouldn't even let me get a clip-on bow tie," Chay grumbled as he flopped down on the bed.

"Sit up. You'll get wrinkled, and my mother will have a fit."

Chay heaved a sigh and sat up, smoothing out his pants.

Keaton threaded a stud through a buttonhole. "We bought the tux because with me getting along with my parents again, you'll likely need it, and you are not wearing a clip-on tie. Trust me when I tell you, my mother will check for a clip-on, and she'll stroke out if you wear one." Keaton finished buttoning up his shirt and tucked it in.

"Okay, okay. God, your family is weird."

Keaton arched a brow as he fastened his cummerbund. "You're just figuring this out?"

"Nah, it was readily apparent when we stepped off the plane."

He chuckled. "It should have been obvious when my brother attacked your friend."

"Well, yeah, that too. Tell me this plan again. Maybe it will make more sense to me this time around."

Keaton grabbed his jacket off the hanger and put it on. "We are supposed to leave the party and go make out in the gazebo in the formal garden. Jake, your dad, my dad, and my dad's betas are going to follow us, hide, and wait."

"It's still a stupid plan. Your brother isn't going to attack you with a house party going on."

Keaton tied his own bow tie and crossed to the bed to position himself between Chay's legs. He pulled his mate to his feet. "My brother isn't the brightest bulb in the bunch. Think about it; he attacked Remi on our property. He had to have known we'd figure out who did it. He hasn't exactly been sneaky." He rose up on his toes and kissed Chay on the lips.

"Mmm. You look good, Bit." Chay nipped Keaton's bottom lip. "My pretty baby."

Keaton wrapped his arms around Chay, tilting his face up for better access.

Chay kissed him, really kissed him. His tongue slid across the seam of Keaton's lips.

He sighed and opened up, his eyes closing automatically. His tongue met Chay's, rubbing together lazily.

"Hey, guys...." The door opened and shut, and Remi cleared his throat.

They ignored him for a few more seconds. Finally, Chay nipped his bottom lip again and pulled back without letting Keaton go.

Keaton snuggled in, laying his head against his mate's chest, and turned to face their intruder.

Remi looked nice in his tuxedo. Keaton gave him a good once-over and noticed his eyes were lupine. Remi's face was pale like he was fighting it. Or maybe that was just his discomfort at finding Keaton and Chay kissing. Keaton wasn't certain which. He and Chay hadn't made any effort to hide their affection in front of Remi, but Remi seemed fairly accepting of Keaton and Chay's relationship since the night he was attacked.

Chay rubbed Keaton's back absently. "You all right?"

Remi shook his head. "No, I'm not all right." He pointed at his own face. "Look at my eyes."

"Are you doing what I told you to do?" Keaton asked.

"Yes. Deep, cleansing breaths, focus on seeing color. It isn't helping." Remi threw his hands up and let them drop.

"What were you doing when they changed?" Chay let go of Keaton and sat on the edge of the bed, facing his friend.

"Jake and I were exploring the grounds, looking for the best places to hide and stay out of sight of the gazebo."

Chay looked at Keaton.

Keaton closed his eyes for a second and took a deep breath. He and Chay were thinking the same thing... *Jake*. Jake's proximity made it harder for Remi to learn control. How in the hell were they supposed to tell the homophobic Remi that Jake was his mate? Keaton opened his eyes. "Remi, come sit down and do as I told you. Deep breath, focus on color. Concentrate. I want you to tell me what color the bedspread is."

Remi crossed the room and sat next to Chay. "I'm trying to make my eyes shift back, but—"

Keaton shook his head. "No, I don't want you to focus on trying to control shifting. Narrow it down, make it simple. Concentrate on color. Your eyes don't see color in wolf form. By concentrating on color, you are forcing them to shift back. It's too complicated to think of it as changing back and forth."

Remi took a deep breath and turned his head to look down at the comforter on the bed. "It's blue." He turned back, and his eyes were their normal human green. "What I don't understand is what is making them change in the first place. I wasn't mad or scared. You said that is what triggers them to change."

"Or arousal," Chay mumbled.

Keaton glared at him.

Remi snapped his head around to Chay. "How did you kn—"

There was a knock at the door, and then Joe popped his head in. "Hey."

Keaton chuckled. *Saved by the bell, or rather by the knock.* "Hey."

Joe came in, closing the door behind him. The man was very handsome. It was easy to see where Chay got his good looks. Joe smiled. "You three look nice."

"So do you," Keaton said.

Joe smiled even brighter. "Listen, I came to tell you guys that there's no sign of Aubrey yet, but Joanna wants you downstairs. Guests are beginning to arrive."

Bit licked a long line up Chay's throat, making him shiver.

"Bit, you are getting way too into this. You are supposed to be paying attention to our surroundings," Chay whispered against Bit's ear.

"I am. No reason I can't enjoy myself at the same time." He nibbled on Chay's earlobe.

"Try to remember we have an audience."

"Mmmm.... Actually, I don't know that we do. I don't smell them." Bit's tongue pushed into his ear.

"You aren't supposed to. That's the point." Chay sighed and relaxed. Well, as much as he could, knowing that at any time Aubrey could pop out of nowhere and threaten his Bit.

Keaton gripped Chay's cock, and he about jumped out of his skin. He was concentrating on the area around the gazebo. He sucked in a breath and realized his cock was hard. Chay might not have been paying attention to Bit, but apparently his body sure as hell was. He luxuriated in the feel of his mate for a few seconds. He buried his face in Bit's neck and pushed up into his hand. Just a few seconds, that's all he had. Someone needed to pay attention, and Bit, despite what he said, wasn't.

Keaton's head jerked up, his eyes wide, startled. His hand left Chay's prick.

Chay sniffed, taking in an unfamiliar scent. No, it wasn't unfamiliar exactly. It was the scent from the night he ran the man off outside their house. The night Keaton's brakes were cut.

"I see it didn't take you long to replace me." A tall blond man came into the clearing, holding a gun. It wasn't Aubrey.

Keaton shook his head. "Jonathon?"

Jonathon? Keaton's ex? Chay positioned himself in front of Keaton. The gun wouldn't do more than hurt a whole lot, unless the bullets were silver, but he didn't want his mate shot just the same.

Jonathon's lips twisted into a nasty smile. "Oh, now you remember me."

"What are you doing here?" Keaton pushed Chay back, maneuvering himself in front.

"You ruined my life." Jonathon shoved the gun forward at Keaton for emphasis.

Chay pulled Bit back again, shielding his body. "Whatever it is you think Keaton has done, I'm sure it isn't too bad. Maybe if you tell us, we can help you fix it." Yeah, it was lame, but he didn't want this bozo to shoot either of them. And it bought time for the cavalry to show up. They were out there hiding, weren't they?

"You, shut up. I wasn't talking to you." Jonathon glared at him.

"Look, Jonathon, I don't know what you think it is I did, but—"

Jonathon scoffed. "You left me."

Keaton scoffed right back. "You had a girlfriend, you dumbass."

Chay groaned. He and Bit were going to have to talk about antagonizing crazy men with guns. The man was a wolf. He had to know a gun wasn't that big a threat to other wolves.

"And you could have had one too, or a boyfriend. I didn't care. I'd have overlooked it. We could've led your pack together. All of it could have been ours. All of this...." He waved his gun around, indicating Reynolds Hall. "We could have been happy. It would have been easy to overpower your father and take over, but you had to run off. And what do you do at the first opportunity? You run off to New Mexico. I tried to scare you by shooting you so you'd come home. But then you replaced me"—he glared at Chay—"with this.... Really, Keaton, your taste is deplorable."

Keaton growled. His whole body tensed, readying for attack. His hands shifted.

Chay stepped in front of Keaton just as he was about to charge.

Jonathon pulled the trigger.

Keaton screamed.

Ouch. Chay staggered back. That bastard shot him.

A blur of white fur streaked past the gazebo and launched at Jonathon as Keaton's arms wrapped around Chay. The gun went flying. Jonathon tried to shift—his eyes and teeth changing instantly—but the wolf didn't give him the chance.

Keaton turned to Chay, his eyes wide. "Where are you hit?"

Chay glanced down at his side.

Keaton's eyes followed. Bit ripped his jacket and shirt.

"Damn it, Bit. We just bought those."

Keaton's hands shifted to claws. "Deep breath. I gotta get it out. If it's silver, it could kill you." He sliced his nails into Chay's side, digging in.

This time it was Chay who screamed. Fuck, he was woozy. That hurt, bad. Chay blinked the tears back and tried to focus on anything but what Bit was doing.

The wolf bit into Jonathon's neck, blood flying everywhere, covering the pale fur. He jerked his head back and forth, tearing the man's skin.

Jake, Joe, Remi, Howard, and his betas, all still in human form, came running into the garden from the direction of the house, the same direction the white wolf had come from.

"Got it." Bit gasped and suddenly the pain from Chay's side receded into a dull ache.

Chay's eyes met his father's. Joe looked worried.

Chay's brain was a little on the foggy side. From the pain, he supposed. His eyes shifted, and then Bit shoved his wrist against Chay's mouth. Chay staggered and his knees hit the ground.

Keaton stood over him. "Drink."

Chay drank.

The wound on Keaton's wrist closed, but Keaton opened it up again, pressing it back to Chay's mouth. By the third time, Chay felt much better. He could think again. The ache in his side was gone completely. He pushed Bit's wrist away and looked down at his side. It was healed.

Oh shit.

He'd been so dazed he'd forgotten about Jonathon. Chay spotted the gun lying on the grass, but before he could say anything, Keaton ran down the gazebo steps, grabbed it, and came back to him. Glancing around, Chay found the white wolf and Jonathon.

Jonathon lay lifeless and pale in a huge puddle of blood. The large wolf still growled and shook the mangled flesh, denying him a chance to heal.

Howard walked up to the wolf and placed a hand on its shoulder. "Aubrey, let go. He's dead."

The blood-splattered wolf released Jonathon's neck, turned toward the house, and left.

Wow. Aubrey hadn't been responsible for any of Keaton's accidents? *Man.* Chay felt like a... well, he felt like an ass. Make that an ignorant, slightly confused ass.

They all stood staring at the limp body for the longest time.

"Chayton? Are you all right?" Joe asked.

Chay frowned. "Where the hell were all of you? Bit could have been shot. You guys suck as a rescue squad. You're all fired."

Bit opened the revolver, and dumped the bullets into his hand. "Silver. Glad I got that out of you." He touched Chay's arm. "How do you feel?"

"I'm fine. I guess we owe Aubrey an apology and a thank-you."

Joe nodded. "Indeed you do. Aubrey talked to us all before we came out here." He shot a sheepish glance toward Jonathon's lifeless body. "That's why we were late. Apparently, Aubrey came to find Keaton as a surprise for his parents."

"The night Remi was attacked, it was Aubrey who ran Jonathon off." Jake held out his hand to Keaton, silently asking for the gun and bullets. "He said he was going for a run. He went back by your house and heard Remi scream. He chased Jonathon all the way to the rez. He recognized Jonathon's scent. Aubrey thought Remi was already dead, so he kept after Jonathon."

Keaton handed over the gun and ammo. "But why didn't he come back and tell us what was going on?"

Howard shrugged. "He tried. He didn't have a phone number. He followed Jonathon all the way back to his hotel and watched him. By then all of you were already on a plane headed here."

"But why the change of heart? Aubrey hates me," Keaton said.

Howard shook his head. "No, he doesn't, son. We all make mistakes when we're younger. He has grown up quite a bit since you left home. Give him a chance. You only have one brother."

Remi groaned, grabbing his face in both hands. "God-dammit! I'm sick and fucking tired of my eyes shifting." He dropped his hands and pointed to Jonathon's body. "And that is just gross. Why do I want to eat it?" He stormed off toward the house.

Chay glanced down at Jonathon. Yeah, it was pretty gross. But he didn't feel the least bit of remorse. That son of a bitch tried to kill his Bit. He glanced up to see everyone staring, puzzled, after Remi's retreating back.

Keaton looked at Chay, his eyes wide. "You're sure you are okay?" He reached up and felt Chay's forehead with the back of his hand. "You don't feel feverish. If you had silver poisoning, you'd be feverish, right?"

"If he had silver poisoning, he wouldn't have healed," Howard said.

Chay shook his head. He couldn't believe everyone was making such a fuss over him. Bit was the one who could have been killed. "Don't even start, Bit." Chay pointed at him. "You're already in trouble."

"Me?" Bit squeaked.

"Yes, you. What the hell were you thinking, antagonizing a lunatic with a gun?"

Keaton sputtered for several seconds.

Chay growled and shoved Bit toward the house, following the others. "You psychotic little Georgia Peach." He put his hand on Keaton's shoulder, needing to touch his mate. "Geez, Bit, you really know how to pick 'em."

Keaton stopped in front of him, turning. He looked Chay up and down slowly, a serene little smile on his face. He rose up and kissed Chay's chin, his arms going around him. "Yes, I do."

Epilogue

Chay sat on the couch, watching his mate dismiss his class of werewolf cubs. Bit had made a life for himself in New Mexico. For a man who proclaimed himself to be socially inept, he had become quite the social butterfly. He still couldn't cook worth a damn, but he'd taken to hosting all their poker games, and inviting more people to boot. The man had his mother's flair for partying.

Chay was so proud of Bit, he could bust. Keaton had also been appointed pack teacher. He was doing such a fine job of teaching Remi control that John Carter had begged him to take the position. Keaton was now responsible for teaching the prepubescent wolves how to control themselves and about pack history—a sort of "How to Be a Werewolf 101"—before they actually changed for the first time. Since the lessons were taught at Chay and Keaton's home, Chay helped on occasion.

"Bye. Have a nice Christmas." Bit waved the last of his class off, all but one at least. From the sound of it, Remi was raiding their refrigerator.

Remi came out from the kitchen with Coke and chips in hand and sat on the couch next to Chay. His friend was getting pretty good at hiding his werewolf instincts, but Keaton continued to work with him. Remi was adjusting well, though he still had no clue that Jake was his mate. Jake fortunately seemed to be taking things in stride, allowing Remi to get used to being a wolf first.

Remi flipped his head up in greeting.

Chay nodded.

"You finish staining those bookshelves?"

"Yup. Looks like I did it at a good time too." He looked at Bit, who had just closed the door. Chay was making the extra bedroom into an office for Bit.

Keaton stopped in the middle of the living room floor, hands on hips, glaring at Remi. "Who said you could eat? You aren't done with your lesson."

Remi groaned around a mouthful of chips and shot Chay a pleading look.

Chay held up his hands in a "you're on your own, buddy" gesture. No way was he getting involved. Remi and Keaton actually got along pretty well nowadays, but that didn't stop them from bickering.

Remi washed down his chips with a swig of soda. "Why did you let everyone else go?"

"They were done for the day. But you aren't." You could practically hear the "duh" at the end of Bit's explanation.

Remi rolled his eyes.

Keaton settled himself into Chay's lap and kissed his chin. "Hey. Did you finish the bookcase?" Bit asked, practically bouncing.

Chay smiled and kissed his nose. "Yes, I did. You want to see it?"

"Uh-huh." Bit smiled.

"Hey. I thought I had more to learn today?" Remi protested.

Keaton pointed at him. "Don't start with me. I voted to let you die. But noooo... Chay and Jake wouldn't have it."

Chay bit his lip to keep from laughing.

Remi's mouth fell open, then snapped shut. "You're an asshole, Keaton."

Keaton blinked. "That is Professor Asshole to you. Now strip!"

"Excuse me?" Remi's eyes widened.

"Strip. I want to see how fast you can shift. If someone were to challenge you, how fast you can change forms could make the difference between life or death. Now strip." Keaton turned to Chay. "Thank you for making me a bookcase. It will be all the better just because you made it for me. Now, if you'd learn to cook...."

Chay pulled his Bit in to snuggle. "You're welcome. And that goes both ways; you could learn to cook too."

Remi was still mumbling in the background, throwing clothes all over the place.

Keaton leaned in, sealing his lips to Chay's, his tongue probing.

Ah yeah. Chay opened, letting him in. He was vaguely aware of Remi shifting into a wolf and back to human. He heard toenails on the wood floor, followed by a deep growl. The doggy door whooshed open, then shut. The whole time Chay's tongue tangled with Bit's, lazily enjoying his mate.

"Dammit, Pita! Give me my underwear back."

Chay and Keaton broke apart, heads snapping around.

Remi stood in the middle of the living room, naked, glaring at the back door.

Keaton started giggling. "Class dismissed."

Excerpt of With Caution

"I fucking love your mouth." Remi dropped his head back to the pillow, his eyes closed, taking in every little sensation.

The suction on his cock increased as the clever tongue danced along the shaft.

"Oh fuck. Gonna come. Stop. Not yet...." Winding his fingers through his lover's hair, Remi fought the growing sensation. He tried to slow the inevitable by pulling those delectable lips off him.

A soft, seductive kiss tickled his stomach, making him loosen his grip. As soon as his hand fell to the mattress, his prick was once again engulfed.

Ass muscles clenching tight, he shivered. His balls drew closer to his body, and his legs tensed. It was absolute torture. A tingle raced up his spine. *No, not yet.* "Oh God, oh—"

The wonderful warmth left his cock.

Remi half growled, half laughed. "You fucking tease."

A snort answered him, and then his dick was gripped, held upright, and laved from tip to balls.

Fisting his hand in the thick hair again, Remi pulled his lover's face closer to his groin. "*Yessss*, that feels good."

His legs were shoved higher, exposing him more, and that wicked tongue laved his crease, snaking down.

Riiiing.

The licking continued.

Remi tried concentrating on the slick caress over his perineum and the breath across his balls. It was so—

Riiiing.

Loud. It was loud, like it was right next to his ear. He looked around, his fingers letting go of the dark hair. He didn't remember there being a phone. It rang again, and the moist warmth disappeared from his cock.

What the—

Blinking his eyes open, Remi squinted against the sunlight coming through the window. *Shit.* He'd forgotten to close the curtain, or rather the quilt he used as a curtain, again. What day was it? Oh yeah, Saturday. He'd just gotten off a twenty-four hour on, twenty-four hour off stretch.

His morning erection throbbed. The wet tip rested against his lower abdomen. Wrapping his hand around it, he squeezed it through the thin jock. "Fuck." *The dream.* He kept having the same damn dream over and over. Well, except for the ringing. The phone was diff—

Riiiing.

My cell phone. Reaching toward the phone on the night-stand, he glanced at the alarm clock—*7:02 a.m.* If that was Chay wanting him to go running, Remi was going to strangle him. He grabbed the cell and flipped it open before it rang a fourth time. "Yeah?"

"Remi." Sterling's voice cracked. "They're at it again. Please come get me. I can't stay here. You gotta come."

Remi bolted to a sitting position. His breath hitched, and his hard-on dwindled, replaced by a knot in his chest. "Where are you?" He threw back the covers and jumped out of bed, looking around for his jeans. "Sterling, where are you? Are you in the house?"

"Hurry, Remi. They've been at it since six."

"What? Why didn't you call me sooner?" Remi snagged a pair of jeans from the floor at the foot of his bed. Loose change flew out of the pockets, falling onto the gray carpet.

"I thought you'd be running with Chay."

He froze, his stomach plummeted to his feet, and a chill raced up his back. "Shh. Sterling, I told you not to mention him in the house. If Dirk hears—"

"I'm outside."

Making himself move again, Remi balanced his phone on his shoulder and shook the pants out. "Sterling, you can't let Dirk know I'm still friends with Chay. If he found out...." He shoved his foot into the jeans, not wanting to think about what would happen if the asshole found out Remi was still hanging out with the "fucking fag." After sticking his other leg in, he tugged his pants over his hips and grabbed the black T-shirt off the computer chair by his bed. "Start walking toward town. I'm on my way."

"But you have to stop him."

Like hell he did. What he *had* to do was get Sterling away from there before the old man decided to start in on him. "Do what I said and start walking." Remi moved faster, putting on the T-shirt and jerking his black baseball jersey out of the closet. The hanger whizzed past him and clattered against the side of the sleigh bed. When he drew the jersey over his right arm, his phone fell from his shoulder. Juggling, he caught it before it hit the floor and put the phone back on his shoulder. "Move it, goddammit. Hang up the phone and get away from the house." Remi winced at the bite in his voice. Snapping at Sterling wasn't something he did often, but he was scared. If anything happened to—no, he wasn't going to think that way.

"I am. I'm going now, but, Remi, what if—"

Wait a minute. Did that say—

Remi pulled the phone off his shoulder and glanced at the caller ID again. Sterling was on his cell phone. If the bastard caught Sterling with a cell phone, he'd kick both their asses. Dirk had forbidden Remi from buying Sterling a phone, saying the kid didn't need it. What a joke that was. Sterling *did* need it. Without it, how could he call Remi when he was in trouble? He damn sure couldn't use the house phone to do it. Which was the exact reason Remi had bought it and told Sterling to hide it. And sadly, he'd used the phone several times already.

Remi placed the phone on his shoulder and looked around for his boots, spotting them at the end of the bed. Socks. He needed socks. "I'm not going to go over this with you again. She doesn't want my help. I've tried to help her over and over. You can't help someone who doesn't help themselves." *Fuck the socks.* Sitting on the edge of the bed, Remi snagged his boots and forced his bare foot into one. He laced it and got the other. *Oh God, Sterling didn't—* "You didn't try to break them up, did you? Did he hit you?"

"No. I hate it when he yells. I went out my window and around back."

Remi laced the second boot and stood, securing the phone with his hand. "Good. Don't you ever try to break them apart." *Keys, keys, keys,* where the hell were his keys? Geez, his room was a mess. Ah, kitchen. He'd left them in the kitchen when he came home from the fire station last night.

"I won't. Hurry, Remi." Sterling's voice hitched like he was crying.

I'm hurrying. Grabbing his keys and helmet off the counter with one hand, Remi squeezed the phone between his shoulder and ear to close and lock the door. He brought his hand back to the phone and jogged down the apartment stairs to his bike.

He hated to get off the phone, but he had no choice. "I'm hanging up now. I'll be there in about ten minutes."

"'Kay. See you then. I'm walking."

"Good, see you in a few." Remi flipped his phone shut and stuffed it into his pocket. Starting the motorcycle, he put his helmet on. His hands were shaking so badly he could barely fasten it, but he managed. He had to get to Sterling. If the asshole happened to leave the house and see him walking—Remi's throat constricted, making it hard to breathe. No, no, it was cool. Mom would cover for Sterling and say she'd given him permission to spend the weekend with Remi. She always did. But if the old man caught Sterling walking and realized he hadn't been picked up earlier—

"Fuck."

Remi backed his bike out of the parking spot under the awning and took off toward the rez.

Sterling got off the bike, unfastened the helmet, and took it from his head, leaving his short black hair sticking up on top.

Remi brushed the spiky strands down.

Sterling was getting tall, almost as tall as Remi now. The kid was growing up and becoming quite handsome too. He had the dark coloring from their Apache father, with his dark skin, hair, and eyes. From their white mother, he'd inherited softer facial features and a straight, narrow nose that turned up slightly at the end. His face was less angular than most Apaches, even though he'd inherited their father's high cheekbones. No doubt about it, he'd have women falling all over him in a couple of years, if he didn't already.

"Thank you." Sterling's lip trembled faintly, and then he took a deep breath and handed Remi the helmet. Raking his fingers through his hair, he composed himself.

"You don't have to thank me. That's what I'm here for." Taking the helmet, Remi fastened the strap before hanging it on the handlebar. He'd completely forgotten to grab both helmets in his rush to get to his brother. Thankfully, the helmet law was only for those under eighteen. Stupid in his opinion—everyone should wear a helmet—but he'd had no choice but to go helmetless.

Sliding his arm around his little brother's shoulders, Remi ushered him toward the restaurant. He squeezed Sterling's neck with the crook of his arm, bringing their heads together. His heart was still pounding, like it did every time he got a call from his brother.

Wrapping his arm around Remi's waist, Sterling hugged him briefly, then shrugged and lengthened his stride. "Okay, dude, you're cramping my style. I'm not six anymore."

Remi chuckled and shoved the little shit's shoulder. Some of the tension left him, seeing Sterling acting like a teenager again. "Brat. I offer to take you to breakfast and this is the thanks I get."

Opening the door of the diner, Sterling nodded and held it for Remi. "Uh-huh."

An array of scents assaulted Remi's nose, making him wrinkle it. *God.* Was he ever going to get used to all the strong smells? Being a werewolf was hell on the senses.

Stepping out from behind the cash register, the hostess greeted them. She smiled and puffed out her chest a little as she went to the podium. Grabbing menus and napkin-covered utensils from the pockets on the side of the stand, she asked, "Two?"

"Yes," Remi answered, studying his brother and trying to block out the suffocating aromas.

Sterling seemed okay, but Remi wasn't fooled. He knew how scary the situation was. The kid was putting up a good front. He was more at ease now that he was away from the house, but shit like this didn't just go away. Remi knew that firsthand. He'd been dealing with it all his life.

Sighing, he took a seat across from his brother at the booth the hostess indicated.

She placed their menus on the table, leaning over way more than necessary to put their silverware down.

Whoa, that's where the overwhelming flowery smell was coming from. Did she bathe in perfume? What was she doing anyway? Remi glanced up and got an eyeful. Good God, the woman was about to pop out of her white dress shirt. Remi averted his attention from her boobs and met her gaze.

"Your waitress's name is Sally." She winked. "But you let me know if there is anything *I* can do for you."

Had her voice sounded that sultry when she'd first greeted them? Remi nodded and gave her a polite smile. Normally, he'd have flirted back, but under the circumstances, he wasn't in the mood. Besides, her scent didn't appeal to him. And that was too bizarre to think about. The weirdness that came from be-coming a werewolf never ceased to amaze him.

Sterling batted his lashes at her, grinning from ear to ear. "Oh, he will, I'm sure."

Biting his lip to hold back a chuckle, Remi furrowed his brow at the brat.

The hostess smiled at Sterling before giving Remi one last look and leaving.

Remi waited until she was out of hearing range. "What was that for?"

Sterling shrugged, but his eyes were bright with mischief. "Only trying to help you out. She was totally into you. Besides, you always used to use me as a chick magnet. I thought I'd bump up the magnetism a little. You need a girlfriend." Sterling unrolled his silverware out of the dark green cloth napkin.

"I did not use you as a chick magnet. You always seemed to attract them." Which was the absolute truth. Remi had nev-er taken Sterling with him to entice female attention. However, he found out real quick a teen lugging around an infant did just that. Hell, even when Remi was in his early twenties and Ster-ling was in elementary school, Remi ended up getting phone numbers and offers that generally had him covering Sterling's ears. "And I do *not* need a girlfriend." Especially not one who doused herself in perfume.

"You haven't been dating much lately."

"And since when did you become my keeper?"

"I thought—" Sterling shrugged again. "Sorry. I was only trying to help. You seem lonely. You rarely hang out with Chay anymore, and you keep to yourself lately, except when you're with me. She was pretty, wasn't she?"

Remi reached across the table and grabbed Sterling's hand. He had to nip this in the bud right now. The last thing he needed, while trying to learn to be a werewolf, was a girlfriend. "She was okay. But I'm serious. If I want a date, I'll get one myself."

"You should go out with Chay's assistant. Tina's nice." Sterling grinned.

For some odd reason, Tina's brother, Jake, sprang to mind. Jake was tall, dark, and handsome, in a rugged way. He was appealing to Remi's nose too. Remi's cock began to fill, and he swore he could smell Jake, but it was only his imagination. Even if Jake was in the restaurant, who could smell anything with all these people around? And why the fuck did he always get hard thinking about Jake? Jake was a guy. Remi groaned. He should be dissuading his sibling from playing matchmaker, not trying to figure out his strange reaction to another man. "Sterling...."

"Hmmm, what do I want to eat?" Sterling looked away, still smiling, and picked up his menu, then flipped it open.

A purplish spot peeked out of the cuff of his long sleeve T-shirt. It looked like—

The sick feeling Remi had banished returned with a vengeance. It felt like someone twisted a knife into his heart. He seized Sterling's hand, and Sterling dropped the menu.

"What—"

Pushing the cuff out of the way, Remi studied the bruises. They were perfectly shaped like a hand. Someone had held Sterling around the wrist, hard. Farther up his arm were bigger spots. Nausea swam in Remi's throat, making him swallow hard. He gritted his teeth, and his vision clouded over. If that son of a bitch hurt Sterling.... "When? When did this happen? Did Dirk hit you? Where else are you hurt?" He growled, trying—but failing miserably—to keep the anger out of his voice. Some of his own past beatings filtered through his mind. The fear, the hurt, and the anger had never faded with age. It was bad enough Sterling had to witness their father's cruelty toward their mother, and even to Remi on occasion, but there was no way Remi was going to allow the bastard to beat his baby brother. "Answer me."

Sterling's eyes widened, looking startled. Slowly, he shook his head. "He hasn't hit me."

Yet. Their father hadn't hit Sterling yet, but he would. Remi was going to throw up. Even now, after all this time, he was terrified to face the old man, and he hated himself for the weakness. Somehow he'd convinced himself, by being the model son, he could make things right. He'd promised to behave as long as Sterling was not harmed, but now because of his own fear, he'd failed his brother. He should have taken the kid years ago and run away. Why had he thought the asshole would stick to his end of the bargain?

Closing his eyes, Remi took a deep breath. A warm, fresh scent assailed his nose, and a sense of peace overcame him. No, not peace exactly, he was anything but calm. It was strange, like a feeling of safety, a lessening of his physical tension, if not his mind.

A hand touched his shoulder. "Remi. I'm glad I ran into you. I've got something for you. Can you follow me outside?"

Remi gazed up into a chiseled face and nearly black eyes. "Jake, hey, uh...." It *was* Jake he'd smelled earlier.

Glancing at Sterling, Jake dropped a hand around Remi's biceps and tugged. "Will you excuse us for a moment?"

Sterling mumbled something, but Remi was too busy try-ing to figure out why Jake was dragging him out of his seat to catch it. His head whirled, barely registering which end was up. That was very rare for a trained firefighter, but given the circumstance and Jake's nearness, Remi doubted anyone could blame him. Not that he was going to let anyone know how Jake affected him, of course.

Staggering to his feet, Remi was given no choice but to go as Jake continued to pull him along. *What the fuck?* Why was Jake leading him out of the diner? Halfway to the door, Remi mustered the strength to draw his arm back. "What—"

"Your eyes. Come on."

Huh? His eyes? *Fuck.* Everything was black-and-white. Which was probably Jake's fault. Every time Jake was within three feet of—

Oh shit. What if Sterling saw?

Following Jake out the door and to his SUV, Remi concen-trated on seeing color, like Keaton had taught him.

Jake opened the SUV's door and motioned toward the seat.

Remi sat, peering up at his... well, his friend. Jake had be-come a friend during the last few months since Remi had be-come a werewolf. Despite his effort to steer clear of the man, Remi usually ended up hunting with Jake on the night of a full moon. "Where'd you come from?"

Leaning his arm against the door, Jake stared at Remi. He took the mirrored sunglasses off the top of his head and held them out.

Damn, Jake was big. Accepting the shades, Remi put them on, then shook his head to clear it.

"I smelled you when you walked in. I was going to come and say hi after I was done eating, but your scent changed, and I figured I better try to help you get a handle on things." Frowning, Jake glanced at the diner, then back to Remi. "Everything okay?"

Hell no, everything wasn't okay. He no longer had the surge of adrenaline his anger had spurred, but now he was fighting off arousal. Remi groaned, dropping his head into his hands. *Fuckin' Chay.* Turning him into a werewolf and making his life even more difficult.

Remi lifted his head. "Everything is fine."

"You always get mad, then terrified in a span of seconds for no reason? Yeah, okay, pull the other leg. What's the matter, Remi?"

That wasn't what he wanted to be pulling on Jake at the moment. And where the hell had that come from?

Remi sighed, and for a second he thought of telling Jake everything, but he didn't. He'd never talked about Dirk. Not even to his friends. No way was he going to risk anyone else, especially a friend, by dragging them into it. He looked right into Jake's dark eyes and hoped Jake would let it go. "That's my baby brother in there."

Jake turned his head, peeking back at the diner. "I kinda assumed. Cute kid. He looks like you."

Following Jake's attention, Remi saw Sterling duck out of sight of the window and scurry back to their table. He grinned. Yeah, Sterling did look just like him, well except for the eyes. Sterling had Dirk's brown eyes. No, he had the asshole's eye *color*. Sterling didn't have mean, dead eyes like the son of a bitch.

"That isn't what I asked, though."

Remi sighed. *That figures.* Jake wasn't going to let it go. "I don't want to talk about it." He had to get a grip and go back inside. Telling Jake what a wuss he was about his father was out of the question. He had to live with his own failures. This was his problem, and he had to fix it. And to do that, he needed to talk to Sterling. *Color. Concentrate.* "Blue."

"Huh?"

"You're wearing a blue shirt." A tight dark blue shirt, which showed off Jake's pecs and—fuck, Remi was seeing black-and-white again. He had to focus on something other than Jake.

Jake chuckled, a low, sexy rumbling sound. The man could make a fortune in radio. "They changed back, didn't they?"

"My scent change again?"

"Yeah."

Could werewolves smell attraction? God, he hoped not. He couldn't. No, that wasn't true, he could smell all sorts of scents coming from people, but he didn't know what they meant. He was still trying to learn to scent prey and the different scents of nature when he hunted. Keaton promised to help him with people next. Until then, he was going to have to be careful. How embarrassing would it be to be caught lusting after a guy? He wasn't gay, damn it.

Remi gazed past the big man to the car parked next to the SUV. What color was it?

"Let me help you, Remi." Jake's deep voice softened into a caress. "I want to help you."

The sincerity was Remi's undoing. He closed his eyes, dipping his head. *Un-fucking-believable.* The slightest show of concern from someone and he was breaking down. No, that wasn't true; it was Jake. Remi had never had a problem putting on a good face when his friends tried to help. He'd always known their help would make it worse for not only him, but everyone involved. But with Jake... there was something about the man that made Remi feel he would always be there for him.

Jake's hand landed on his shoulder. "Deep breath. Relax. Getting worked up again isn't going to get your eyes back to normal."

Nodding, he focused his attention past Jake again and took a deep breath.

Something brushed past his cheek, startling him.

Remi sat up straight, trying to figure out what had happened.

Jake stared at him, wide-eyed, and stepped away.

Oh fuck. He'd leaned into Jake's hand, rubbing his cheek against it. What the fuck was he thinking? He glanced down, trying to act cool. "I'm sorry, I uh, I—"

"No big deal. You just surprised me. Tell me about your family. What happened to Sterling?"

My family? Remi's head jerked up. *How does he know it has something to do with Sterling?* How had he forgotten Jake was a PI? Maybe Jake *could* help. "Can you follow someone for me and gather info on them?" He knew damn well his father was a dirty cop—which was what made him dangerous—maybe if Remi could prove it, he could get the information to the right people, and no one would have to know he or Jake were involved.

Jake cocked his head. "I think you need to tell me more, but yeah, I can do that."

Remi relaxed, feeling better now that he had started thinking of a plan. He had no idea how he was going to come up with the dough to hire Jake, but he'd figure out something. Keeping Sterling from suffering what Remi had gone through was worth it.

He stood and Jake stepped back farther, but not before Remi got a good whiff of the man. Damn, he smelled raw and masculine and—he was doing it again. If he was going to let Jake help him, he was going to have to rid himself of this infatuation.

Remi shut the door and tried to hand the glasses back to Jake, but Jake shook his head.

"Keep them, you may need to put them back on."

Nodding, Remi shoved them on top of his head. It was probably a smart idea, considering Jake's nearness always made him go haywire. "Come on, I'll introduce you to my little brother. You can bring your breakfast over to our table."

About the Author

J.L. Langley said her first words at six months of age. By the time she was a year old, she was talking in complete sentences and, as most of her family and friends will tell you, she hasn't shut up since. After becoming an accomplished motormouth, J.L. set out to master other avenues of self-expression, including art, and dance.

She attended the University of Texas, where she majored in art, and worked as a dance instructor on the side. Her love of artistic expression in dance landed her a career in which she taught and performed for over twenty-five years. After marriage to her junior high school sweetheart and the birth of their children, J.L. decided to try her hand at writing. To date, she has several successful novels and a handful of novellas to her credit.

She lives in Texas, where she was born and raised, with her real life hero, their rowdy two boys, two even rowdier German Shepherds and ten goldfish, one of which is named Jaws. When she's not writing, she can usually be found with her nose in a book, appreciating the communication skills of other writers.

Learn more at www.jllangleybooks.com[1]

---

1. http://www.jllangley.com

Books by J.L. Langley

Sci-Regency Series
My Fair Captain
The Englor Affair
My Regelence Rake
Diplomatic Relations
My Highland Laird

With or Without Series
Without Reservations
With Caution
Without Abandon
Without Secrets (coming soon)

The Ranch Series
The Tin Star
The Broken H

Stand Alone Titles
His Convenient Husband
Horsing Around
With Love